EVIL AT THE CORE

EVIL AT THE CORE

VINQUITA
ROMAINE

Matador
Unit E2 Airfield Business Park,
Harrison Road, Market Harborough,
Leicestershire. LE16 7UL
Tel: 0116 2792299
Email: books@troubador.co.uk
Web: www.troubador.co.uk/matador
Twitter: @matadorbooks

ISBN 978 1803130 835

British Library Cataloguing in Publication Data.
A catalogue record for this book is available from the British Library.

Printed and bound in Great Britain by 4edge Limited
Typeset in 12pt Minion Pro by Troubador Publishing Ltd, Leicester, UK

Matador is an imprint of Troubador Publishing Ltd

Dedicated to
Kumkum, Lavanya and Shalini

To the children, who are our future
To our future, which is our Earth
In the name of my little cherub, Figgy aka Inaya
That it may help to redress our shame of
The oppressed, the exploited, the dispossessed
That it may help to support and nourish
The downtrodden children and women
That it may help sustain our nature
And reverse the environmental carnage
I pledge my personal profits from this book

CONTENTS

*Sometimes, it takes a terminal fall
to restore freedom
Sometimes, it takes a terrible mistake
to achieve restitution
Sometimes, it takes a leap in the dark
to land in the light
Sometimes, it takes a killing
to establish justice*

1

THE SNAP

Everything in the material world has a finite limit, be it size, energy, strength, wealth, possessions.

The immaterial – love, patience, tolerance, compassion – may be infinite, but even they, when stretched beyond a limit, snap.

I had been going downhill for some time, really. Oh, the heady days when fresh from university I had got myself a well-paying job as a pharmaceutical representative for a big multinational. It seems scarcely possible now, but I believe there was a time when I was an attractive hunk who charmed many a fair lady. And I did, though I was never a Casanova.

And along came gorgeous Harriett, who charmed me fatally! Harriett, who was paranoid about spelling her name with a double 't' – I could never understand then, but now thinking back, I can see that the double 't' really did define her. Harriett, who never failed to declaim about the merits of female emancipation and the need for equality at work and pay, but had a singular aversion to hard work (or indeed any work at all). Harriett, who loved to go out, eat out, dance, be the life and soul of the party. Harriett, who wore designer clothes and jewellery, even dreamed designer dreams! Of villas and yachts. She had me in the palm of her hand. In retrospect, the mention of a rich, landed grandmother in Scotland I am sure played a huge role in her interest in me.

Harriett Whittaker and I had met in a pub, through mutual friends, and I was quite simply captivated; infatuated to be precise. We met for our first date a week later, when I learnt that she had recently broken up with her boyfriend. (That man must be a ginormous loser, I said to myself.) Much later I learnt that he was the last in a line of distinguished losers. We dated for a couple of months, before Harriett 'yielded' to my deadly charm and we started on what I considered to be a torrid love affair.

After a whirlwind romance, we ended up getting married in what was a rather modest affair. Her ailing mother attended in a wheelchair but there was no sign of the father (who had decamped twenty years earlier with a younger model). I never thought of it at the time, but at the wedding, Harriett had no other relatives (not her fault), but just two bridesmaids, and no other friends. Surely that must have said something about her social skills, but I was much too besotted to engage in such analysis at that time. That was Saturday, 17 January 2015, the day of our fairy-tale wedding, suitably embellished by heavy snowfall.

My only remaining relatives were my grandmother and my cousin Jack, neither of whom I expected would grace the occasion, and I was right. I did, however, have thirty-odd friends from school and university, who did attend, and I have always been hugely grateful for that. Harry and Kevin were there, but I was not as friendly or effusive as I should have been. Shame on me that over the years I had slowly dropped them all, one by one, in part thanks to Harriett.

I had enough money saved up to buy a small semi-detached house in Portchester, in Hampshire, in a quiet little enclave. The honeymoon did not last long. The career trajectory that I had imagined (sales director in five years was what Harriett had assumed, and demanded) did not come to fruition and after a year, my pay scale suddenly seemed woefully inadequate to my dear wife. Harriett's spending was progressively ahead of my income, and on one occasion I had the temerity to suggest that perhaps she should take a job. Her response was short, sharp and fierce, and I never mentioned it again. Harriett's mood and temper deteriorated steadily, in direct proportion to our finances.

I have always been keen on family and wanted to have a child, a suggestion that went down like a lead balloon with Harriett. Oh no, things like motherhood would never appeal to the brand of feminism that she represented. I have to admit, however, that in that one sense she was absolutely right. In retrospect, I would never have forgiven myself for having brought a child into our marriage. Harriett became more secretive and I never really knew where some of the money was going – not that there was a lot of it. At some point, I became convinced that she had found herself another man, and I think this must have been some time in 2017. I did not have the guts to ask. On the odd occasion that I did venture to ask where she had been, or what she had done on the day, or where she was going, she would simply ask me to mind my own effing business. She made it blatantly clear that I was a loser and a failure as far as she was concerned.

The last straw made its appearance today. I lost my job.

☦

"I am really sorry, Quentin, but there really is no other way. Our profits have been dropping for three years. We are surviving, but only just, so we have to cut back. We scrutinised the performance and reports of all the staff of your grade and I'm afraid you are one of those that did not make the cut."

I looked on speechlessly, and after a pause, seeing no response from me, he continued. "We will provide you with a lump sum as compensation, of course, and provide any additional remedial training that would enhance the chances of your next employment."

When I came home, I could hear Harriett humming in her bedroom. Yes, *her* bedroom, as I had been banished to the smaller single bedroom over a year ago. I knew this would be the mother of all showdowns, and I wondered how I was going to muster up the courage to give her the news of my 'early retirement'. How else, but to fortify myself with whisky! I opened a bottle of J&B and downed a couple of shots.

There in front of me, looming large, stood this terrible apparition. An overweight hulk with a protruding belly, collapsing tissues, dark bags under the eyes, an unkempt head of hair, a thirty-six-hour stubble and bloodshot eyes. Swaying to the sound of tinnitus. Looking at my reflection in the mirror, I felt sick. I felt drained of just about everything, with not even the desire to live, not even the motivation to try and kill myself. It would be safe to say that my life was at its nadir, well below zero. I was full of self-loathing and self-pity, both fuelled by the whisky.

Harriett came out of her room and down the stairs, looking like the million dollars that neither of us could dream of. As usual, her expression hardened when she saw me and it was obvious that she was just setting off on one of her trysts.

"Harriett, I have something to tell you."

She gave me a look of disdain and was plainly not interested. "Well, what is it?"

"I've lost my job."

Harriett went red and her eyes widened.

"You fucking loser, are you ever going to be anything more than a waste of space? That's it, I've had it. We are done. I want you out of here, out of my life. I am going out now and will be back in two hours, by which time I expect you to have vanished. Off the face of the earth, preferably."

She stomped back into her room, and just for a moment, I felt this enormous sense of relief that I had got through the most difficult part of it. I went back to the comfort of J&B, wondering what my next move should be. She wanted me out, *I* wanted me out, who could ask for more? I was going to be liberated. Feverish thoughts raged through my mind, but with a thud, I came back to earth. She was still here, and I was dreading her return down the stairs. I hurried up the stairs, hoping to disappear into my room before she came out of hers. The plan was to quickly stuff a few things into a suitcase and get ready to go. But where?

Harriett came out of her room and caught me on the landing. To my slight surprise, she looked calm and there was a look of smugness that caused me some unease. "I am off to meet the love of my life."

I feigned surprise.

"Never suspected, did you? It's been going on for a couple of years now."

I wished I had the guts to punch her in the face and wipe off that look of self-satisfaction.

"Congratulations, it couldn't have happened to a nicer man!"

The sarcasm got to her and for a moment I thought she was going to slap me, but I think my clenched jaw must have put her off.

Harriett walked down the stairs to the door, opened it and turned around to me. She had a curiously taunting expression on her face, as she said, "We met at the Health Club, and I thought it was just a nice accident. Turns out it was all predestined. He's the one with whom I've spent the New Year's Eves, not to mention all those other evenings and nights. And all right under your nose…" She stopped herself, and with that she was gone.

✣

So, I am now back to where I started. Tipsy, swaying on my feet, looking like a decomposing troll, miserable as sin. It was at that point that something snapped inside my head. The wild idea exploded in my head that I would walk away this minute, once and for all and forever from the current self-inflicted hell. Over the next few minutes, I tossed a thousand ideas around and settled on one course of action.

I picked up my passport and my wallet (with £45 and a Mastercard). Then, filled with an uncharacteristic bravado, I entered Harriett's room and rummaged through her possessions, being careful not to displace anything. Even at that point, my fear of her temper was such that subconsciously I was trying to hide my actions. There was something at the back of my mind which was bugging me and I knew I was looking for something that she had been hiding from me for a while. And then I found it – a little electronic safe camouflaged under a pile of scarves and jumpers. What number could she have used for her code? I tried a few random sequences, with no luck. What about her date of birth – surely she wouldn't be foolish enough to use that? Nevertheless, I tried, and bingo!

I opened it with a real sense of excitement and achievement. What I found was no surprise – jewellery, but surprising amounts of it. I had no idea just how much she had managed to squirrel away. I was no expert in assessing any of this, but looking at the number of gold items and precious stones, I reckon there must have been at least £20,000 worth. I know for a fact that Harriett would absolutely never ever use any costume jewellery, and had insisted on nothing less than 14-carat gold, and semi-precious stones. I recognised some items I had lovingly bought her in the first two years, and some that she had forced me to pay for, but at least three-quarters of them were new to me. I assumed they were acquired through a combination of my earnings and gifts from her boyfriend.

I was more intrigued, however, by a little stack of letters, which even without inspecting, I knew was related to this unknown lover of hers. Not that it bothered me one bit, so much so I decided to skip them altogether. And then I found a manila envelope, which yielded a wad of £50 notes – again I could not be bothered to count, but I reckon there were probably a hundred of those. What the hell was going on? She had been screwing me every possible way, except in the literal sense. I picked up the box and in its place I substituted a couple of boxes of tissues and then replaced her camouflage. I took the box up into the loft (using the pull-down ladder) and secreted it away behind the water tank. I had an overwhelming desire to picture her reaction upon discovery of her loss.

I carefully shut her bedroom door and hastily put my stuff together in the battered suitcase I had under my bed. I had barely made it down the stairs, when the door opened and Harriett walked in. She was flushed, and agitated. She looked at me and her eyes narrowed. "I'm glad to see you are all set to go."

I looked at her insolently and then shrugged my shoulders and walked into our small lounge, heading for the J&B.

Harriett continued. "Right, this is crunch time. I want you to leave now and find yourself a place to stay. The Red Lion in Cosham should be good enough. I am going to keep the house. I'll send all your remaining stuff to the hotel tomorrow." Even today, I marvel at the fact that she took it for granted that the house was hers, and that I should be evicted, never mind her adultery!

I took a slug of the golden nectar, facing away from her towards the French window that led from the lounge to the patio at the back.

As an afterthought, she said, "I am feeling really generous, so I won't ask to share any of your money."

I turned around and looked her in the eye, still saying nothing. She was visibly annoyed at my nonchalance. "Where the hell are you going, anyway?"

I looked at her squarely without the slightest tremor and was astonished by the sudden dissolution of the trepidation that I usually felt with her. I heard myself saying, "None of your bleeding business. I sure as hell don't want to see you again."

Harriett surprised me with a complete change in tactics, saying, "You know, Quentin, it's not all that bad. We tried to make a go of it, but sadly it just didn't work. I won't hold it against you!"

Harriett was mostly Mr Hyde, but could occasionally play Dr Jekyll, which she was doing with consummate skill. But I had crossed a mental line, and emboldened by the alcohol, there was no stopping me.

"You won't hold it against me, eh? You sure as hell won't hold *it*, or anything else of yours, against me, that's for certain. In fact I won't even let you within three feet of me, that's how desirable you are!"

"Quentin, please! There is really no need for unpleasantness. Deep down I do care about you, you know."

"Yeah, right. The way a school of barracuda might."

Harriett stepped up to me, and I was acutely aware of the delicate perfume and her generous cleavage.

"It's too late for seduction, baby," I said. "I've got other plans, and perhaps the odd surprise for you."

She was visibly taken aback, and snarled at me, saying, "Then just get the fuck out of here and my life!"

Mr Hyde was back!

"Shit, you haven't been messing around in my room, have you?"

The question found its mark in my expression and she turned and ran up the stairs. I knew I had to get away, and I rushed out of the house into the driveway. On the spur of the moment I turned, took out my key and locked the door. I jumped into my old banger and that's when I heard her scream from her bedroom, through the open window sash. "Quentin, you bastard…!"

I remember the date well: 20 October 2019.

2

FLIGHT TO OBLIVION

Flight is always thrilling, be it
Flight on holiday
Flight to one's home, or
Flight from danger!

I wasn't going to wait around listening to her vituperation, much as it would have given me satisfaction. I eased the car into gear and it moved away noisily. The damned vehicle was twelve years old and falling apart, but that is all I could afford. Not so Harriett, who had bullied me into buying her a two-year-old Volkswagen Golf convertible, which she drove with a frenzy reminiscent of Messala at the chariot race in *Ben-Hur*. I knew every second counted, as she could overhaul me in no time at all. My only hope was to get out of sight and hope that she would take a wrong turn, if she did, indeed, decide to come after me.

I turned out of the estate and left onto Dore Avenue, accelerating as hard as I could. On tenterhooks, I reached the next cutting and turned left onto Nyewood Avenue, at which point Harriett's car had not yet appeared in my mirror. Barely thirty yards away I came to the T-junction and turned left on Hill Road. I accelerated uphill, certain that if by chance a police car happened to be around, I would be dead meat, speeding and under the influence! The next hundred yards were the most anxious ones in my life, as I was in plain sight if she had guessed my turns correctly. Fortunately, it was almost dark and she would not have been easily able to identify my car from a distance, or differentiate it from other vehicles travelling in both directions. As I cleared the motorway bridge, I breathed a sigh of relief because I had got through the first hurdle. I rapidly turned into Nelson Lane and went over the hill past the Nelson monument, into the tiny country lane that would take me down towards Wickham. With the ongoing traffic it took me about ten minutes to reach Wickham and turn north onto the A32. As the adrenaline surge gradually settled, I became acutely aware of two facts – first, that I was probably well over the limit for alcohol, and second, that I was ravenous. Fortunately, within a few minutes I came to the Roebuck, one of my favourite local haunts. I turned in, parked my car where it would not be easily visible from the road, and went in.

"Hello, Quentin, long time no see!" said Brian, whom I had come to know over the years, serving behind the bar. Without waiting for me to respond, he started filling a pint of my usual local beer.

"Not today, Brian. I'm afraid I've already had one too many. I need food, desperately. And I still have some way to go tonight. I'm heading for Heathrow."

Brian looked disappointed.

"Heathrow, at this time? Isn't it a bit late?"

"Actually, I plan to crash out near the airport and take a flight in the morning. Before you ask me where, I am not very sure as it is a surprise waiting to be unleashed on me. But firstly, can you please rush through an order for your outstanding fish and chips?"

Brian controlled his curiosity and rang the order through.

I continued. "Things have come to a head, Brian, and I need some time away from everything. I just made a spur-of-the-moment decision to go."

After exchanging a few pleasantries, the inevitable question came up.

"And how is Lady Harriett?" asked Brian, with mischief in his eye and a single raised eyebrow. I thought for a second and decided there was no point in dissembling.

"It's over, Brian. I have finally broken my shackles. She's out of my life. In fact, I'm semi-free, semi-white and thirty-six going on sixty-six."

Brian chuckled at my warped humour, but was clearly delighted and made no attempt to conceal his approval. "Long overdue, mate. Heaven knows why you stayed with her this long."

No idea, no idea at all. I wolfed down my dinner and it was around ten-thirty when I said bye to Brian and walked to my car. And then the phone rang – Harriett! I revelled in not answering. By the time I was sat behind the wheel and about to move, the phone rang again. I was feeling particularly defiant, so decided to answer. "What do you want?"

"Quentin, you drove off like a bloody lunatic. Where are you now?"

"Not far, actually – at the Roebuck. Why, are you worried about me or something?"

"Well, yes, but… there's something of mine that's missing. You bastard, you've filched it, haven't you?"

"Ha, ha, wouldn't you like to know? Anyway, I haven't got time for this crap. I'm heading off to Heathrow so goodbye!" I disconnected and turned the phone off.

Whatever else was deficient about me, I was second to none when it came to directions, and I knew all the shortcuts and countryside roads in Hampshire. It was dark and the road was relatively free of cars by this time, so I drove to Alton, and from there took the road towards Odiham. It was pitch-black, and as there was no hurry, I decided to pootle along at thirty miles an hour. I thought I would find accommodation at one of the inexpensive hotels on the A4, east of Heathrow, park my car there and disappear. I hadn't quite worked through what I was going to do with the car – or maybe I'd park it in the long-term car park, and head off. I could worry about its retrieval when (if) I got back. The damned thing was probably only worth a few hundred pounds.

The extraordinary events of this evening resurfaced in my mind, and I wondered what exactly Harriett was up to at this very moment. Had she really given up on me? Most unlikely, knowing her. She would move heaven and earth to get even with me and retrieve her precious worldly wealth. I wondered who her mysterious boyfriend might be. The exertions of the day and the heavy meal were making me distinctly soporific.

I must have been driving for about half an hour since leaving the Roebuck, when I became aware of a bright set of headlights behind me. It was a big SUV, probably a Range Rover. The driver was obviously in a hurry, so I slowed down and flashed my left indicator light, so he could overtake. That was exactly what happened, except he was intent on taking me out! As the nose of the SUV car passed mine, it swerved violently to the left, and a split second later, I did the same. The result was that he caught me hard, but nothing like what it could have been. My car jumped and juddered off the road and I jammed on the brakes. The car came to rest in a ditch, tilting at a forty-five-degree angle. The first thing I did was to move all four limbs to make sure there was nothing broken. I unbuckled the seat-belt and straightened myself, whilst at the same time opening the car door. It creaked and protested loudly, and I had to force it open.

Shaken and slightly dizzy I tried to pull myself out, when I noticed that the SUV had come to a halt about fifty yards ahead and a dark figure was emerging. I was sure he was not exactly coming to offer me succour, when providence came to my aid. Flashing orange lights of a car became visible, approaching us from the other side. The man turned back and jumped into his vehicle and took off. The approaching vehicle screeched to a halt near me and two men scrambled out and came up to me. It turned out to be a motorway maintenance vehicle, and the two men had their hi-vis jackets on. With their help we got the car back onto the road.

"You're lucky, sir. What really happened?"

I related the details of the accident, all the while hoping that they would not smell alcohol on my breath.

"Right, so this was a hit and run. He obviously got out of the car to help you, but decided otherwise when he saw us approaching. Not sure if your car is safe to drive, or indeed if you are. Perhaps we should ring for an ambulance."

I thought rapidly and decided it was probably best not to complicate matters by telling them exactly what my plans were. I had absolutely no intention of being foiled by events.

"Oh no, thanks, I'm fine. I'll just call the rescue service, and wait for them to check out the car. Hopefully drive home soon. I would much rather you guys went off to finish whatever you were planning to do."

They were ever so solicitous, but I managed to persuade them all was well. I turned on my phone and made a pretence of calling the AA.

As soon as they departed, I turned on the ignition and was delighted to find that the banger was still alive and kicking. Of course, the right side was badly dented, but I didn't care. All I wanted to do was to get to my destination, but first I needed to gather my thoughts and come up with an action plan. And then the phone rang again – Harriett again. No, I wasn't going to oblige. I drove onto the M3 towards London, and pulled into the first services that came along. In the meantime, I had decided on a change of plans. No hunting for hotels, I was going to do something quite insane.

I bought myself a large Americano from Costa and then went online on my faithful old HTC and applied for an ESTA to enter the US, which was remarkably quick and successful. I then located the address of a scrapyard, not far from Heathrow. I then bought some paper and a biro from the shop. I drove off half an hour later, and in this time, Harriett had rung me three or four times, all unanswered. I drove to Hounslow and discovered the whereabouts of the scrapyard, and parked outside it. I got into the back seat and dropped off, remembering to turn off my phone, knowing for certain that Harriett would hound me. I had no definite time in mind, thinking I'd just wake up whenever.

When I woke up it was six-thirty in the morning and still dark. On the A4 sheet of paper I printed 'FREE TO A HAPPY HOME!', which I was sure would lead to a quick adoption by the dealer, and placed it on the dashboard. On the driver's seat I placed the vehicle registration document, signed on the dotted line, so the dealer would have no problem scrapping the car legitimately. I walked out, and onto the main road, which was just about fifty yards away. Traffic was already building up, and I called for an Uber, and found myself walking into the airport half an hour later.

The first stop was at the ATM, where I drew £250. I picked up a travel kit from Boots in the airport concourse, and proceeded to freshen up in the toilet. I still looked terrible, but there was a rare gleam in my eye! I then went to the ticketing desk of Virgin Atlantic, which at that early hour was manned by just one surly-looking young lady. One look at me and her expression became even more surly. Well, no more Mr Nice Guy, I said to myself, and glowered back at her.

I paid a ridiculous amount with my Mastercard, comfortable in the knowledge that there were enough funds to cover that. I also knew that my severance pay of £22,500 would be in my account within a couple of weeks. And it would be safe from Harriett's sticky fingers, as it was in my sole name.

By the time I got through immigration, I was dead beat, and plonked myself in one of the seats and snoozed. Announcements woke me up and I saw that I had a little over an hour to depart. That's when I remembered to turn my phone on, to find twelve missed calls from Harriett. I was seized with a sudden desire to confront her, even taunt her. I knew she had discovered the loss of her little treasure trove and would be desperate. I was not sure whether to tell her where it was, or keep her hanging on a bit longer. After some deliberation I decided to call her anyway. She was breathless when she answered the phone.

"Quentin, just where the fuck are you?"

"Ah well, if it isn't my dear spouse! Do you really care? Or is it that you are after something you have lost?"

"I know you found my little secret. I really am sorry, but you know I was so insecure, not knowing how long you would have the job, and thought I would start putting a bit away every month, just to secure my own future. It was completely wrong of me and I do apologise. I can't really ask your forgiveness, Quentin, but please do consider my vulnerable position and I'd be eternally grateful to you if you could return the stuff to me. Listen, even if you don't want to return my things, I'll understand. Can we at least meet and talk about it?"

I had never known Harriett to be quite so pliable and helpless! Could this really be happening? Or was it just Harriett playing her usual games? I was on the verge of telling her where I had hidden the loot, when I thought the better of it and decided to continue to be no-more-Mr-Nice-Guy.

"Listen, sunshine, don't try and pull the wool over my eyes. I am not really that desperate to keep the stuff, even though arguably it's all mine. In fact, I will give you at least half the value of it, if you behave yourself for a whole year. By that I mean, *don't* come back to me, don't even *think* about it, and *please* stay with this poor sod you have found for yourself. But I'm going to disappear for a year and when I come back, if you haven't created any mayhem, I'll give you your share."

"Quentin, please, let's just meet at least once. Just where on earth are you, anyway? You're not really at Heathrow, are you?"

"Well, I suppose I might as well tell you. I *am* at Heathrow and flying out within the next hour. Never mind where, all I can say is I don't plan on being back any time soon."

"Please, give me just one opportunity to speak to you face to face. I can be there within a couple of hours; we can have lunch together and you can take a later flight to wherever it is you want to go."

There was a hint of desperation in her voice, which I could not understand. Harriett must by now have realised that I was not bluffing. She must have assumed that I had the loot on me, and perhaps, planned to take it off me, with the aid of her new boyfriend. Or perhaps she was planning to use her feminine charms to recover her lost treasure, but I was not in any mood to give her a chance. "No go, baby. I'm *outta* here."

"Look, everything here is a mess. I can't sell the house without you being here, and think about it, you could get half the value of that. Secondly, I have no regular means of income and now you have stolen my nest egg. Last but not least, I am not too sure of Monty, who for all I know, might send me packing if things don't work out. So, what am I going to do?"

I never thought I would get to repeat these famous words in real life: "My dear, I don't give a damn!" Apologies to Margaret Mitchell and Rhett Butler ('Frankly' was an addition in the film, which in my opinion, was pointless). And with that I rang off, and powered the phone down. So, the boyfriend was called Monty. First name, shortened surname or nickname? I could not recollect meeting anybody of that name.

The flight left on time. I found myself in a corner seat, as all the aisle seats were taken by the time I checked in. I groaned inwardly as my two neighbours turned out to be a loud and cheerful middle-aged American couple. The man sat in the middle, next to me, and bestowed me with a patronising smile and a nod. There was also a spare tyre which was competing for space with mine.

"*G'die, mite!*" he said to me. "That's how you guys say it, isn't it?"

I was annoyed. "How did you know I was Australian?"

He looked confused and I had the satisfaction of seeing his discomfiture. He tried to make up for the faux pas by saying, "Ah, I see. Jolly good day to you, old top."

"And the same to you, old cock." He looked distinctly uncomfortable and a bit offended. He turned away, much to my relief. As I said before, no more Mr Nice Guy.

I leaned against the window and lost consciousness for the next couple of hours, until lunch was served. My neighbours looked generally miffed and averted their faces from me, which suited me absolutely fine. I closed my eyes and slipped into a reverie as I went over the events of my life.

3

REVERIE IN SPACE

Why, when exertions should lead to exhaustion, does the mind explode with memories, regrets and remorse?

I was born on 4 October 1984, and have never had any recollection of a mother or a father. There are exactly five faces that I remember from my early childhood. The first, and by far the most wonderful and angelic person, and the only one who truly, absolutely, cared for me was Aunt Charlotte. I was not entirely sure how exactly she was my aunt, but relationships matter nothing when a child finds love and tenderness in the midst of icy relationships, and overt animosity. I later learnt that she was the sister of my late father. I can only describe her as having a face that I wanted to look at, and keep looking at, forever. She had golden hair, a regal nose inherited from her mother, a set of beautiful white teeth, slightly sloping from left to right, and deep blue eyes. She was tenderness and gentleness personified.

The second equally powerful memory was that of Uncle Charles, Charlotte's husband. If ever a man could terrify and terrorise simply by his looks and words, Uncle Charles was that man. He was a big man, built like a bull, with a craggy, though handsome face. His laughter boomed, and had the paradoxical effect of cowing down, rather than uplifting. He loathed me, and I could never define why. His son, Jack, was around my age and I used to think it was in some way related to that, but none of it made any sense. Jack was actually a year younger than me, but was my nemesis. His was the third face etched painfully in my memory. There is much to say about Jack that will unfold in the succeeding pages.

The fourth face that will always remain with me is that of Jimmy Clayton, a shadowy ghost who came and went. Superficially he could look scary. With his protruding black eyes, he was dark, brooding, rough and unkempt. His devotion to Aunt Charlotte ensured that we had a strong rapport, and soon I came to believe that he was always there to protect me, my guardian angel. He didn't have any family, and lived by himself with a dog that he adored.

Last, but not least, was my formidable grandmother, Lady Winifred, tall and gaunt, who never allowed a smile to mar her noble mien. She had a striking nose, and iron-grey hair, with eyes to match. The one constant in my life during my childhood years was my grandmother, who was like a sculpture in ice. I often questioned whether she really was my grandmother, for she seemed to have no desire to have anything to do with me. But when you're a child you don't ask questions and simply accept what you are told. All I remember being told from the word go was that I was essentially an orphan. It seemed I owed my grandmother a huge debt of gratitude for her generosity of spirit in taking me in. My father, her son, was supposedly a tearaway and older than my aunt, Charlotte. Never a devoted student, he absconded from university when he was twenty, and two weeks later my grandparents received a postcard from the island of Lanzarote, reassuring them that he was alive and well, and warning them not to try and get him back. It seemed he ended up in India at some point. He was effectively excommunicated from the family. That was until the High Commission in Delhi contacted the family to regretfully inform them that their son and heir had been killed in a climbing accident.

Evidently, 'they' travelled to India to identify the body and whilst there, discovered that he had been cohabiting with an Indian woman, who had borne him a son, a mere three months earlier. They pensioned off the woman with a handsome settlement, in exchange for the right to adopt me. I have no idea what my original name was, but I became Quentin and was 'repatriated' within a few weeks.

My grandmother seemed more to me like a robotic and unfeeling caretaker. She made no secret of her dislike for me, most particularly in contrast to her favourite grandson, Jack, who was the obvious heir to the fortune. It was only later, much, much later, that I saw the human side of her, when it was far, far too late. My grandfather died, I believe, long before I was born.

✚

By the time I was five, I was completely obsessed by, and besotted with Aunt Charlotte. She could see and sense my isolation, growing up in this great estate in remote Scotland, with the grand name of *Gorm-Faire*, with neither companion nor friend (except for Jimmy). She (they) lived somewhere else, possibly in London, but I cannot be sure. She certainly made it a point to visit us every month. She would bring Jack along every time, but as the interactions between Jack and me were not particularly pleasant, she brought him less often as time went by. Much to my relief, Uncle Charles only visited a couple of times a year, and believe me, I dreaded every visit of his. Harry Potter had not been created then but in retrospect, Uncle Charles and Jack, for me, were the equivalents of the Dursleys and the Malfoys rolled into one.

I was sent to the local primary school, which frankly, was my salvation. I remember a few friends from there, though I have lost touch with them, with the exception of Kevin McArdle. Kevin sought me out and we became very good friends. Jimmy often managed to 'bump into me' when school finished. I was meant to come straight home by the school bus, but always managed to get a few minutes with him, which I really looked forward to.

"Don't you worry, laddie, you'll be a'righ', you'll be a'righ' as long as your auntie and I are around. But you just keep away from that uncle of yours and his nasty little boy." Jimmy would shake his head to make the point. Not that he needed to advise me on that.

There are some snippets that impregnated themselves on my memory indelibly. There was this occasion when my aunt and uncle were visiting, and for once Jack was behaving reasonably. This was most unusual, but I presumed this was because my aunt had warned him not to step out of line. No such luck. After dinner, we were both packed off to bed and no sooner had the door shut, than he turned on me. It was a very large room, so there was plenty of space for me to flee from his attentions. Even though I was supposed to be older than him, he was as tall as I, and a whole lot stronger. Being light, agile and fleet-footed I dodged him for as long as I could, but finally he did corner me.

The commotion, of course, attracted the attention of the elders, and I was rescued in time. My aunt gave a tongue-lashing to Jack, while my uncle looked at him with a slight smirk of pride, and at me with complete contempt. However, he could not say anything at the time. Pretty soon we were both settled into our beds with a strict warning not to engage in any further shenanigans. Soon Jack was away with the fairies, but I could not sleep. I always had a glass of water by my bed, but in all the excitement I had forgotten to get one, so I tiptoed downstairs to get it. That was when I overheard the conversation.

I heard my uncle saying, "I know that twerp is supposed to be your brother's son, but did they have to bring him back here? Surely the half-breed bastard would've been better left to fester in India?" I was hurt and shocked by his words, the contempt and the crudeness.

"Shut up, Charles," Aunt Charlotte retorted. "Have you absolutely no humanity in you? In fact, you may be right in that this poor boy would've received more love and caring in a poor shack in India, than in this great big estate, with my imperious mother as his caregiver. Anyway, why don't you just get the hell off his back? What has he done to offend you? If anything, he just gets beaten up and dominated by Jack."

"And so he should, the little parasite. He really has no place here. And who knows, one day he might try to claim a share of the estate and I'm not having that. All of this goes to Jack, and the bastard can have a settlement appropriate to his station. Do you realise that I would do anything, absolutely anything, to ensure that our child gets it all?"

"But, Charles, for heaven's sake be reasonable. This poor child is also an heir to the estate. It's not his fault that he was born out of wedlock, and to an Indian mother. In fact, it could be argued that as the son of the son, he deserves the lion's share."

I did not realise that my grandmother was sitting in on this conversation, until she intervened. "Over my dead body. Charles, don't worry yourself. The estate is all mine and mine to dispose of as I see fit. Jack will be the inheritor and this rather unfortunate creature that we have been landed with, will get a small settlement to keep him going."

The floorboard creaked, and I froze. There was complete silence downstairs and I tiptoed back to my room, left the door slightly ajar, to avoid the click of the door locking, and crept into bed. I heard footsteps come up and could almost sense someone at the door, and wondered which one of them it was. I froze, almost not daring to breathe. After a little while, which seemed like an eternity, I heard the door click shut. That night was one of the worst in my memory – sleep, exhaustion and conflicting emotions all churning me around.

They left the next morning. My grandmother was standing at the top of the steps as the three of them departed in my grandmother's Bentley, which was used to ferry visitors to and from the airport. None of them had so much as said a word to me that morning. I was stood behind the door, like a frozen statue, with a sensation of total and utter depression.

Aunt Charlotte suddenly stopped and turned around, exclaiming, "Oh dear, I have left my scarf behind." She ran up the steps, past my grandmother and came in. She grabbed me in her arms and kissed me on both cheeks and whispered, "I love you, Quentin. Just remember that, whenever you feel down."

Even then I knew that she had planted it there as an excuse for coming back. How could I not love her? Why did she marry this brute of a man? I could never fathom this, until much, much later.

So, who was this father of mine? Clearly a bastard (metaphorically) who begot a bastard (literally). Why the hell did he have to die in an accident? I would have been so much happier living with him and my real mother in India, sleeping rough on the road with her rather than this supposedly lavish living I was enjoying. At some point it struck me like a fatal blow, the thought that my real mother had abandoned me in return for cash. I hated her, hated her more than even Uncle Charles. The one thing I absolutely swore to do, was that when I was grown up, I would get all the details from my aunt, and travel to India and seek out my natural mother. I would be her nemesis, and show no mercy. And then another side of me would kick in and I would argue on her behalf that faced with poverty and destitution, did she not make the noble sacrifice of giving her child away entirely for his benefit? What mother would willingly give a child away? Maybe she did a really noble act, at least in her mind. Such conflict ravaged my thinking for so many of my early years. And my later years.

☦

CHARLOTTE GRAYLING

Aunt Charlotte was born on 15 June 1962, the one birthday that was indelibly etched into my brain. Her presence transformed the general atmosphere of gloom, which was unrelenting. The sunshine that she brought with her was tempered by the presence of Jack or Uncle Charles. On the occasions when she came on her own, even though she was so much more loving and communicative with me, there was an air of underlying tension between her and her mother. For some reason my grandmother disapproved of her special relationship with me, pretty much as she did with Jimmy. I tried desperately to get her to like me, but nothing seemed to work. I came to the inevitable conclusion that my grandmother simply did not want me to experience any form of happiness.

I remember asking Aunt Charlotte about her childhood and her parents.

"I was born in London, Quentin. I saw little of my father, who was flying high in the business world and became quite wealthy by the time he was forty. Your grandmother was wealthy in her own right, always a bit of a recluse, and she had decided to get out of London to somewhere remote as soon as it was practicable. I was sent off to boarding school when I turned eleven, and Mummy relocated to this wonderful estate in Scotland, *Gorm-Faire,* where we now are. My father commuted to London, staying there three to four days a week, and returning to *Gorm-Faire* for long weekends."

"Aunt Charlotte, is there something wrong with me? Why does Granny hate me? I try so hard, but she is just so awful." I could not stem the flow of tears at that point, and Aunt Charlotte grabbed me in a bear hug. There was just silence but I felt as if I had suddenly found refuge from all my tribulations. I looked up to find her eyes brimming and a look of such love I did not know was possible.

"Darling, there is absolutely nothing wrong with you. You are a fine little boy, extremely clever and sensitive. You are just very unlucky in not having parents like most other children do. Your grandmother does not really hate you. She is unable to show any affection; she is just made that way. She shows me no more affection than she does you, in case you haven't noticed."

"So why did my real parents abandon me? I know my father died in an accident, and maybe I can't blame him for it. Knowingly or not, he did abandon me. But so much worse is the fact that my mother truly abandoned me. What kind of mother would do that?" My aunt clasped me to her chest and broke down. We both wept.

On another occasion I asked her, "Aunt Charlotte, I think I know the reason why they don't like me. It's because I'm half-coloured, isn't it?"

She looked at me with her great big sad eyes and said, "You may be right about that, Quentin. You must know that in this big bad world that we live in, people have dreadful prejudices. That means, my darling, that they hate someone for no good reason, other than that they are different in some way – they may be a different colour, or from a different country or follow a different religion. Many of them don't care and will never change. Some of them are aware of their prejudices, but unable to come to terms with them. However, it is vital that you do not give in to these human weaknesses and react with negativity, the same negativity that people display towards you. In the end that makes you a much better person and in time you *will* triumph over the prejudices. If it is any comfort, you should know that people who hate, for whatever reason, are really the most unhappy people in the world. The old saying that love makes the world go round is actually true and you must believe in it, my darling."

My aunt got me into the habit of reading from a very early age. On all the occasions that she came to visit on her own, she would slip into my room after I had gone to bed, lie beside me with my head cradled in her arm, and read. Thanks to her induction and my own state of loneliness, I became a voracious reader by the time I was six. The library, which was stocked with at least a couple of thousand books, became my favourite haunt. Particularly on long, dark days, or grey, cold and rainy days (both of which were in plentiful supply in Scotland), I lost myself in the world of books and imagination in that library. Thanks to her I read a lot of the literary classics, and watched a lot of her favourite old classic movies like *Gone with the Wind*, *Ben-Hur* and *My Fair Lady*.

"Aunt Charlotte, what was my father really like?"

She shrank visibly and could not hold back her tears. I hated myself and said, "Oh, I am so sorry. I didn't mean to upset you. You must have been very fond of your brother."

She composed herself and said, "Quentin, you have no idea just how much I loved your father. The fact is he was unlike most people in our family. People considered him a maverick, which I suppose he was. What clearly matters is the fact that he was a fine human being. He absolutely charmed everybody he met. He was physically handsome and extremely brainy. I still really don't know the exact reason why, or what drove him to take off and abandon you."

"But he died in an accident, didn't he?"

She bit her lip and was at a loss for words for a couple of seconds and then replied, "That is what I meant by abandoned. As you yourself said to me some time ago, knowingly or not, he did abandon you."

"I hate them, my parents. They abandoned me, sold me into slavery!"

I remember the look of regret and horror on my dearest aunt's face. "No, Quentin, my darling, no. Hatred just begets more hatred. Yes, what they did was wrong; yes, they should have committed themselves to you over everything else, particularly your mother. There is no excuse and she is living through hell, I am sure. Just try and leave a little room for forgiveness, not because they deserve it, but because forgiveness is an act of greatness, which you are capable of, and an act of healing, which you richly deserve."

Those words of Aunt Charlotte's have stayed with me all my life and I truly believe that she was the one who got me through my wretched childhood. I did, however, refrain from saying to her that I hated most of my living family, in the form of her mother, her husband and her son! I daydreamed about being cast away on an island with Aunt Charlotte and Jimmy as the only survivors, the rest of the family having drowned.

For whatever reason, I stopped thinking about my natural mother. Perhaps she sold me back to the family for *my* own future and prosperity. Perhaps she sold me simply because the money was more important to her than me. In either case she was dead to me and I made up my mind never to think of her, far less try and make contact with her in the future. Another time I asked Aunt Charlotte about my mother; if there was anything known about her at all. Was she a beggar? Was she someone my father worked with? Was she someone from a good family?

"I can't really answer those questions, Quentin. All I would say is that she must have had some really compelling reason for giving up the care of her child."

"I don't care what the reasons were, I think she was a rotten human being!"

Aunt Charlotte looked at me long and hard, and I really could not quite interpret the expression on her face. "You know what, I think you are right. She was a rotten egg, and I hope she spends the rest of her life regretting her decision."

"I don't care, Aunt Charlotte, as long as I have you. You are better than the rest of the world put together."

Her eyes were swimming as she clasped me to her bosom.

Aunt Charlotte never missed a single birthday of mine; Jack and Uncle Charles never attended one. Those were the happiest days of my life, when I would be pampered with gifts, a cake and games which featured Jimmy. The one day when Gran would look the other way, literally. But with Aunt Charlotte around, did I care? The most memorable was my tenth. She was almost manic, in retrospect. After the most wonderful weekend, just as she was about to leave, she whispered, "Quentin, there are things I wish I could tell you, but not just yet. Just have faith, my darling."

☥

JIMMY CLAYTON

Jimmy goes back into the mists of time in my life. I suppose he was a kind of odd-job man, who lived somewhere in the village, outside our lofty estate. He turned up almost every day on some pretext or other, and ran errands for the lady of the house. His arrival was unquestionably the high point of my day. He was in mortal fear of my grandmother, but had nothing but sheer adoration for my aunt. And dare I say it, he was incredibly fond of me. In the late morning, once he had finished doing whatever he had to, he would beckon to me and I would trot after him to the edges of the estate. Playing catch, of course, was an eternal favourite and there was nothing better than running through the woods, either chasing or being chased by Jimmy. I never thought of his age, but looking back I guess he must have been somewhere between thirty and sixty! He had a craggy, lined face, very brown and very kind. There was a permanent crinkle of a smile, which only disappeared at the sight of my grandmother, or at the sight of Jack. For me it was a double disaster when Jack visited, as Jimmy would disappear very quickly.

On one such occasion, Jack said to me, "Hey, twit, was that the bloody gypsy I just saw slinking away? Why do you suck up to him, anyway? Birds of a feather flock together, I suppose," he sneered.

"Shut up, Jack. Jimmy is a great guy. You'll never make half the man that he is."

And of course, I paid the price right there and then. But that did not faze me, because I was prepared to risk anything to defend my Jimmy.

Periodically, at weekends, Jimmy would allow me to sneak out with him, and take me back to his little cottage in the middle of nowhere. This had to be absolutely secret, as my grandmother would almost certainly have dismissed him had she come to know. He grew flowers around the house and the tiny cottage itself was spick and span. He would brew his own brand of tea which was amazing to me. It was spicy, sweet and strong, with just a dash of milk allowed.

"This, laddie, is a very special blend from a faraway land. You'll never taste anything like this."

He was right. He never failed to spoil me with a cake or a couple of biscuits. Sometimes he would have a delicious stew containing venison, along with boiled potatoes. At the time it never struck me he was probably spending most of his hard-earned money on these treats for me.

One time, when Jack had come up to the manor and I was out playing with Jimmy, Jack decided to ambush me. He hid himself behind the trunk of a tree with a stout stick in his hand, intending to deliver it straight onto my back as I passed. Unfortunately for him, Jimmy had crept up behind him. He got Jack by the neck and believe it or not, lifted him off his feet. His strength was formidable and Jack was petrified. He pinned Jack against the tree and motioned me to silence. We stood there for probably a good thirty seconds. He then put Jack down and sent him away with the words, "Say nothin' to no one, or else." What a hero!

Like everybody else, Jimmy was terrified of the mistress, my grandmother. In her presence his only communication with me was a little nod and an occasional wink. However, he was my best friend and playmate when we were not being watched. I am still unable to put an age to him. On the occasions that I would ask him about it, he would look at me blankly and say, "I don't know, laddie, but I am very old." I remember breaking out into peals of laughter at this, that it was possible for a person not to know his age. So I made it a point to ask him that question at periodic intervals. He was certainly a lot older than Aunt Charlotte, but younger than my grandmother. I therefore arbitrarily decided that his birthday would be 1 May 1940. Jimmy was truly delighted at this and hugged me as if I had actually given him something valuable, and I said as much. His reply was touching, and has stayed with me all my life.

"What is of real value for me, laddie, is that you care."

Jimmy was fit as a fiddle and certainly able to outrun me when we raced each other. I loved getting 'lost' in the woods, playing hide and seek with him. When I was around twelve, there was one occasion when we talked about survival in the wild, and how the army and marine recruits had to train. I remember saying, "Jimmy, is it possible for people to hunt small animals with just a knife? After all, they are not given bows and arrows, are they?"

All of a sudden he grabbed something from his bag and the next thing I saw was a knife embedding itself with some force into a tree, some thirty feet away. Suitably impressed, I asked if I could try, and Jimmy reluctantly agreed. The real surprise was my innate ability to handle the knife-throw. After that, at least once a month we would have a competition and soon I was challenging Jimmy's ability successfully.

Jimmy lived alone, but for the love of his life, his dog, Lily. Physically, she was anything but a lily, a big, strong mongrel full of beans and boisterous at all times. I can now see the irony in her being named Lily! My grandmother, however, had strict rules about animals and she was not to be brought onto our estate, much to our regret. Sometimes he would take me to his house, under the pretext of taking me for a constitutional walk to the village. I could not wait to see Lily, who would come bounding towards us and then launch herself full pelt at me. The inevitable result was that I would be flat on my back and she would be standing over me licking my face. I cannot actually remember wanting to do anything more than being with Jimmy and Lily. Though my grandmother disapproved of my association with Jimmy, I think she realised that it was probably better to let me have a few hours away with him, than hang around the manor, lugubrious and miserable.

There were occasions when the three of us (Lily, not my grandmother) would go down to the rocky coastline using a circuitous path that would wind its way down, ending up a hundred feet below the estate. We would generally try and keep close to the foot of the cliff, even when the tide was out, for fear of being seen by my grandmother who often used to walk out to the edge of the cliff and stare out to sea. I must mention that *Gorm-Faire,* in my memory, was quite simply, vast. It was as wonderful physically as it was depressing psychologically.

⊕

IMPLOSION

I remember that day as vividly today – 14 March 1997.

"Quentin, you need to be strong. There has been an accident. The car in which Charlotte and Charles were in fell off a cliff."

My grandmother struggled to maintain her composure and even her formidable self control gave way as her eyes welled up. She even awkwardly put her arm around me. I could feel myself choking as I said, "Is Aunt Charlotte…?"

"Quentin, I am afraid Charlotte has left us. She is no more. You know how much she loved you. For her sake you need to be strong."

I was thirteen, and I had lost my aunt, my bulwark, my friend, guide and philosopher, my angel, my entire world. I have little recollection of the next couple of weeks, as I descended into a black mine of despair. That is perhaps the only spell that I can remember when my grandmother actually seemed to care about me. The details of the funeral are nebulous, and I think my mind had shut down. Jimmy, bless him, was a source of great support during this time and was allowed to drop in almost every day to spend time with me. He would frequently shake his head, saying, "Not right, laddie, just not right." I never knew what he meant, but by this time I had got used to his cryptic sayings. I expected Jack might come to live with us and that depressed me even more. Fortunately he elected to go and stay with Uncle Charles' parents.

One day I decided I could not stay indoors any longer, and on a sudden whim, set off for Jimmy's cottage. When I got to within a few feet of the door I suddenly heard him shouting. Shocked, I stopped in my tracks, unsure what to do. "No, no, no," Jimmy kept repeating, at full pelt. There was no sign of Lily, and I assumed she was indoors with him. I crept up to the door and listened.

"Charlotte, my baby Charlotte, how could you leave us?" Jimmy was shouting and sobbing at the same time. I could take it no more, and fled silently, my mind in turmoil. Jimmy in love with Aunt Charlotte? I knew he was extremely fond of her, indeed that they were very fond of each other. But actually in love? And did Aunt Charlotte reciprocate this? He must have been twenty years her senior by my estimation. I did not know whom to turn to. I knew that any mention of this to my grandmother would result in serious consequences for Jimmy. Not in a million years would I allow that to happen. I could not help making the comparison with the situation of

Heathcliff and Cathy in *Wuthering Heights*, though the differences were stark. Jimmy was as gentle and compassionate as Heathcliff was not.

So it came to pass that I was packed off to boarding school, and much to my dismay, so was Jack, to the same one. Fortunately he was a year below me, so at least I did not have the displeasure of interacting with him in my classes on a daily basis. In fact it was only then that I came to realise that he was actually younger than me. I was enormously relieved to find that we would be travelling separately to the school, Jack from his grandparental home, and I from Scotland.

⊕

HARRY RICHARD

"Hi, I'm Harry."

"Hello, I'm Quentin."

"Quentin? That's a rubbish name. Let me think… it ought to be Quincy, which sounds so much more classy."

I was a bit overwhelmed by this eccentric introduction, but Harry had stuck to his own version of my name ever since, at least privately, though in company he always referred to me as Quentin. I was thinking of a nickname for him, but he read my thoughts and broke in.

"Anyway, I got in first, so you can't try the same trick with me, at least not today."

"So you won't object if I get you another day?"

"Ha, you wish," said Harry, with mock contempt and a twinkle in his eye.

Harry Richard was born into a family of modest means. Though I had never met them, I knew that his father worked for the navy, but not as an officer, and his mother worked in a shop. People of that ilk could not usually afford the boarding in a private school that we were privileged to have. It was a mark of their overwhelming dedication to Harry that they spent every spare penny on him. Harry really was the nicest person you could ever meet. While he was full of mischief and pranks, there was absolutely no doubting his genuine goodness. His sense of humour was boundless and fearless. He could laugh at himself as much as anyone else could, always able to disarm his worst critics at a stroke.

I started off as one of the quiet and diffident children, but fortunately found the studies pretty easy-going. I had to make very little effort to keep up my grades and by the end of the first year I had levitated up to the top of the class. My lack of confidence in other areas left me vulnerable, particularly to Jack. As I may have mentioned earlier he was big for his age and physically very strong. But more than all of that he had this street-fighter mentality, which meant that he would often prevail over bigger boys. He certainly did prevail time and again over me. I did my very best to avoid him.

In retrospect I have to say that the boarding school was my salvation. Had I stayed in *Gorm-Faire*,

I am pretty sure I would have jumped off that cliff. The memory of Aunt Charlotte haunted me every night and on more than one occasion I would have to try and smother myself in my pillow to conceal my sobs. The only one who was privy to my secret and my weaknesses was Harry. He was so wise beyond his years, so mature and such a blessing to have as a friend. How I regret the way I treated him later.

I distinctly remember the day I had organised a surprise birthday party for Harry. As he entered an unlit room and turned on the light, the whole dormitory started out with the chant I had primed: "Hairy Dick, Hairy Dick, Hairy Dick." Without turning a hair, he jumped up on the nearest table, quietened us down by gesture, and said, "It's not hairy and I can prove it. Who wants a closer look?"

He pulled down his trousers to reveal his privates scantily covered by a pair of briefs. There was a collective groan as everyone backed off. Nobody could ever get the better of Harry when it came to words. I have ever since been an ardent admirer of his.

We remained steadfast friends right up until the time we left school. I was his private tutor and he was always hugely grateful to me for the extra tuition he received from me. It was ironic that during classes Harry would be playing the fool and distracting everyone, but then ended up frantically getting tutored as the exams approached. He was actually very clever, with a natural gift for computers and electronics, which had very little attraction for me.

Sadly, and to my great shame, I made little effort to keep in touch with him. He returned to his home town of Norwich, where he went to university. In the early days we used to communicate regularly by phone and I learnt that his father had had a stroke, and his mother was occupied full-time looking after him. So it fell to Harry to support the family, which he did admirably, as one would expect. He had to drop out of university and he joined an insurance company, at a rate of pay that would at best have been modest. None of that of course in any way subdued his ebullience and he remained the wonderful man he was. I was flying high in Cambridge at that time and my feet were slowly getting too big for my shoes. Even then we met at least once every couple of months, and I'd really look forward to visiting him for a weekend of easy conversation, dark humour and local ale.

Sadly, I moved on in the world and with the typical arrogance of a successful young man, full of himself, I began to neglect my dear friend. Having landed a well-paid job with a promising career in 2007, I was walking on air. Even now I cringe when I think about it. Despite Harry's attempts to keep up, I basically dropped contact. The next year I got an invitation to Harry's wedding, and was quite miffed by the fact that he had not bothered to call. Bloody cheek, in retrospect, given that I was the one who had basically terminated communications in favour of my social ascent. Even more to my shame, I did not make the effort to attend the wedding, electing instead to make a feeble excuse, sending him a card and a bouquet of flowers on the day. How I wish I could go back in time and make reparations.

Harry then moved on to work with the Driver & Vehicle Licensing Agency, while also freelancing as a computer techie. Two years later I got a card with the photo of a newborn, proudly introduced to the world as Quincy. That felt like a needle through the heart. I winced as I thought back to the time when we met each other for the first time on joining school. I thought to myself, why on earth would he name his precious new baby after a loser like me? It only made me feel worse. I then rationalised by telling myself that Quincy was the name he had always liked and would probably have named the child that regardless of whether he had met me or not. Whatever the case, I felt like a heel, and yet was paralysed by an egocentric state of mind, which would not allow me to make contact. Why could he not call me, I asked myself. And so on it went for a day or two until I took the easy way out, and sent him a congratulatory card with a voucher for £50 as my first and only gift to Quincy.

Harry never failed to send me a birthday card, but after I failed to reciprocate for three years running, he stopped too. Bang. It's a stupid bind and a chore, sending cards and all that, I said to myself. Over and over again. And so it was that Harry dropped out of my life. Of course, the crowning glory was that Harry did attend my wedding, in his usual irrepressible style, with no reference to my neglect of him. He was only apologetic that his wife could not come, as she was down with the lurgie. The nascent guilt was swiftly overpowered by my adoration of Harriett and I largely ignored him during the event. How lucky was I to have lost Jack from my life? How stupid was I to have ejected Harry?

✠

KEVIN McARDLE

I got friendly with Kevin about three months after joining the boarding school. Interestingly, we discovered that we had actually been classmates back in Scotland, seven years earlier. Kevin was a great friend, generally serious, nothing like Harry. When most people laughed at a stupid joke, he would seriously ponder it. His statements were incisive and usually correct. Where we were stupidly conforming, he would stand apart and analyse the situation. Sometimes I felt that the poor boy was missing out on the fun of being a child. But then, who was I to judge? I had had a lifetime of misery by that stage. I often felt that I was a combination of David Copperfield and Oliver Twist. Having said that, I was hugely heartened by the fact that all the Charles Dickens protagonists had managed to achieve very satisfactory endings, and in my childish fantasies I too imagined some happy ending, though at that stage I could not even begin to imagine what such an ending could be.

Kevin had something about him that was hard to define, a certain *je ne sais quoi*. He was a dark horse, and one could never fathom his thoughts, in contrast to Harry. But nobody could consider him dull by any stretch of the imagination. He had some truly distinctive characteristics. He adored westerns, which he had watched as a child, with his father. He had brought with him a toy gun, which he would stick inside his belt and spend time practising the draw. He claimed he was the fastest draw in the land, and he was probably right! The other gift he had was in acting and doing impressions, which propelled him into the limelight in the school's performing arts. The third unusual thing about him was his strong streak of socialism. He quite simply could not accept that people were allowed to have different levels of wealth and possessions. When he castigated me for my elite status, I disabused him very quickly, pointing out that everything would go to the official heir, Jack.

"You watch me, Quentin, I'll strip your filthy rich cousin of all his wealth and we'll redistribute it!"

Kevin, after school, went back to his native Scotland, and attended the University of Dundee. We used to speak once a month or so, but never did meet up, and after a couple of years we lost touch. My last contact with him was when he came for my wedding, at which time he was working for a charity. He was still single at the time, and was a focal point for the few single women at the wedding. Kevin had matured into a very handsome young man, two inches taller than me, with ginger hair and blue-grey eyes, which bore deep into your soul. He also let slip that he had pursued his childhood flair and had become a crack-shot with the hand gun. Harriett was most impressed! I promised him I would keep in touch, but never did. Shame on me.

⊕

JACK HILLIER

Jack loomed larger than life in my formative years. He was christened John, and was officially John Hillier. Ever since he was taunted in primary school as 'little Johnny,' Jack had learned to detest that name. Nobody, but nobody, called him Johnny and got away with it. He was Jack, that is what he expected to be called and he would have it no other way. Like all children, my earliest feelings were one of awe and admiration for this brother, who I thought of as being the same age as me. The fact that he was generous in doling out regular blows and kicks never seemed to make a dent on that. Oh, don't get me wrong, I was frightened of him, but it was that inexplicable mixture of fear and thrill that one feels when being attacked by a predator! He used to visit us at the manor once every few weeks, usually with his wonderful mother. We played the usual games, until the inevitable confrontation. My only saving grace was my fleet-footed ability to outrun him. So this then led to him waiting to ambush me and soon it came to the point when, if I did not have him in my field of vision, I would be treading warily and keeping a sharp lookout. Of course, there was no point complaining as my grandmother was totally besotted by Jack, and had little time for me. This was more than compensated for by Jack's mother, whose seraphic presence made everything tolerable.

I still remember one time when Jack jumped me from behind and pushed me down a short flight of steps, resulting in me cutting my forehead. Jack realised he had gone too far, and said to me, with his teeth clenched in his usual threatening way, "You better not say anything to anyone, dummy, or else it'll be much worse the next time."

Unfortunately for him, his mother had stepped around just in time to watch the 'accident'. I glanced at her and sensing this, Jack turned around and realised he had been caught in the act. Aunt Charlotte said nothing, but I still remember the flash of anger in her eyes and her jaws clenched in a manner not dissimilar to that of Jack's. She hurried down the steps, and realising that he was in trouble, Jack tried to make a run for it. Alas, he was too late and she caught him by the scruff, turned him around and delivered a resounding slap on his face. I can still hear it like a pistol shot! Jack fell in a heap next to me, with a look of complete shock, and could not stop the tears springing from his eyes. She said, "And if I ever see you doing that again, it will be a lot worse." I worshipped the ground she walked on.

Those early days I discounted our skirmishes as the kind of thing that happens between brothers, albeit cousins. It was only much later that I realised that Jack had a real loathing for me. This became pretty obvious once we were in boarding school, even though he was in the year below me. Whenever he got the chance he would certainly have a go at me, but by then I had become wise enough to devise various means of avoiding him. Furthermore, he had to establish himself as the alpha male of his own year and wouldn't receive too much credit for picking up a fight with an older 'brother'. I was considered a fairly mild and wimpish sort of a boy in my own year and had enough trouble with the macho classmates. My best friends, Harry and Kevin, helped to pad my defence sufficiently to deter troublemakers. Kevin in particular seemed to have no fear, and his demeanour had the mysterious quality of dissuading would-be assailants, including Jack. When I commented on it, Kevin simply replied, "That, my lad, is because they can see the killer instinct in my eyes." Harry produced a fake fart and all three of us laughed.

Another interesting episode was when one of my rowdier classmates lost his temper with me over something stupid and wrestled me to the ground and was in the process of delivering punches to my head, which I was avoiding with my head tucked in, and arms around. Much to my surprise and delight, he was dragged off me by Jack, who then proceeded to thrash the boy until he fled. I couldn't believe what was going on, until Jack turned and said to me, "Don't think I did this to help you, creep. I just felt like a punch-up. Why the fuck don't you ever defend yourself?" With a contemptuous snarl, he stomped off.

The other thing which came to my aid as I progressed, was my rather unexpected sporting prowess. Much to everyone's surprise, I became a bit of a star at cricket, tennis and swimming. Despite his size and brute strength, Jack was mediocre, at best, at these sports. He excelled in what one might have expected – bodybuilding and boxing. My rapid progress in the sports arena brought with it a certain *cachet*, which more than made up for my previous status of a woose. Even Jack had to be careful not to overstep, for fear of facing the wrath of the teachers if they found out. So his assaults on me were relatively infrequent and short-lived, ranging from a rap of his knuckles on the back of my head, to a friendly kick on my backside and the occasional hard shove. Even then I don't think I actually bore him any serious ill will, telling myself that he just could not help being a bully. I have no idea why I was making excuses for him, but there was something in me that still impelled me to accept him as a brother (as if that was the standard behaviour to be expected of any brother). I wonder if subconsciously I was so desperate to have a family, that I was accepting of Jack, whatever the circumstances.

By the time I was sixteen I really had shot up and was actually an inch taller than Jack. Where I was lean and wiry, he was built like a bull. In a scrap I wouldn't stand a chance, and we both knew it. By then of course it was much too late for him to engage in any physical rough stuff, though on more than one occasion I could see it in his eyes that he would like nothing better than to land a punch on my jaw. So he made up for it with jibes and verbal insults, which I ignored for the most part.

Harry said to me once, "You really don't have to take this bullshit, Quincy. Give it back to him, there is nothing he can do about it. The more you take it, the more he is going to dump on you."

"Oh, don't worry, Harry, all this is just fraternal messing around. I am sure in the long run we'll end up quite close to each other."

The school had a tradition of having a prefect, and a deputy from the top year, along with a junior prefect from the year below. The junior prefect would usually end up as one of the two prefects in his final year. Jack had always assumed that he was going to make prefect in his final year. Much to his fury, and not a little due to the reputation he had built up over the years, he was passed over for junior prefect, to be superseded by a much more rounded and popular young man by the name of Christopher Whitlow. Christopher was one of those boys who had an air of confident calm as he went about his life, excelling in academics, but not particularly sporty. Jack, on the other hand, was highly intelligent, probably more so than Christopher, but would never buckle down to do the hard work it required to excel academically. With pretty minimal effort, he always managed to produce surprisingly good results, but was just not there at Christopher's level. Though he did have a faithful band of followers, it was pretty clear to everyone, including the teachers, that Christopher was the obvious leader. To cap it all I got appointed as the deputy prefect, which went down like a lead balloon with Jack. When I commiserated with him on his failure to land the junior post, he growled and the only word he could find to say was 'bollocks'. On the next couple of occasions when I attempted to say anything to him, he would just walk away, leaving me a bit miffed.

I used to wonder what the source of his antipathy was, because it clearly exceeded all 'physiological' rivalry between siblings, cousins or even friends. The one thing that always stayed with me was the kindness and love shown by his mother to me, and I saw little of that towards him. I became convinced that his hatred was really an expression of this jealousy, carried to an extreme.

Jack and I had some similarities, at least superficially. For a start, we were both tall and well built. We were both intelligent in different sorts of ways, though I can scarcely believe now that I could have been intelligent at any time. On the other hand, our contrasts comprised a much longer list – his nose was sharper and more delicate than mine. He was broader and much more muscular, where I was lean and wiry. Although he was intelligent, he was feckless and lazy. I used to work reasonably hard and generally managed good grades and a high rank in the class, much to his annoyance. I was dead straight and did not believe in cutting corners or breaking rules, whereas he was exactly the opposite. I hated bullying and always took the side of the underdog, of which I was one myself, of course. He was a born bully, and cunning in the way he went about it. I never cheated or stole, whereas he was at it all the time. Above all, there was the colour – his milky whiteness and my honey-tinged pallor (which often misled people into thinking I was Spanish or Italian).

Jack's misdemeanours were carried out with such calculation and design that he rarely, if ever, got caught out. He had started smoking by the time he was ten and alcohol soon followed. Needless to say he was a smash hit with the girls. Rumour had it he was having it off with girls of sixteen-plus when he was barely thirteen. He had a sort of fatal charm which drew the young and innocent to him. Many a poor trusting soul gave herself to him, only to find that they were unwelcome after a short spell of passion. Again, he managed these unions and separations with such consummate skill that he got away without any overt row or scandal – he certainly never got anyone pregnant, to the best of my knowledge.

I still remember the day the results came out – it was the last week of school before the summer break. I had achieved A's in almost every subject and had come out in third position in the entire year of 120 students. Jack came twenty-third in his year. He was in a particularly evil state of mind that day. I came out of the class at the end of the day with Harry and Kevin. When the three of us were together there was safety in numbers and though we were no match for Jack and his three sidekicks, at least we could ward them off long enough for someone to intervene. Their frustration was pretty obvious when they saw the three of us coming out. I was expecting the usual glare, sneer and insulting remark from my cousin, but he turned his face away and muttered something to his mates. I accompanied Harry and Kevin to the gates and we chatted for about ten minutes, at which point Jack and friends sauntered up from behind us.

"Well, well, if it ain't the clever clogs, with the extra set of brains in his arse."

I turned around and looked, and was struck by the particularly malevolent look on Jack's face. Normally, I would just ignore him, or block out the insult and defuse the situation and make a quick getaway. To my own amazement I found myself saying, "Well, well, if it ain't little Johnny, the boy with the extra arse in place of his brain."

Kevin and Harry erupted in laughter, and looked at me with undisguised admiration. Well, that was that, it was the four seasoned thugs against the three of us. Fortunately for us a passing teacher intervened and broke it up, but not until we had sustained some beating. I must confess the pain was not a match for the pleasure and pride that we felt in doing what we had just done.

Around the time I graduated from school, Jack 'invited' me to a round of boxing, which I politely declined. However hard he tried he could not engage me in any kind of a combat, so it ended with his usual insults.

"Have you no balls at all, you creep? Is there nothing at all that you dare risk in life?"

His sidekicks sniggered, while Kevin and Harry glowered beside me.

I said, "Listen, weasel, anyone who knows anything knows that I am no match for you physically. Even your dumb sidekicks know that you could not begin to match me for brains. So why don't you cut the crap and piss off to your sleazy world! I don't have to do anything that I don't want to!"

The look on his face was ugly, but he knew he could do nothing at that moment, when students were bustling all around, as well as some teachers.

"Born yellow, living yellow, forever yellow." He spat the words in complete contempt and stormed off.

I still remember his final words when our paths crossed for the very last time, when I was leaving my room, on my way to the train station – "I'll get you, you fucking creep. You think you can hide behind your brains, but you'll see, you're no match for me either way. I'll get you if it's the last thing I do." His eyes burned into mine, malevolence personified, and without any warning his clenched fist slammed into my solar plexus.

It gave me considerable satisfaction to learn that his attempts to enrol in Oxbridge had failed. My grandmother, when I saw her during one of my infrequent visits, was not keen to talk about Jack for reasons I couldn't fathom. Much later, I heard on the grapevine that he had gone to Bristol, and then into business, having predictably decided that higher education was only for idiots. I believe he went to the US for a couple of years. I also heard that he was involved in a number of shady deals, which came as no surprise. By the time we were thirty, Jack was well established in the East End of London with his fingers in a few dirty pies and I was told that he had become someone either revered or dreaded, depending on which side of the divide you were on. I wanted to know nothing about Jack and prayed I would never ever meet him in the flesh.

And then this letter arrived from Jack, a month ago, which literally bowled me over.

☥

Dear Quentin,

This might come as a bit of shock to the system! Please don't panic, or tear this up, just bear with me. Ever since Gran's death I have been through a low. Maybe I've been re-evaluating my life and re-setting priorities. The point is, I would like to put our differences behind and refresh our non-existent relationship. Let me hasten to add, I am not about to offer you a share of the inheritance, or a bribe of any sort. I simply wish to establish an amicable relationship.

If you are amenable to this, why don't you give me a call on the number appended below? If it goes to voicemail, just leave me a message and I'll get back to you. I do travel regularly on business to the Pacific region, and may not always be immediately available.

I really do look forward to hearing from you.

Sincerely yours,

Jack

PS. How about a boozy mates' long weekend in France, where we can have a bit of bachelor-type fun and try bonding!

⌖

That really shook me and I didn't now whether to be pleased (at his transformation) or furious (that he thought he could just coolly walk back into my life). Most of all, I was very suspicious of his motives. What could he hope to gain? I was almost broke, in every sense. A weekend with Jack sounded as enticing as a cosy dinner with a black mamba.

THE DARK AGES

The years between graduation and meeting Harriett represent a period of nebulous degeneration. I was in this make-believe world of high living, partying life away, secure in the knowledge that my career was on a stratospheric trajectory. I was dismissive of my dearest friends, Harry and Kevin, as well as a couple of good mates from Cambridge. I had even developed a certain aversion to Jimmy, dear Jimmy, who was everything a lonely child could have wished for. Ever since the day I heard him anguished, after Aunt Charlotte's death, I had a kind of cringing revulsion after the fact that they might have had a history. My visits to Scotland became less frequent, and each time I could see the reproach in Jimmy's eyes, which only served to unleash my sense of guilt. I was living the 'good life', with no eye on the direction of travel. When Harriett crashed into my life, I was replete with my own sense of importance and faith in my infallibility.

LOVE, MARRIAGE AND BEREAVEMENT

I met Harriett in April 2014, in circumstances I've already outlined. She was physically striking, just under six feet in height, with a beautiful rounded face, a small nose and liquid brown eyes. Her auburn hair was always cropped short. She was a complete extrovert, and demanded attention. I was captivated, infatuated! The second time we met was in a pub. Our eyes met in mutual recognition, and my nod was reciprocated with a devastating smile.

"Hello, handsome stranger!"

"Hello, gorgeous lady!"

That was a really exciting evening, at the end of which we fixed our first date three days later. We went out twice a week for the first few weeks, until we'd got around to kissing goodnight, kisses that were getting steadily more passionate.

"Quentin, stop being such a gentleman and a bore! Come on up."

It took no effort at all for her to seduce me within a couple of weeks, and I was enslaved! She soon moved in with me, and I thought I had finally 'arrived'. I had precious few real friends at this time, just some superficial acquaintances with whom I enjoyed going out. Harry and Kevin were simply not there in my mind. Soon, Harriett made sure I wouldn't fraternise with anyone at all, and demanded my total attention, which I gladly gave. When I proposed, she graciously accepted, reminding me that I was a very lucky man indeed.

I have already mentioned my wedding. I thought it went splendidly. Harriett charmed everyone into submission! My friends, old and new, were absolute sports. Despite my neglect of them, Harry and Kevin were just brilliant. But the one who gave me most pleasure was Jimmy! He turned up in a suit, with a bow-tie and a fashionably grizzled beard. His eyes were full of life and mischief, and as my best man, he insisted on kissing the bride. I sensed an immediate discord between him and Harriett, a mark of his unfailing prescience.

The most amazing postscript to that wedding was a thick envelope which landed on my doorstep. It was a card from my grandmother, inside which was a cheque for £25,000 and a letter.

⊕

17 January 2015
Dear Quentin,

My heartfelt congratulations on the occasion of your wedding. My absence will have neither surprised, nor upset you. I am afraid I would have felt out of place and out of sorts, and probably cramped your style, such as it is.

Please accept this small gift as a token of my affection, and convey my best wishes to your bride. I wish you both a long and blissful married life.

I have not been the best of grandmothers, but perhaps I am finally making amends. Please forgive me, and knowing you, I know you will, though I am entirely undeserving of such an act. In my fading years, I suddenly long for the sound of chatter, for the sound of a child's laughter.

Sincerely yours,
Winifred Grayling

☦

I was dazed, and more than a little touched. I thought of Aunt Charlotte and could not stop my eyes filling up, imagining how wonderful it would have been to have her to felicitate us. I wanted to travel north right away and proudly introduce my ravishing new wife to my grandmother, but Harriett was having none of it. "Quentin, stop being such a wet rag. The old woman's given you nothing all your life, and you fall for the first little crumb she throws at you. No, it's time for you to play hard to get. And don't ever forget that you are getting half the inheritance by right." I did not dare tell her that I was expecting to get nothing, whatever my rights.

Harriett's penchant for celebration was peerless. On New Year's Eve of 2015/16 she insisted I take her to an expensive venue at a fancy London hotel. She got thoroughly drunk and proceeded to demonstrate the famous cancan, followed by a striptease and finally went mental, hurling abuse at the staff, who were trying to bring her under control. It was so traumatic that I swore never to accompany her again. We argued about it, and it was one of those rare occasions when I stood my ground. Harriett simply spat in my face and said she would find someone else to take her. And she did. The next year she said she was going with a couple of girls she had met at her health club, but in retrospect I suspect she had gone with her boyfriend.

'Under your very nose!' – I remembered her parting words. What did she mean by that? One of my work colleagues? She had flirted overtly with a few of them at our biannual work parties. There were two of them who were on the hunt; Ethan James, who was single, and John Vickers, who was married-but-game-for-more. I knew they were still with my erstwhile employer, the latter my line manager, who had so kindly let me go. Damn! Could it really be that he did the dirty on me because of his liaison with Harriett? But Harriett had mentioned a Monty – who could that be? I cursed them all and gave up.

By the end of 2017 I should have given up on Harriett, but some stupid voice in my head persuaded me to persevere. Her physical appearance just had this effect on me. I could not get myself to give up on her. Over the next year our relationship deteriorated steadily. Despite being convinced of her infidelity, I could not get myself to confront her, basically because I didn't want it confirmed. The humiliation that would follow…

My grandmother had, over the years, mellowed, and if she wasn't actually warm, at least she was no longer frosty. Harriett accompanied me just once to *Gorm-Faire*, and it was an unqualified disaster. The two women developed an instantaneous and mutual disdain!

"Ah, Harriett, it's so nice to meet you finally."

"Thanks, Lady Grayling, likewise. You are just as Quentin described. Forbidding, I believe, was the word he used!" Harriett faked a laugh to make it sound like a joke.

Gran responded with a tight-lipped smile, and a sharp glance directed at me. Over dinner, conversation moved to other things, including careers.

"I'm a hardcore feminist, you know. I believe we women should support each other and stand eye to eye with men, don't you?" Gran looked entirely sceptical.

"What exactly do you anticipate doing with your life in the long run, Harriett?"

"I can put my hand to just anything, actually, even if I say so myself. Let me assure you, I can very easily slip into the role of the lady of the manor, which I expect I would have to in due course, Quentin being your eldest heir, and all!"

I could scarcely believe my ears, and certainly did not dare to venture a glance at Gran.

"You seem to be taking things for granted, my dear. Are you sure you'll ever be up to it?" It was withering contempt.

Harriett realised she had met her match, and went into a sulk.

I tried to visit Gran twice a year, though after the first visit Harriett declined to accompany me. I only stayed one or two days, which was hard enough. There were several occasions when I got the feeling there was something she left unsaid. On occasions when I asked about Jack, all I got was a vague answer, and clearly she didn't have an appetite for it.

It was the summer of 2018 when I last saw Gran and Jimmy. It was a routine visit, by myself. She seemed withdrawn and I was sure she was depressed. When I hesitantly suggested that she might take something to help her mood, she brushed it aside, saying, "My mood is what I have earned over the years, Quentin. Pills aren't going to fix it."

I visited Jimmy, who was delighted as always to see me. He caught me in a bear hug, and his spirits soared further when I handed him a bottle of single malt, which I always brought for him. We spent a couple of hours catching up and reminiscing. I was careful not to mention Aunt Charlotte, as that always brought him to tears. He asked me about Harriett, and I tried to be diplomatic and noncommittal, but there was no hiding from Jimmy.

"Listen, laddie, sounds like that was not your best decision in life."

"I know, Jimmy, but I have to keep trying to make a go of it."

He shook his head and said, "Sometimes you have to cut out the weeds. The same goes for Jack."

When it came to my grandmother, Jimmy was surprisingly conciliatory. "She ain't what she used to be, laddie. She does have a heart buried under all that shit. I keep an eye on her, a'righ'. I cannae forget that she's what's paid to keep me alive all them years. I don't know how much longer she's got. If she goes, I ain't got nothin' to keep me here, laddie. Not if that Jack comes back, lording it."

I looked at his wonderfully kind, sad, ugly, lined face and felt a physical pain when I thought to myself, *"And how much longer have you got, Jimmy?"*

The new year of 2019 dawned dull and dreary, with not much to look forward to. I barely saw Harriett for the first few days, but one day she suddenly turned amorous and insisted that we head off for an impromptu holiday to Tenerife. She cracked on with the bookings and we left a couple of days later. Rather annoyingly, I lost my mobile phone, or at any rate couldn't find it when we landed in Tenerife. Harriett was dismissive, saying it was of no importance, and I too decided I could well do without the damned contraption for a week – particularly as I was hoping to have an intensely romantic week! My hopes were short-lived, as Harriett soon returned to form, though she was at least civil during that week. I enjoyed time on my own, travelling around the island, while Harriett worked on her physical aspects, lying around by the poolside. I even wondered if she was meeting secretly with her boyfriend, who could have travelled over. Maybe even on the same flight!

When we got back home I found my phone lying in the kitchen, where I must have left it on the morning we departed. I turned it on to find two missed messages from Jack. That came as an ominous surprise. It was only then that I got news of Gran's demise, just the day after we had left, and the funeral four days later, which I had obviously missed. I felt no real sadness, but felt guilty because I was not sad, and annoyed that I felt guilty. I wished I had at least been present for her funeral. I realised that I had not seen Jack in many years, and did not relish the prospect of even talking to him. I called the number, which rang for a good thirty seconds, and just as I was about to give up, Jack came on the line, sounding his usual gruff self. His voice had matured to a deeper tone, and perhaps his accent was more polished.

"Quentin, where the fuck have you been hiding? I know you hated the old woman, but at least you could have made an attempt to attend the funeral. After all, she did bring you up in some way."

I apologised, explaining the reason, and then asked him how Gran had died.

"Officially an accident. She was found at the base of the cliff, on the rocks, broken to pieces. My own suspicion is that she had decided she had had enough. She has been depressed for a long time, as you might have noticed yourself."

I did not reply, but concurred with Jack's thoughts. Gran had become increasingly withdrawn. I felt a sudden surge of pity for the lonely and sad woman, living in that remote estate, with no human company.

Jack continued, "I did try to contact you, Quentin, and sent you the messages. Anyway, that's water under the bridge. As of now I am the sole proprietor and you need to understand that. I don't want any unpleasant contests." Some things never change.

"Don't worry, Jack, I have no interest in any of it."

"However, I'm prepared to consider making a one-off settlement of, say, £50,000."

Was I surprised? No, I was shocked!

"Awfully generous of you, but no thanks. I'll manage."

☦

Jimmy, my guardian angel, hanged himself on 2 March 2019. It brought back vivid memories of our last time together, when he hinted that he would have nothing to keep him going after Gran's death. I did make it to his funeral, on my own, as Harriett wasn't the least bit inclined.

I was pleasantly surprised to see some forty to fifty people congregated for the service. He had been much more popular than I had realised. Everyone had nothing but praise for him. I did the eulogy and at the end of it I felt totally alone and wretched. I cannot begin to describe the effect this had on me.

I became a zombie for the next few weeks, much to Harriett's amusement. All of a sudden I realised that Harriett, for whatever she was worth, was the only person in my sad life. I considered more than once, re-establishing contact with Harry and Kevin, but a combination of shame and pride got in the way. I kept telling myself that in time Harriett would see the error of her ways, leave her boyfriend and return to me. Ha!

PRELUDE 1

THE TALE OF THE REBELLIOUS PRODIGY

The scamp was turning out to be quite something unexpected. Out in the streets as far as he could, playing games with his innumerable friends, he was never to be found. He attended school under sufferance, and regularly failed his exams, to the despair of his parents, who lived in a modest little house. He was, however, the main event amongst his mates. His greatest ally was his maternal grandfather, who often egged him on, and beamed with pride at his antics and limitless ability to get up to mischief. All that was until the grandfather died, when the boy was ten.

The lad never fully recovered from the bereavement, and underwent a change, which came as a mixed blessing for the parents. They welcomed his more disciplined approach to school and studies, but were seriously concerned about what they perceived as a loss of his indomitable spirit. They held education above all in life, but equally realised that the boy had the kind of fearless spirit which would be invaluable in succeeding in life. They wanted him to shine, but shine brightly, like a shooting star.

They need not have worried. The boy turned out to be as clever as anyone could have hoped, and graduated from school a year ahead of his peers. The trend continued when he entered college, opting to study history, geography and philosophy for his BA, much to the dismay of his father who had set his heart on his son taking up sciences and ending up as a doctor or an engineer – the only two professions which really counted.

Any regret was short-lived, as the young man exhibited extraordinary prowess at everything he touched. It was then that the extraordinary offer arrived. He had achieved a scholarship to study in Cambridge. The father was delirious with pride, the mother terrified of losing her son.

Parting was all sorrow, nothing sweet. The entire neighbourhood was at the airport, from where he would fly first to Bombay, and then onwards to London. The young man kept up his external calm as far as he could. His father's last words were, "God bless you, my son. May He grant you eternal success and a long life. I know you will make us proud!"

His mother, barely able to speak, said, "How will I live without my precious son? Please come back safe, my child. And you won't forget your old mother, will you, Avi?"

That's when he broke down, unable to get out his words.

4

THE BIG BAD APPLE

*When all seems lost, all seems lifeless, all seems
pointless, something inexplicable supervenes. Call
it fate, call it destiny, it opens out a new world. Of
friends, of enemies, of opportunities.*

By the time we landed in New York I was exhausted
and the only factor that was keeping me up was the
realisation that I had no clue about what I was going
to do. I knew I had enough in the bank to sustain me
for a few months and that was enough to satisfy me
for the moment. The official at the immigration was
a pain.

"What's your business in New York?"

"None."

"Why exactly are you here?"

"No particular reason, it seemed like a good idea."

The man behind the counter was now getting distinctly annoyed and I realised I was asking for trouble.

"How long are you planning to stay in the US, and what are your means of support?"

"I haven't quite decided yet, but I was intending to travel across the country ad-lib. I'll just get into town and find myself a place to stay. As for means of support, I have my credit card."

The man looked unconvinced and unhappy, but did not know what he could do about it. He stamped my passport with a grunt and nodded me on. My ageing suitcase had arrived by the time I got to the carousel.

I got out into the open and was looking around to see where I could pick up a taxi, when I was jostled rather rudely and felt a hard item poking into my ribs on the right side. A terse voice said, "Don't make any stupid moves and just walk."

He had his left hand on my left shoulder and directed me towards a car waiting at the kerbside. It was a dark blue sedan (a Chevrolet when I got closer) and there was a man sitting in the driver's seat. As the initial shock wore off I suddenly realised that there was no reason why I would have to follow this goon's instructions and get abducted. I stopped to turn and look at the man, who was about my height and the most obvious thing about his face was his bulbous nose, remarkably redolent of a large garlic.

"Get in, you sonofabitch."

Someone with my voice replied, "Get stuffed and shoot me if you dare, with all these witnesses around."

It was a combination of bluff and bravado, but I really could not see what anybody could gain by shooting me there and then. I could feel his grip tightening on my shoulder and I reacted with a sudden extension of my right shoulder, which delivered my elbow with some force into his solar plexus. I then walked swiftly towards the kerb away from the Chev, where a taxicab had just pulled in around twenty yards away. It suddenly struck me that any second a bullet could plant itself into my back, or worse, my skull. I held my breath, but nothing happened and I made it safely to the taxi, and got in.

The driver was startled by my entry. "Hey, man, you seem to be in a hurry!"

"Yes, my friend, I am in a bit of a hurry. I'm trying to escape some unwanted attention. So, can we make a quick getaway, and you can drop me off at any motel of your choice, but one that is in a reasonably well-populated area?"

Even as I was speaking, the man stepped on it and accelerated away. "You got it. There is one about eight miles from here. A friend of mine runs it and charges eighty bucks a night, but for me he'll drop it to seventy." I thanked him.

"By the way, my name is Mitch. You sound British. Travellin' light?"

I was not in the mood for conversation, but knew that I had to be civil and sociable. Besides, this Mitch seemed extremely affable to say the least.

"Yup. I left London in a bit of a hurry and couldn't be bothered with trivial matters like decent luggage."

Mitch came out with a throaty laugh, which was infectious. "I've seen all sorts, man, in my twenty years of cabbying. On the run from someone?"

"I suppose you could say that; I'm actually running away from a very scary woman."

Mitch's guffaw was truly infectious and I joined him.

It struck me that the would-be abductors could still be on my tail. The only explanation I could think of was that they saw me as a potential target for a ransom. Really? The poor sods would have truly landed a damp squib if that was the case! Or, could this have been related to the earlier car incident last night? Surely not!

"Hey, Mitch, is there by any chance a dark blue Chevrolet following us?"

"Yup, and I was just thinking that it may have something to do with you, the way you jumped into my cab."

"So, I'm going to ask if you could try and shake them off. Sorry to ask this of you, but I am prepared to double your fare."

Far from protest, there was real excitement in Mitch's voice. "Oh man, I haven't done this in years.

It will be my pleasure to shake these assholes off your tail!"

Mitch continued to drive sedately for the next ten minutes or so. As we approached a set of traffic lights which were turning red, Mitch suddenly accelerated at full pelt, with a scream of tyres, and swerved left. I turned around and felt a wave of relief when I saw that the blue Chevrolet was stuck behind another car which had stopped at the red light. "Nice work, Mitch. So how long to get to this motel of yours?"

"Guess what, man? I got a proposition for you. Wanna try staying at Motel Mitch? Things are tight for us, so we try and rent out a room as and when we can. It's clean, it's got an attached bathroom and breakfast is included. I'll do it for sixty bucks a night. As long as you don't mind sharing the living space with me and my family."

I took less than a second to make my decision. "I'll take it, Mitch. By the way, I'm Quentin Grayling, recently unemployed, recently separated and recently assaulted."

Another one of Mitch's booming laughs.

"Mitch Cassidy, at your service, sir!"

He drove expertly, weaving between lanes and using several shortcuts to finally get to his home.

Mitch fished out his mobile phone and punched a series of numbers. "Hey, darlin', guess what? I got us a paying guest. We'll be up in five. Can you check the spare room is presentable? Oh, and make sure the kids are on their best behaviour. Our guest is an English lord!"

Mitch's laughter boomed, slightly to my embarrassment. When he had locked the car, I extended my hand, saying, "Thanks, Mitch, I really appreciate this."

He grasped my hand in a firm grip. He was a bit shorter than myself, around six foot, I reckoned. The corners of his mouth were slightly upturned, giving him a permanently cheerful expression. I was quite excited by the recent turn of events, and the prospect of living in with an African-American family. Mitch opened the door to his apartment and ushered me in. Hands outstretched, there stood his wife who greeted me warmly.

"I'm Matilda. Welcome to our little home."

"I am Quentin. A real pleasure to meet you, Matilda, and thank you for taking me on board."

"And those two there, are our twin children, Nelson and Toni – Toni with an i."

The two were huddling in a large armchair, looking at me with unconcealed interest.

"Are you really an English lord?" exclaimed the girl.

"I am nothing of the sort. I think your dad was having a bit of fun."

"You speak just like the people who appear on the English TV programmes," said the boy.

"I'm afraid so. Sorry to disappoint!"

Mitch intervened. "All right, kids, that's enough for now."

I said, "Nice choice of names. Any significance?"

Mitch replied. "Actually, yes. 1993 was the year Matilda and I got married. It was also a unique year for black people the world over – two of them received the Nobel Prize. The twins arrived much later, when we had almost given up hope. So, when it came to the choice of names, we picked those two."

"Nelson is after Mandela, and I presume Toni is after Morrison?"

Matilda exclaimed, "Wow, I'm impressed that you know of Toni Morrison. Why, even most white Americans don't know who she is."

"Hey, take it easy, Matilda. We don't want to scare off Quentin before he's had a chance to look around. But it's true that over here we have an issue with no recognition of achievements by black Americans."

"No worries, Mitch. I know a little something of the social injustices, not just here, but the world over."

"Right, Quentin, I am going to show you to your room, and give you a couple of hours to settle in and rest. And then I'll knock on your door and we can have an early dinner."

"Mitch, that is extremely generous of you, but after all the excitement of the day's events, all I really want to do is crash and burn."

Almost in unison the twins cried, "Crash and burn, crash and burn, like the phoenix in *Harry Potter*?"

"Ha ha, yes indeed."

Mitch led me to the room, which was probably fifteen feet square, with a comfortable-looking double bed and a built-in wardrobe. A door led into a small, attached bathroom, which, however, was perfectly adequate, with a shower cubicle. I realised that in all the excitement I had not turned my phone on. After a moment's reflection, I decided to keep it that way. I took a quick shower and keeping to my word, 'crashed and burned'.

☧

EXPLORING THE BIG APPLE

I spent the next two days wandering the streets of New York City. It was aimless, tiring and most enjoyable! I felt liberated and almost intoxicated by the atmosphere. New York was very much what I had expected of it. No surprises, given the amount of publicity that the city enjoys, a combination of fame and notoriety. There was a terrific energy pulsating everywhere, with virtually everybody appearing to be on a mission that their lives depended on. Everything was intense. The people were manic, as I had imagined Americans to be, but by and large very friendly. The grid pattern of the streets made it relatively easy to find one's bearings in Manhattan. There were, of course, considerable similarities with London. I guess all the megacities of the world would have a number of things in common.

I visited the iconic site where once the Twin Towers stood and which was now occupied by the New World Trade Centre. I loved the variety of food that was to be had, and much as I frowned on fast foods back in England, in this setting I could not deny myself the pleasure of consuming the classic New York street food, which included hamburgers, hot dogs, bagels, etc. I developed a particular weakness for the 'chili dog'. I travelled on the bus, the subway, and by taxi, all for the experience. I wandered through Greenwich Village, did the boat trip across to Liberty Island and did the statue. I visited the famous stores, and bought myself some clothes. Central Park was a bit disappointing; it was not quite as green and picturesque as I had imagined, although without it, New York would have been considerably diminished. I contemplated seeing a show, but decided against it as I just was not in the mood. I simply enjoyed being an absolute nobody, lost in a great big alien city. By the third day I had managed to forget everything that had happened since I left home, and it all seemed like a distant dream.

I would return to Mitch's quite late, by which time the kids would be in bed. I would then relate my activities for the day, providing considerable amusement to Mitch and Matilda. Inevitably the talk came around to my past and what brought me here. I just gave them the bare bones of the story, including my recent loss of employment and spouse. They were very sympathetic, and more than a little surprised when I said, "Actually, you guys have no idea how good I feel right now. After thirty-five years of suppression, repression and sometimes depression, this is the first time I have ever been truly in charge of my life, the captain of my ship, and totally liberated! I have enough money to keep me going for a few months and I fully expect everything to come crashing down at the end of it, but frankly I don't give a hoot. Enough of me for the moment, for the rest is really boring. How about you two love-birds?"

"Well, we've had pretty boring lives, haven't we, Matilda? We were both born in Brooklyn and have lived here all our lives. Neither of us could afford to go to university, and ended up doing what most people in this situation do. We make just about enough to survive and as you can see, try to supplement our income with paying guests like you."

Mitch cleared his throat and continued, "Well, I am pushing fifty and Matilda, forgive me, darlin', has just turned forty-eight."

I expressed astonishment at this because Matilda, in my opinion, looked in her thirties.

Mitch continued, "We've been married now twenty years and believe me I couldn't recommend anything better for anyone. We met when I was bumming around doing very little and Matilda was going to evening school. When we decided to get married, there was no end of opposition, particularly from Matilda's family, who were relatively better off and educated. But no, sirree, my Matilda stood firm and there it was."

They clasped hands, and I was overwhelmed with a sense of awe at their obvious love for each other.

Matilda interjected, "That was the beginning of a long and happy marriage. When I was young, I used to fantasise about this tall, distinguished scholar, who would come and scoop me away in his arms and we would live happily ever after. The reality has actually been slightly better than that! My Mitch here did not pursue education; nor did I for that matter. We certainly haven't ended up rich or famous. On the other hand, we have a full and happy life, with two children who are worth their weight in gold. Well, let me rephrase that, no amount of gold or anything in the world can equate to even one of them. That's all there is to say, except that in the last four or five years we have both been thinking seriously about moving out of New York."

Mitch continued, "Quentin, this is a great city to have fun in. I used to love it, but you know what, over the last few years we've been increasingly worried about the level of violent crime and drug use with kids in school. We decided five years ago to move, but just haven't had the guts to make the move. But one of these days we certainly will. So that's us. Now, coming back to you, I get the feeling there's more to it than you're telling us." Mitch's shrewd remark was blocked by Matilda.

"Hush, Mitch. Quentin's our guest and you will not pry!"

I pleaded exhaustion and retired.

On the fourth day Mitch informed me in the morning that he would be working late, and offered to meet up for dinner. At nine o'clock we met at a restaurant of my choosing and I made it abundantly clear that I was hosting the dinner. As agreed, Mitch and Matilda met me at Greenwich Village and we went to an upmarket seafood restaurant. They were initially ill at ease and it was very obvious that they were feeling uncomfortable at a place like this that they could never afford.

"Listen, you two, you've just got to suspend reality for the next couple of hours. The simple fact of the matter is that I can afford to do this today. Of course, I'm no millionaire, but I have a plan and I have a budget. I have enough to keep me going for a few months and I intend to spend every penny of it before I return home. So, tonight is just a drop in the ocean. I want you to let your hair down and really enjoy."

They reluctantly acquiesced and by the time we had downed our first drinks they had relaxed completely. We talked about a topic that was dear to our hearts, namely travel, which we had done precious little of.

"My life's dream is to travel to Europe," said Matilda, with Mitch nodding his agreement.

"You must have travelled a lot, Quentin. From what I hear you guys travel a lot more than we Americans here."

"That may be true in general, but I'm a bit of a failure in that department. I have wanted to, but circumstances have got in the way. Incidentally, my first desire is to travel to Africa, and experience nature in all its glory."

Conversation flowed easily and I reflected that I had not felt so relaxed and happy in anyone's company before. It was a startling revelation.

As he was driving, Mitch stopped with one drink, so Matilda and I shared the remainder of the bottle of Argentine Malbec that I had ordered. The meal was excellent. I was taken for a walk around that iconic area. The atmosphere was all that it was cracked up to be, and I was not disappointed. There were people from all corners of the world it seemed, speaking a dozen different tongues, and the whole place was buzzing. Mitch dropped Matilda home at around eleven, and I elected to stay on as his companion during his late-night shift.

It was a great experience driving around the various quarters of New York. One of the drop-offs was in the Bronx, and it was even more forbidding than what I had come to expect from movies. It was fascinating to get a late-night view of the ends of the social spectrum. The frequent screams of the sirens, mostly police, some ambulance, were inescapable. It was just after four in the morning when we got home.

☥

CRUISING TO A WET GRAVE

And so it was, the next day, at the spur of the moment I decided to take one of the popular cruises on the Hudson River. I had the day free and decided to explore a bit of Long Island. Following Mitch's advice, I walked to Jamaica Station and took a train to Long Beach, which took about half an hour, and was most pleasant. I ran for about an hour on the beach, taking in all the sights and sounds. I got back to M&M's around three and showered. I rang Mitch to let him know of my impromptu decision, and he was most amused. I took the train again, to Penn Station and from there I found my way to the Chelsea Piers. It was a beautiful autumnal evening and the boat was not very full. I wandered through the decks and finally approached the bar, with every intention of getting pissed.

As I looked around, the scene unfolding itself in one corner was inescapable. The centre of attraction was a slim man of medium height, obviously well-to-do. He was dressed in an exquisitely tailored suit, headed by a handsome face with fine, delicate features and a shock of curly black hair, the whole effect offset by a thin moustache. There were three burly men hanging around him, clearly his minions, and it suddenly struck me that he was probably a local gangster.

The last, but by no means the least, member of this little troop was a tall, anorexic woman, with a face like a scarecrow, heavily made-up. The skeletal face made her eyes look enormous, made more so by their extraordinary shade of violet-blue. Or purple maybe? I thought she looked revolting, and wondered why some women ruin their natural looks by resorting to hideous artifice. I couldn't help contrasting her with my gorgeous Harriett, who was minimal in her use of make-up, and optimal in her dietary habits, such that the end result was truly something to behold.

There was an obvious altercation going on between them, stimulating my curiosity. Pretending to ignore them, I went up to the bar and stood just a few feet away, close enough to eavesdrop. The man was facing away from me, while the woman was in my direct line of vision. She was a good four inches taller than him, and even allowing for her heels, she must have been taller. I ordered myself a large Glenfiddich.

I heard the man behind me say, "If you don't shut the fuck up, you're gonna feel the back of my hand right now."

"Fuck you, Marty. I've had enough of your crap. I'm not going through a weekend of misery with you in Vegas, while you do your business with your mob, gamble and pick up stray sluts." Her accent was different and softer than the New York drawl, and I wondered where it was from.

I was beginning to enjoy this hugely and felt a real thrill of excitement. I downed my first drink and ordered another. I turned my head around and caught her eye and rapidly looked away. Marty followed her eyes, turned, took a look at me, and turned back. I heard him say, "Don't create a scene here, and you ain't drinking any more."

"Just watch me."

To my surprise and delight, she came around and stood next to me and said, "Sorry to intrude, sir, but I just heard you ordering your drink. Glenfiddich, I believe?"

My initial surprise was further accentuated by her sudden shift into a perfect English accent. Marty had turned and the look on his face was not pretty.

I put on the biggest artificial smile I could and said to her, "You're absolutely right, mademoiselle. Do you like whisky?"

"Yes, I would love a wee dram of whisky. And by whisky, I mean proper Scotch, preferably single malt. Unlike the local whiskey, with an 'e' in it, that people drink around here," she said, pointing to Marty.

I duly guffawed in appreciation of her joke and she giggled. The flash of her beautiful white teeth made that scarecrow face much more bearable. It was obvious she had had too much to drink, and was probably a regular tippler. There were big black circles under her eyes, the nose, though sharp, seemed too big for her wasted face, with cheekbones that stood out like scaffolding, from which the hollowed cheeks descended to her wide jaws, leading to a dimpled chin.

"I'm Claire."

"Quentin. A real pleasure to meet you."

"*Enchanté*, Monsieur Durward."

She surprised me again, not only with the French response, but also the obvious literary connotation. I had not expected someone like her to be familiar with Walter Scott. My surprise must have shown, because she went on, "A bit surprised, are you, that this tart seems well read?"

"Oh, please forgive me, that was not my thinking at all. I was just caught off guard, probably because of the company you keep!"

Her response was just as I had hoped, evoking an uninhibited laugh. Marty decided it was time to intervene and came around, put his arm around Claire's shoulder and gripped her right arm. Claire winced.

Marty said, "I see my girl's tryin' to pick you up, mister, something she does all the time. And when she is not trying it on, she is dead drunk."

Claire retorted, "Do you blame me, being forced to live with this apology of a man?"

My goodness, this was turning out far better than anything I had anticipated! Under normal circumstances I would have politely excused myself from the situation and escaped, but not this time. This was no normal situation, I was no normal man and clearly these were not normal people!

"Considering that this is a free county and all that, Claire, would you allow a gentleman to buy you a glass of the golden nectar?"

Before she could answer Marty interjected, through gritted teeth, "Listen, asshole, you heard me.

Keep out of this or you won't even live to regret the day."

I had visions of a real punch-up, of the sort that I had seen in so many Hollywood westerns. He was a good four inches shorter than me, but a lot leaner and fitter. Nevertheless, I thought I could take him on, fortified by the two large whiskies I had downed. However, given that I would have to face the rather large minions in attendance, I was relieved when Marty suddenly simmered down. He turned to the bartender and said, "You better not serve any more to these two here. They are the sort who would keep drinking until they're wasted, and go for a swim in the river."

I rolled my eyes at Claire. He marched away and nodded to his henchmen, who glowered at us and duly followed him out.

"That's Marty Nero, my so-called boyfriend. He is more like my keeper and I hate him. I would kill him if I had half a chance."

Her face dropped and for a moment I thought she was going to cry. She pulled herself together and turned to me with a real effort to smile. "Well, I don't care anymore. I am leaving him, and I don't care what he threatens me with. In the meantime, I am going to flirt outrageously with you!"

"I am sorry he spoke so disparagingly of you," I said. "That was pretty awful."

"Actually, what he said was true," she replied with obvious bitterness. "I would happily pick up any man, in preference to this animal. And I'm probably drunk half the time. So, anyway, what's any of that to you? Let's just have a good time tonight and screw tomorrow."

"In a funny sort of a way I am in exactly the same situation, though our backgrounds are totally different. Actually, it would be interesting to exchange stories."

"What's the point, brother? Let's just have a good time," said Claire, pressing herself to me. I was again reminded of the contrast between Harriett and this woman, whose perfume reeked, and her low-cut blouse had little to reveal.

"You obviously mean business, don't you, Claire? Are you really suggesting that you and I make sweet music tonight? Or maybe right here and now?" I said with a combination of amusement and sarcasm.

"Oh no, how could I expect that of a tight-assed Englishman like you? Forget it, brother, you are not exactly Brad Pitt in his prime, are you? No, all I want is some fun company and anything to piss Marty off."

"That sounds just fine by me, lady. I'm afraid you don't exactly appeal to me either." She looked daggers at me and knocked back her drink.

She perked up again the next second. "So tell me, Tintin, what brings you to our shores?" By now her accent had reverted to her usual American, which I still could not place.

"It's Quentin, actually. I presume you created this nickname purely to annoy me," I said, without any rancour, but with a hint of amusement.

"Not really. You just seemed such a contrast to the famous creation of Hergé. On the other hand, you do resemble the canine version. I hope you are offended."

Again, I was impressed that someone with her phenotype should be so knowledgeable about things un-American.

Claire continued. "Stop looking so goddamned surprised at everything I say. There was a time when I ..."

Her sentence tailed off and her face fell. I was getting more curious by the second.

I said nothing, waiting for her to continue. After a couple of seconds, I said, "So who is this canine version, then?"

"Ah, you don't know? Never heard of Rin Tin Tin? The famous German shepherd of the old movies?"

I shook my head and Claire was visibly pleased.

"Oh, fuck it, all these recollections are pointless. Let's just continue to drink. My round," she said, opening her purse. "So, going back to what I was asking, what brings you to these shores?"

"I'm not really sure where to begin, and I don't think we have the time, nor do I have the inclination. Let's just say I made a sudden decision on the spur of the moment and left England to come over, with absolutely no plan. I am just taking each day as it comes."

"So how long do you plan on staying? Are you going to tour around?"

"I have absolutely no idea, and no plans. I was thinking of making a trip to Atlantic City and gambling my remaining pennies away!"

"What kind of a loser gambles? I'm afraid you're rapidly falling in my esteem."

"Oh dear, that sounds like a fate worse than death! So, what exactly would you have me do, Lady Claire?"

"How about taking Marty out? I can probably raise enough money. Would you consider it?"

It was clearly tongue-in-cheek, though I think I detected an underlying note of seriousness.

"You really do not like that man, do you? What beats me is, why leaving him is such a big deal. He is obviously a lowlife thug, but in modern America surely you have the freedom to walk?"

"You have no idea, do you? You don't just walk away from a guy like Marty. Nah, it's all about exploitation and fear. But now I don't care about the consequences, and I really am going to walk out. Of course, if I do, he'll come after me and I could be in a whole lot more trouble. Or dead."

"Surely that's a bit melodramatic?"

"Listen, sunshine, it should've been obvious, even to your senses, that Marty is no ordinary lowlife thug. Have you seen his clothes? Have you seen the gorillas who hang around him? Marty is the boss of a big operation in New York and people don't mess with him. I really don't rate my chances of a permanent escape one bit, but it's just come to the point where I really do not care if he puts a bullet between my eyes."

By this time, we were both quite tipsy, Claire more than I, as she had had a head start.

"Come on, soldier, let's go and get some fresh air. If I don't, I might throw up."

She clung to me as we walked out of the bar and she pulled me up the stairs to the top deck, where we stepped out into the open.

It was a beautiful, mild night, with clear skies. We were cruising along at a steady pace and there was a light breeze fanning our cheeks. Claire pulled me towards the balustrade, and we looked over into the swirling black waters of the Hudson River. She turned towards me and threw her arms around my neck. "At least kiss me goodbye on my last night with this lowlife – who knows, maybe my last night in this world!"

Even in that dull light I could see fear and hopelessness in her eyes, which were welling up, and I suddenly understood the depth of despair that Claire was in. Suddenly, my own tribulations seemed far less daunting than what she was facing. And so, I did her bidding.

It was a most strange sensation, kissing a woman, something which I had not done for at least a couple of years! After the first year of our marriage the kisses between Harriett and me became token gestures and soon simply disappeared. Harriett's disregard for me was such that even the perfunctory kiss on the cheek was banished. I have to admit this was the worst possible reintroduction to a romantic kiss. It was just the physical apposition of two pairs of lips, with absolutely no other human interaction. I am sure Claire felt the same, but nevertheless she was determined to keep it going as long as she could. It was then that I noticed four men striding briskly towards us. Marty and his henchmen.

I pulled away from Claire and turned to him, saying, "Well, well, if it ain't the jealous husband."

Claire immediately followed, "You know, Marty, this guy here can kiss like you never can. I can't wait to see what he can do for me in bed!"

Marty nodded his head at the man standing near me and before I had even time to be surprised his fist rammed into my abdomen. I buckled over, winded, and at the same time I could see that one of the other men had clamped his hand around Claire's mouth to stop her screaming. And then the most terrifying three seconds of my life, as I was physically hoisted by two of them and hurled over the side!

The shock of hitting the cold waters of the Hudson River cannot be overstated. However, there was a substantial element of excitement and an adrenaline surge that was already pumping me up, which unquestionably contributed to my survival. I kicked strongly and surfaced for air. It probably took me about a minute to get control of myself and the thought flashed through my brain that this was probably as good a time as any to give up the ghost and depart this world.

I heard a splash and there was Claire about fifty feet ahead of me. She came up thrashing for air and screaming, or trying to scream. It was obvious that she was in a state of panic and I realised that she would drown within a matter of minutes. I struck out towards her and my natural swimming ability kicked in. As soon as I reached her, she flung her arms around my neck and tried her level best to drown me along with herself. With some difficulty I pulled us both back to the surface and yelled in her ear, "Stop struggling and just relax." Within a minute it also became clear that she actually could swim and with my help, pulling her along, we swam painfully slowly towards the shore.

Thinking back, I am surprised that we did not drown, as the current was swift. Fortunately, it was pushing us towards the shore, and with our efforts, we nevertheless managed to get there. I cannot be sure, but it must have been not more than ten to fifteen minutes, but seemed like a lifetime. Once on the bank we simply lay there for almost half an hour, exhausted. Finally, we dragged ourselves up, soaking wet and shivering in the chill. We found our way to the nearest road and realised there was no way of contacting anyone. Both our mobile phones were waterlogged and dead.

Providence intervened and a yellow cab came along, which we flagged down. The taxi driver was obviously astonished by our appearance and looked askance. Claire took over and said to him, "No questions, pal. Just take us to the nearest motel, and you'll get a twenty-dollar tip." Ten minutes later we were deposited in a rather down-at-heel motel, the sort in which they ask no questions. We booked into their only remaining 'deluxe' room at ninety dollars a night. "Hey, listen," said the guy behind the counter, "I don't want all that wet stuff on my bed, you understand?" A wink and a nod.

The deluxe bedroom turned out to be all of twelve feet square and the double bed occupied a substantial proportion of it. The attached bathroom was probably six feet square and not in great shape. We looked at each other, taking measure.

I shook my head. "I can't believe what just happened. I can't even believe that we are alive. I am not sure that we really should be alive, given the prospects of what's to come."

Claire looked at me expressionlessly, too tired even to respond. She just shook her head and went into the bathroom. She came out a few minutes later and said, "You better go in and do what you have to."

So, I went in and relieved myself and went back into the bedroom to find Claire's clothes draped on the chair and she was on the bed and under the sheet, fast asleep. There was nothing else for it, but to do the same. I stripped off completely and tiptoed into bed and got under the sheet. Claire's naked form was obvious, but believe me, the prospect of any sexual stimulation was about as attractive as an invitation to get back into the river! I was out for the count.

I have no idea what time it was when I woke up. Claire was not in bed and I could hear her in the bathroom. She came out of the bathroom a few minutes later, back in her less wet clothes.

"Good morning," I said. She flushed.

I thought I would make light of it by saying, "Don't worry, nothing happened between us!"

She gave me a dirty look. "If you had tried anything, wise guy, you would've been singing in a falsetto, if you get my drift."

I put my hands up. "Hey, that was just a joke. Neither of us was in any condition to engage in anything more than a coma."

Her look was positively petulant. "And even if we were in any form or shape, nothing would've happened, let me reassure you."

"Don't worry, baby, you're not exactly my type. In fact, I don't even know what Marty could've seen in you."

That really got to her and fire flashed in her eyes as she turned towards me. For a moment I thought she was going to strike me, but she controlled herself and turned away with clenched jaws.

I did regret saying that, as it really was not called for. She did look like a scarecrow, but I had no right to say what I did. "Hey, I'm sorry I said that. Sometimes we say things when provoked, particularly when tired and hungry. Why don't we concentrate now on what to do next? Actually, before we do anything else, I need some food and I am sure so do you. So, why don't I head out to the nearest fast-food place? We could sit, eat, and plan our next move. Unless of course you wish to come with me."

Claire shook her head. "You go. Get me any burger you like, with fries and a Diet Coke."

Fortunately, we both had our resources intact. In my wallet, in addition to the credit card, there were a couple of hundred dollars in various denominations, all of which were of course still wet. Similarly, Claire had some cash, I am not sure exactly how much. She had paid with her credit card for the room last night. It took me ten minutes to get to the fast-food outlet, with the quirky name 'Burglar King'. It was fortunately quiet at that time. I ordered two mega-burger meals and paid with my credit card. Twenty minutes later I was back in the room, where I found Claire asleep again, this time on top of the bed, fully clothed. She awoke when she heard me and got out of bed, leaving an outline of her half-wet clothes on the sheet, and exclaimed, "Shit, I have wet the bed."

"Don't worry, it can happen to anyone, there is no shame!"

My attempt at humour did not go down well. Without any further exchange we both sat on the rickety chairs and proceeded to wolf down the food I had just brought back. I can even today feel and remember the taste of that burger, which was literally a lifesaver. Ten minutes later both of us were feeling much better.

"So, young lady, as the local resident expert on hiding or escaping from New York, what would be your plan of action?"

The two of us sat together in that cramped room, contemplating our next move. After the excitement of last night, and having survived the river, we had come off our highs and were hitting the ground hard. Not just downbeat, but edgy.

"I need to retrieve some vital stuff from home, without which there is no chance of escape. Fuck!"

"I know a quick short-term solution. I am staying as a paying guest with a wonderful couple in Queens, and they will put us up for sure. He drives a taxi and I should call him right away."

"Yeah, why not? Whatever we do, I suspect our days are numbered. At least mine. Marty will find us for sure. If you make a run for it, you just might get away, as he has no interest in you."

"OK, let's cut the negativity, shall we? I started out this journey by thinking I don't care where and when I die, but having got close to it, I am beginning to feel otherwise. I see no reason why I should sacrifice my existence for a lowlife like Marty, or for that matter, Harriett…"

I stopped mid-sentence.

"Oh well, that's a story for another day. Just stay here for a minute, while I go down and give Mitch a call, given that both our mobiles are waterlogged and dead."

"Mobiles? Is that what you guys call cellphones?"

I nodded and left the room. Down at the reception desk I explained that we had no means of telephone communication and asked the girl behind the desk whether she would be kind enough to allow me to use their landline and call my friend in the city. I put on my poshest upper-class English accent, which I had heard was considered impressive in America. It worked!

✠

FINDING REFUGE

One of my facilities was the ability to remember numbers, useful or otherwise. So, I had no difficulty in rattling off Mitch's number and I got a prompt response, much to my relief, instead of the dreaded voicemail.

"Hey, Mitch, it's me, Quentin. I need help."

"Hey, Quentin, man, where've you been? I've called you a dozen times."

"There's been some major excitement, but I'll explain everything in due course, Mitch. Right now, I need you to come and pick me up from a location across the river." I picked up the motel's card and read out the address to him.

"What the hell are you doin' out there? I'm going to be busy for the next couple of hours, so I probably won't be able to get down to you till around seven."

"Thanks, Mitch, and I do apologise for being a pain in the arse."

Mitch guffawed and said, "I like the way you say arse! I'll give you a call when I'm ten minutes away, and you can give me an exact location."

I went back up to the room to find Claire scowling at nobody in particular.

"Right, so that is sorted. Mitch is going to pick us up at seven and we'll get back to his place. I really owe that guy."

"I've been thinking," she said, "I need to disappear fast. Marty's men are probably scouring the district even as we speak and it is only a matter of time before they get to this motel."

"Hey, hang on; he would've assumed that we drowned in the river. Why would he send his men out looking for us?"

"For a start, if two bodies had been recovered from the river, that would have made the news. Yes, it is possible that the bodies are still floating somewhere in the sea, but Marty wouldn't gamble on that. In fact, nothing would give him greater pleasure than hunting us down. That's the kind of animal he is."

"So, what have you in mind? My own plan was, after New York, to take the train across the country. It has always been one of my desires to do this trip and see a complete snapshot of America. Perhaps this is the time to do it."

Neither of us said anything for the next few minutes and clearly Claire was mulling over my idea.

"What the hell? I might as well join you. It sounds as good a way as any of getting away and staying under the radar. If nothing else it will buy me time to formulate a plan. Juanita is my only hope of getting my stuff from the house. She is our domestic help, and will do just about anything for me. I'll have to ask her to bring my stuff over to me on the quiet. Assuming the bastard hasn't discovered my cache." And then Claire started.

"Oh shit, I have to warn my mother. She is the first person Marty will get to if he does not find me."

"Where does she live?"

"In Boston. Alone and vulnerable." Claire's eyes welled up and I thought to myself, how a hard-nosed gangster's moll could suddenly melt when faced with the love for a mother.

"I have to warn her and get her to move in with someone until all this blows over. Let's stop wasting time and get a move on. First of all, I need to get a new cellphone and change of clothing."

I nodded and we left the motel ten minutes later. A cab took us to the local shopping mall, where we headed straight to a telecoms shop. Claire, after confirming that her phone was indeed, dead, paid cash to obtain a mobile phone. I was astonished to find that my phone was still functional, and rather sheepishly realised that I had (for no clear reason) got myself a phone that was water-proof. Without checking any details of incoming calls, texts or WhatsApps, I powered the phone down, and took out the SIM card.

I bought and installed a new SIM and also bought a universal charger. When we got out, Claire walked a little distance away from me and made her call to her mother. There was an animated conversation for about five minutes and it was obvious that she was having difficulty in convincing her mother to do what she wanted. I sat myself down at the nearby café and ordered a coffee.

Claire returned to me shaking her head. "My mom can be stubborn as hell. Anyway, I have managed to convince her to lock up and disappear for a few days. Fortunately, she has a couple of really good friends, who are not known to Marty. One of them lives in Montreal, which is not too far to drive. She has agreed to do that." I still found it a bit far-fetched that Marty would go to all this trouble, but then what did I know? Claire saw the look of askance on my face. "Don't go there. I can't be bothered to explain."

"Looks like we both have histories to exchange. If we do get on that train, I guess we're going to have all the time in the world."

Claire grimaced. I shrugged my shoulders. "Not my first choice, either."

Using her phone, I called Mitch again to redirect him to the mall we were at. I then said to Claire, "Given that we have nothing to do for the next hour, other than mope and moan, I think I'll go to that ice rink and see if I'm still any good."

I was pleasantly surprised at how well I could still skate. At the same time, I realised just how unfit I had become, and got into a bit of a rage, which propelled me to try and burn off as many calories as I could in the next forty-five minutes. I was sweaty and smelly, but knew that as soon as I got home to Mitch's I would be able to shower and change. I must have looked a real sight in my current clothes, but I did not care. I came out to find Claire in the same café, with what looked like a fresh mug of coffee. On the chair next to her was a bag, with some clothes.

"You managed to get yourself some clothes, I see."

"Yes, Einstein. You look hot and sweaty."

"And smelly."

She gave me a withering look and rolled her eyes.

"I hope this friend of yours isn't going to keep us waiting."

"Oh no, he couldn't possibly keep your ladyship waiting."

"Oh, shut up."

I ordered a coffee for myself and sat down across the table. She had a new pair of shades on, so there was no way of knowing at whom or where she was looking. I leaned back and closed my eyes and tried to just be in the moment and avoid all negative thoughts. A lifetime ago, I had tried engaging with yoga and meditation, to no avail. Mitch rang on Claire's phone at 7.10 and directed us to where he was waiting. He got out of the car and greeted me with the warmest smile one could imagine, and gave me an uninhibited hug, which both startled and slightly embarrassed me.

"Mitch, I'd like you to meet Claire."

"Very pleased to meet you, ma'am. Old friends?"

"Hey, Mitch. No, we are not old friends, but perhaps this is not the best place to start the story. I'd feel much happier if we could get going and we'll fill you in on the details on the way."

Mitch was taken aback, partly by her abruptness, and partly by the fact that I had not warned him that I was going to have a co-passenger. Gracious as ever, he acknowledged her request and we both got in the back of his car. There was silence for about three minutes, at which point Mitch gave up the struggle. "Quentin, pal, are you going to spill the beans or what?"

Mitch's infectious laugher caused both of us to join him. I looked at Claire and she nodded, so I recounted the events of the previous twenty-four hours. Mitch's various reactions were delightful to behold.

"Fuck me, Quentin – pardon my language, lady – I can't decide if you're making all this up, or if it really happened. Is all this true, ma'am?"

"Call me Claire, Mitch. Believe me, I'm no fuckin' lady. And what you heard is exactly what happened. Now what your friend Quentin failed to mention is the fact that my boyfriend, Marty, is the ultimate psycho. He will be on my tail and frankly I don't rate my chances. So, if it came to his knowledge that you were helping me, the chances are that you will be in danger yourself. So, it might be best if you could just drop me off at some out-of-the-way motel and leave me to take my chances."

"Claire, you are absolutely right. Whatever happens, the last thing I would want to do is to jeopardise Mitch and his lovely family. So yes, Mitch, drop us both off and we will plot our escape together. You could drop my stuff off at some point."

"You kiddin'? I ain't gonna leave you two in the middle of nowhere just like that. No, sirree, you are coming to my place and that is final. I don't care who this Marty is, I don't scare easy. In any case, the chances of you being traced to my apartment is zilch. So, I suggest you settle in, chill out for a day or two and work out a plan."

By this time, we had more or less reached Mitch's place. As we got out, he said, "Quentin, man, in my fifty years I ain't seen nothing like this! Thanks for bringing in some excitement!"

Ah, what can I say, Mitch was an absolute gem.

"There's just one problem, guys," Mitch continued. "I only have the one bedroom to spare, so either you have to share it, or, Quentin, you'll have to use the couch."

I looked at Claire, who flushed, and then said, "We shared a bed last night, Mitch, and I can tell you this guy is the safest guy on earth to sleep with!"

"Sadly, I have to agree, Mitch. Any possible natural desires I might have had were totally decimated by this young lady." Mitch laughed. To my surprise, Claire chortled.

When we entered the apartment, Matilda was predictably surprised and her eyes widened when

Claire was introduced as my roommate for the next few days.

"That was fast work, Quentin!" said Matilda with a twinkle in her eye, which did not go down well with Claire.

"Can I please make it absolutely clear that the two of us are neutral in gender towards each other. Circumstances have just forced us together," she said with a touch of acerbity.

Matilda looked abashed and apologised immediately. By this time, I was really annoyed with Claire, but before I said anything she replied, "I'm sorry, Matilda, I didn't mean to snap, but I'm on the run from a wild animal, and frankly I'm shit scared."

Matilda's eyes widened again and she looked at Mitch.

"Baby, you'll hear the whole story in a minute. Shall we let these two go and get ready for dinner? Quentin, you look like something the cat dragged in. Go and clean up, man!"

"Where are the kids?"

"Oh, they've gone to their friends and will be having their dinner with them. They will get dropped back here by nine."

Claire and I went into our room, and I let Claire use the bathroom first, while I kicked off my shoes and collapsed on the bed. I think I must have dropped off, and only resurfaced when I found myself being shaken.

"OK, time to wake up." Through my sleepy eyes I noticed that she was looking dramatically different.

She was still skeletal, but all the make-up was gone from her face, which was a huge improvement – not that I would have the temerity to say so. She wore a short dress, which hung loosely on her frame, no doubt due to the total lack of adiposity. I suddenly realised I was staring at her, and before I could avert my eyes, she gave me a *look* and walked out.

I opened the tiny cupboard and pulled out a change of clothing. I had bought myself some clothes during my wanderings in NYC. In the bathroom I threw off my clothes and stood in front of the mirror, imagining that I had lost a bit of my belly! I tensed my pectorals and deltoids and pulled my stomach in, then tensed my lats and finally my traps, looking hopefully at the reflection. It was no use, I still looked like a slob. Maybe the dark circles under my eyes had regressed a little, the bags less filled out, maybe?! I got into the shower and felt a sensation of real bliss as the steaming water cascaded down on my skin. By the time I had finished, the bathroom was completely fogged up. Feeling the stubble on my face I realised that I had not shaved, so I did just that. When I joined the others, Matilda and Mitch were suitably complimentary about my much-improved appearance, though Claire pointedly avoided saying anything, or even making eye contact.

We sat down to an excellent dinner, consisting of broccoli soup that Matilda had made, followed by roast chicken, potatoes, vegetables and finished off with an apple pie. Mitch, in his generous way, offered to serve wine, but I quickly declined before Claire could respond, as I knew this would add to their hardship. I had already decided that at the time of parting I would leave him with a generous 'bonus' in addition to the agreed daily rental. During the dinner, various aspects of our recent misadventures kept resurfacing and Matilda sounded positively awestruck.

"Just wait till the kids hear of this," said Mitch.

"No, Mitch," said Matilda. "We don't want any of this to reach their ears. At least, not just yet. Maybe a year down the line, when all this is done and dusted."

The children came back later than expected, and looked delighted to see me and Claire.

"Is Claire your girlfriend, Quentin?"

"No, not really. We are just friends and we thought we would hang out for a couple of days."

They looked at Claire and were rewarded with a winning smile, and again it made me realise that there was a side to Claire which was very human and could be appealing. Before long they were packed off to bed and Claire announced, "Guys, I'm bushed. But before I crash out, can I just say again, Mitch and Matilda, you are absolutely the best couple in the world and I really would like to thank you. In the dirty world I live in, we don't get good genuine folks like yourselves."

For once, Mitch was tongue-tied and looked totally embarrassed. Matilda shook her head and said nothing, but her eyes were moist.

I rescued the situation by saying, "Don't believe her, she says that to everyone she meets."

That produced general laughter and Claire headed off to the bedroom. I followed a few minutes later.

When I went in, she had changed into her pyjamas and was brushing her teeth. When she came into the room, we looked at each other, with the same unspoken words. How were we going to sleep?

"I'm happy to take the couch."

"Thanks, I appreciate that."

So, I changed, brushed my teeth and went out to occupy the couch in the lounge. Anticipating this move, Mitch had already furnished it with a pillow and a light duvet. I lay down and was soon lost to the world.

I woke up at a little after nine in the morning, to find the apartment in complete silence. The family had gone to their respective work/school. I knew we had to finalise our travel plans. I made two mugs of coffee and mustered up the courage to knock timidly on the door. Claire came out bleary-eyed and we exchanged 'Good morning's. We sat sipping coffee, without a word, yet knowing exactly what the other was thinking.

"Shall we get ready and crack on with our escape plans?" I said.

Claire nodded. "Yup. After that, I have to meet someone at a restaurant called Zoilita's at two o'clock. It's a fifteen-minute walk from here and I'd like you to come with me." I made no attempt to hide my surprise and curiosity. Claire pre-empted, saying, "I called Juanita yesterday and arranged it. Believe me, it's crucial for me."

I was alarmed, and said, "Look, you're not delivering me into Marty's arms in return for your life, are you?"

Even as I said it, I regretted it, and more so when Claire pivoted and punched me hard in the centre of my belly. She was surprisingly strong, but fortunately I'd had enough time to tense my muscles, with the result that I was able to take it with nothing more than a wince.

Claire screamed at me. "Is that what you take me for, you fuckin' asshole? Damn your suspicious English mind!"

Her eyes were aflame, the startling purple now imbued with red, and brimming. Words failed me, but instinctively, I cupped my hands around her face, and let my eyes do the apologising. After ten seconds, we returned to the present, and almost simultaneously apologised.

"Don't you remember me mentioning Juanita? She's the one who has kept me sane and going for the last five years."

I nodded, and Claire outlined what she had arranged, as part of her escape plan.

At eleven, we went online and did the bookings on the Amtrak website. There was a train that would be leaving Penn Station in forty-eight hours, on 28 October. We booked our seats, and I insisted on booking on my credit card. We were able to get tickets through to LA, which we decided would be our next port of call, and it would give us enough time to devise a definitive escape plan – for Claire, particularly. As for me, I'd decided to fly out to a Pacific island, and from there keep moving west until I'd gone full circle.

✠

JUANITA

At 12.50, we set out for Zoilita's, a name I loved, and I was intensely curious, and not a little uneasy. My doubts about Claire's intentions had, however, vanished by now. There was something of her integrity that I now believed in. I asked her how she had come to know Juanita.

"Juanita was born in Lanzarote, a Spanish island in the Atlantic. Do you know it? At the age of twelve, she came over to America, with her family. Her poor father, who came with big dreams and hopes, found that life was not as easy as he had imagined. Her mother became pregnant quite late in life, with her second baby. As you may know, immigrants get second-class treatment, and she was not looked after well. Her blood pressure went out of control, and they called it pre-eclampsia. Things went badly wrong when she was about eight months pregnant and she died."

There was a delicate pause, and then Claire continued. "Juanita's father worked his guts out and finally dropped dead with a heart attack. Luckily, Juanita had completed school by then, and could at least look after herself. She worked as a cleaner and cook in a number of places, until she met this guy Joe and fell head over heels in love with him. He worked a bar in Manhattan and they got married. They were together for a good four or five years, at the end of which he walked out with another woman. So, Juanita returned to cleaning and after a year or so, managed to get a job in the Nero household and that was when we met. Believe me, Tintin, she has been my salvation. Just her moral support, her encouragement and her empathy have kept me going. Not to mention this final act of redemption."

We reached the café, and I ordered a coffee, while Claire decided to have a pizza. I saw a delighted smile break across her face, as she stood up to welcome her Juanita, and they embraced for what seemed like a long time.

"How are you, my Clarissima? I've been so worried. There has been so much chaos at home, with Marty goin' crazy and yellin' at everybody."

"I'm good, Juanita, as you can see. Let me introduce to you the man who saved me – Quentin."

I raised my hand for a shake, but Juanita grabbed my shoulders and planted a kiss on either cheek.

"First of all, Chiquita, here is your bag. Thank God you gave it to me three days ago, otherwise I wouldn'a been able to take anything from the house."

"Juanita, that animal hasn't harmed you, has he?"

"No, no, he has no idea that you have been planning your escape. He guessed that you had survived the river, and thinks you are just on the run. Oh, he gave me the third degree about where you were hiding, but I can act real well!" she said proudly. "Anyway, I did not know until you called me."

Juanita was petite and attractive. I said to her, "Claire has told me all about you and how wonderful you are. Are you going to tell me that the feeling is mutual?"

She required very little encouragement. "Claire is now like a part of me. I found someone with whom I could share my feelings, and you don't know how much difference this girl makes to my life. But it was hell having to watch her go through life, in the grip of that animal Marty. I prayed that Claire would be free of this curse. I haven't told you this, Claire, but I even think of killing Marty in his sleep! Anyway, my flight to Spain is booked and I will be home for good."

It was time to part. "Goodbye, Juanita," said Claire, eyes brimming with tears. "I promise I will come and visit you in Lanzarote one day."

"Yes, *mi querida*, I wait for you. Who knows, by that time I even find a good man. I don't know what you two are going to do, but I pray God for you. And *you* take care of her, mister."

We parted company. Claire was clearly overcome, and we were silent all the way back home. It was only after we arrived, that Claire revealed the contents of the bag. They included her passport, a credit card and a cheque book (of a bank account that Marty had no knowledge of), and a number of secret bank account details that she had squirrelled away over the previous year.

"This bag is my insurance. I've been siphoning money out of one of Marty's many accounts into one I created under a different name, preparing for this day. I'm now going to do some stuff to hide my trail, so you can go amuse yourself elsewhere."

I needed some space and fresh air. I put on my newly acquired trainers, and went out for a run. On my way back I picked up a case of prosecco, which I'd heard Matilda mentioning. The evening was another pleasant affair, and Matilda was over the moon when I presented her the case – by now properly chilled. She promptly cracked open a bottle and we had a kind of celebration for just being alive. Finally, Claire was able to relax, after a couple of glasses of the bubbly. We went to bed relatively early, with the same arrangements as the night before.

✢

PLANNING THE ESCAPE

The next morning the entire family left at the usual time, leaving Claire and me to our own devices. I had decided to skip breakfast, whereas Claire gorged herself. Afterwards we decided to proceed with our plans and got onto the Internet, and booked some extras, this time using Claire's new credit card. We had the rest of the day to kill and I was getting restless.

Claire refused to go out and plonked herself in front of the TV. I spent some time scouring the Internet to see if there was any interesting news from old Blighty, about a hit and run, or an abandoned car, or a missing person, but there was none. Not that I expected any, but was still relieved. I realised that I had not once thought about Harriett.

I went for another run. I realised again how unfit I was, as I jogged along, determined to use my misfortunes to some physical benefit. Two hours later I came back to the apartment, drenched in sweat and worn out. Claire let me in without a word, and returned to the sofa, resuming her TV, and eating out of a tub of ice cream.

"We owe Mitch and Matilda big time," she said. "How much are you paying?"

"Sixty dollars a night, but now that you've joined the party, I'm thinking of doubling it."

"That's still not enough, Tintin. I'm not going to embarrass them by offering money directly, but I'm going to leave some extra money in an envelope for them."

"That's generous of you. I had already decided to do just that."

I showered and came out to join her in front of the TV. By this time, I was ravenous, so I helped myself to some muesli and fruit from the fridge. Claire looked up and said, "Looks like you are trying to lose a few pounds."

"Looks like my loss will be your gain!"

I meant it as a light-hearted comment, but it came across as sarcastic, which did not go down well. Claire's nostrils flared and she responded with, "Whatever." We sat in silence and watched the second half of *Brief Encounter*. Again, I was surprised by her choice. I didn't think an old English classic in black and white would appeal to a young American woman of her description. It struck me that there was a lot about her that was intriguing, and I found that annoying.

The children came home at six o'clock and were both excited and curious about the two of us. Claire underwent a transformation again and became very animated with them, asking about their school, their friends, and their activities. I was a bit wary of children in general, mainly because I had had very little exposure to them. Matilda returned a few minutes later and fussed over us. When the children were out of the room, she said to us, "I really can't wait to hear the full life stories of you two. There's so little excitement in our lives and all of a sudden, the two of you have transformed it! But not just yet, we need to wait until Mitch is back. He'll never forgive me if I left him out of it."

"Matilda, listen, we're leaving in the morning and will settle our dues tonight, if that's all right," I said.

Matilda looked crestfallen. "Hey, don't worry about what you owe us. If you are short of money, we are quite happy to host you for a few more days."

Claire interjected, "Listen, darlin', I didn't even know people like you existed. I would give anything to just spend a month with you guys, and money is absolutely not an issue. However, as I said last night, I am in considerable danger and I need to disappear fast. On the other hand, Tintin here can stay as long as he wants, but for whatever reason has decided that he needs to escape as well. Believe me, I have made absolutely no attempt to lure him away, and on the contrary have warned him that he is in much greater danger in my company."

Matilda dwelled on this for a few seconds and then turned to Claire. "I thought his name was Quentin!"

The twinkle had reappeared in her eyes and Claire flushed. "Oh, that. It's the name of a character from a European comic-book series and refers to a smart-ass kid, who gets it right every time."

I responded tartly, saying, "Well, this is one dumb-ass kid, who gets almost everything wrong, so I suppose the name is appropriate in reverse."

Claire couldn't wait. "Exactly my meaning."

"Come on, you two," Matilda said. "Stop behaving like my kids. How about we all get a hot mug of coffee?"

While we settled ourselves around the table with our mugs of coffee, Mitch walked in, beaming. I asked him about his day and he shrugged his shoulders, saying, "Just the average day. I have cancelled my service for tonight, so we have some more time together." I was touched by the hospitality of this big lovable character, who reminded me of Baloo from *The Jungle Book*.

"You know what, Mitch," Matilda said. "These two have decided that they are leaving town tomorrow. Though they haven't told me exactly where they are heading to."

Mitch sounded outraged. "Oh no, you guys. I was really looking forward to having you for a few more days. You're not really in any danger, as long as you are here. How the hell is this psycho guy going to trace you?"

Claire replied, "Mitch, I love you both dearly and would like nothing better than to enjoy your hospitality, but you really have no idea how dangerous Marty is. He has his spies all over the city and I really cannot afford to hang around New York any longer than absolutely necessary. That's why we have to go."

Mitch looked up at me enquiringly.

"So we're catching the train and heading west," I said. "That is as far as we know at the moment, because beyond that everything is nebulous."

Claire chimed in. "Yes, Mitch, we have to go. I wasn't intending to drag this guy along with me, but he seems to think that would be best for him as well. I have to work out a plan to deal with the situation in one way or another."

Mitch nodded reluctantly. "Yeah, I guess you guys need to do what you need to do. But just remember we are here to offer any help we can. Not that we are particularly useful in terms of advancing any money, but anything else."

"Mitch and Matilda," I said, "you two are the best things that ever happened to me, with apologies to a couple of my old friends whom I have deserted. We *will* meet again, I promise you, in much happier circumstances."

Famous last words, I thought to myself.

Later we talked about our lives. In brief, without going into too much detail. I recounted the bare facts of my life – the fairytale marriage that went pear-shaped, Harriett's infidelity and my sudden break with convention and reality.

Mitch then said, "But, Quentin, you haven't told Claire about the subsequent adventures!"

So, I then recounted the eventful drive to Heathrow and the arrival at JFK. Claire looked amazed. "Just who the hell *are* you? Are you in possession of some serious loot that people are after?!"

"Ha ha, Claire, if only you knew. My entire worth at the moment is probably of the order of £30,000, which is, what, 40,000 U.S? Killing me isn't worth the trouble, is it? Though having said that, if I were to die, that money would automatically go to my dear, recently estranged but not yet divorced wife, Harriett."

Claire raised an eyebrow and tilted her head significantly, and I shook my head. "No way, not even Harriett would go to such lengths to have me bumped off, all for that little sum of money. Besides, it's too far-fetched to think that she would actually employ a hit man to go after me. And knowing her, I'm positive she is shacked up with a guy who is loaded." It was at that point I remembered the phone call I had made to Harriett from the departure lounge at Heathrow. I felt a sensation of real discomfort, for no clear reason, and could almost feel her looking at me from behind. It was as if she could get her tentacles into me any time and from anywhere.

Claire contributed a condensed version of her own life. "I'm not proud of much in my life, guys. I've just been a prisoner of this bastard, and don't want to say any more…" The bitterness in her voice was palpable. "For the last year I've been planning to make a break for it, and three days ago I decided how. I would have executed my plan yesterday and would by now be somewhere in northern Canada, if I hadn't become over-confident and flirted with Tintin here! I have to give it to Marty, even I never dreamed that he would be audacious enough to throw me in the river."

I lost myself for a couple of minutes, and when I returned to present company, Claire was saying, "But for my drunken stupidity, I'd have escaped and our poor friend here would have only one, instead of two maniacs looking to kill him! As it is, I guess I probably would've drowned but for my…" She turned and there was an awkward silence while we looked at each other. I did not know what to say and just shrugged my shoulders nonchalantly. Claire's voice was low when she said, "I guess I really owe you, Tintin." I glanced at her and I saw genuine gratitude in her eyes.

Dinner was very quiet, and the mood was downbeat. I slept on the couch again, but not very well. I woke up several times, troubled by bizarre dreams.

5

ON TRACK TO NOWHERE

There are times when haste will not do.
Best to find shelter, find space and find time
And let the brain do its work.

The next morning Mitch insisted on driving us to Penn Station. Rather reluctantly he accepted payment for the room, which I insisted I would boost because of Claire, but Mitch refused to accept more than a hundred per night. Unbeknown to him we had left two little envelopes under our pillows, one containing Claire's rather more generous contribution of a thousand dollars and mine of five hundred. Matilda would discover the gifts after her return from work.

We agreed that we could not put a monetary value on what Mitch and Matilda had offered us – their unstinting hospitality and warmth. All the same, I was bowled over by Claire's generosity, and felt a bit small that I could not match her. When I mentioned it, Claire simply replied, "Thanks for the compliment, but as far as you are concerned, I guess you have been as generous as you could in your circumstances."

Matilda had to leave for work and gave us both a tight hug and a kiss, one for me and two for Claire. She made us promise that we would keep in touch and see them again. Claire was dubious about it, but I was not.

"Matilda, if I don't succumb to another assassination attempt, I solemnly promise that..." – imitating Arnie, the Cyborg – "...I'll be back." Everyone laughed, including Claire.

It was a dull, drizzly day and it took us a good hour to get to the terminal. Claire and I were quite subdued as I suppose we were both feeling slightly intimidated by what might lie in wait for us. Mitch, on the other hand, was full of beans and did his level best to keep our spirits up. He regaled us with some of the hilarious moments he had experienced in his life as a cabbie. The best was the one about this slightly inebriated passenger he had picked up at La Guardia Airport. He said he wanted to be taken to the Hancock Tower. Puzzled by the request, Mitch asked the man if he could tell him the location or give him the co-ordinates, as he, Mitch, was unfamiliar with this building. The man became rather irate at this, saying, "Hey, man, are you a cabbie or what? What kind of moron doesn't know where Hancock Tower is in Chicago?!"

At which Mitch had exploded in laughter and retorted: "The kind of moron who lands in New York looking for a building in Chicago!"

We finally arrived at Penn Station and it was time to say goodbye. Despite having known him for barely a week, I felt I had known him for a lifetime. He grabbed me in a bear hug and I tried my best to reciprocate. He was a bit more restrained with Claire, who, however, gave him a hug and a peck on the cheek.

"Remember, Quentin, we are here for you. You better keep that promise and come back to see us."

"Or maybe you can come and see me sometime in England, Mitch?"

Mitch shook his head regretfully and the look on his face really touched me. "Well, you know, Quentin, that's never going to happen. Not in this life of mine."

I swore to myself that I would make it happen. We were all very much on edge and just wanted to be on our way. "Get the hell out of here, you two," were Mitch's last words as we crept away, heads down.

Claire and I walked briskly towards the platform from which the Amtrak train was due to depart. The station was very busy with hordes of people heading in every different direction. That was when I heard Claire hiss, "Fucking hell!" I was not a great admirer of people who swore, particularly women (am I being sexist?), even though I had had plenty of experience with Harriett.

"Now what?"

Claire replied, "I've just spotted one of Marty's men, the one called Bronco." She gripped my arm, turning her face away to the right. "Don't look to the left, as he just might remember your face."

"What the hell is he doing here? Is it likely to be a coincidence?"

"Like hell it is. He is clearly searching for me and I can bet there are at least two others scouring the area. How the fuck could they know?"

"Online booking, Claire. He must have access to the systems. Or maybe simply random searches. Who knows?"

We kept our faces averted, while trying to locate any other henchman who was likely to ambush us. Thanks to the crowds, we managed to get through the barrier and onto the train.

"Whatever you do, just don't look back or turn around," said Claire. I complied with some difficulty, particularly as I was about to board the train, but managed to control myself.

The conductor greeted us cordially and after the initial welcome said, "You're light travellers, aren't you? Is this a honeymoon or something like that?"

"Something like that," Claire said, and her abrupt tone turned him off immediately. We got into our 'Superliner roomette', sat down and heaved a huge sigh of relief. We were safely ensconced in our cabin, which was very comfortable, indeed. We were on tenterhooks until the train departed. I was expecting someone to burst in any minute, but Lady Luck was with us. By the time the train had travelled for ten minutes or so, we were both in a curious mood of elation, apprehension and excitement, all rolled into one. We sat back and said some meaningless things, whilst in the back of our minds, I'm sure, we were both worried about the next phase of our escape. We both knew that this was nothing but a short respite before the hunt continued in earnest.

"If indeed our route has been hacked, Marty could have a reception committee for us at pretty much every station we might try getting off at. We just have to hope that he expects us to get to LA, and lie in wait there. So we need an alternative plan, like getting off at an earlier station."

"They will be looking for us as a couple, so it might make sense for us to split up and once through the barrier meet up when it looks clear." Claire nodded gloomily and said nothing.

I decided to take my mind off the situation, telling myself that my suggestion was probably as good as any. Claire's face would be easily disseminated from photographs that Marty would have had, but not mine. That gave me a sense of safety, and I felt ashamed. I knew I could not walk away and let her fall prey to her hunter. I watched the world go by as the train rolled through the pretty, if flat, countryside.

I think I must have dozed off, and when I awoke, I found it was just past four thirty and realised I was feeling peckish. Claire was wide awake, looking into the distance, her face expressionless.

"Oh, I'd love a cream tea at this moment," I said.

"Scones and clotted cream? Not a chance in hell. But I wouldn't mind a nice hot mocha."

We ordered, and the beverages were delivered within ten minutes.

I decided to open with, "Any bright ideas?"

"As a matter of fact, yes. This is a real long shot, but maybe the only one that will take care of Marty permanently."

I was amused at the thought of Claire bumping off Marty! She saw my amusement and glared at me. "What's so fuckin' funny?"

"Certainly not your language. I was just wondering if by that you meant to kill off Marty, a prospect which seems a wee bit unlikely."

She was miffed and went into a petulant silence. After about ten minutes I relented. "Look, I'm sorry. I didn't mean to be rude or dismissive. Tell me what you had in mind and I promise to be serious."

For a moment she looked as if she was going to deliver her usual epithet, but she relaxed, saying, "You see, there is this guy called the Salamander, whose real name escapes me. Everybody just refers to him as that, or Il Salamandro. He just happens to be one of the bosses controlling Nevada. This was probably ten years ago, when he got into a deal with Marty, who ended up screwing him for a lot of money. Millions, I believe. Being the devious bastard he is, Marty set up a fall guy and pinned the blame on him. The guy of course was conveniently killed in a car accident and the money was never recovered. Now if I were to get to the Salamander and tell him the truth, there might be a realistic chance that he could help me get away from Marty, and who knows, he may even be ready to take him out."

"Claire, I can't believe I'm hearing this. You are not seriously suggesting that you collude with one gangster to eliminate another?"

"Of course, you ass… I mean ass!"

We laughed simultaneously.

Claire continued, "Do you think Marty's looking for me to fulfil his unrequited love? I know for a fact that he has killed at least a dozen guys, some of whom were innocent. I would eliminate him with as much hesitation as stepping on a cockroach."

There was fire in her eyes and I realised that she was neither weak nor stupid. I heard myself say, "If that's the way it has to be, I guess that's that."

I sat and listened quietly while Claire outlined her plan in detail. There was a deafening silence for a few minutes, while we both mulled over the plan. "Claire, I really am impressed that you have thought through all of this."

A rare smile appeared briefly. "All that remains is now for me to contact the Salamander. I hate to have to do this, but my mom is our best bet."

I looked at her, surprised. Claire shook her head, picked up her phone and punched a few numbers in.

"Hello, Mamma, it's me. How're you doin'?"

After a few exchanges and reassurance that her mother was safe and well, Claire continued: "Mamma, I'm on the run from Marty and this time he is out for blood. I need to contact the Salamander, who is my only hope. I hate to bring the past back, but do you have any contacts who might get me to him?"

Claire listened intently as her mother spoke to her, and jotted a number down.

"Thanks, Mamma, I knew you would come up with the goods. I'm really sorry I have to rake up the muck from the past. I love you."

She listened for another minute and then closed the conversation with, "I'm not all alone and scared, Mamma. The guy I told you about, Quentin, he's with me and we're in this together. He's a tough guy and an ex-con, so you don't need to worry!"

She laughed into the phone, while giving me a cheeky wink. "I love you so much, Mamma. Just don't go back to your place. When all this is over, I promise I'm going to take you away for good."

Claire was struggling to control herself and her eyes were swimming. For a moment I felt a real connection with her, and a deep visceral longing for a mother I never had. However unfortunate, at least she knew her mother. What would I not have given to have known a mother? Somehow, I had never felt a longing for a father, possibly because my mind was somehow poisoned against my father, as represented to me.

We went over the plan a few times and I tried to play devil's advocate trying to find holes, and succeeding, until we had a plan which seemed watertight. It was around 8 p.m. when we arrived at Pittsburgh, where we had to transfer. We discussed the possibility of a reception committee, and decided it was most unlikely, and in any case, we should be safe inside the station. There was a four-hour break, which gave us ample time to eat and drink. We started at the bar and I ordered a whisky. I looked at Claire, who said, "I'm in the mood for a cocktail – what would you suggest?"

"Skinny bitch?" I said, and for a moment, I thought I'd done it again. Fortunately, she took it the right way and chuckled.

"That would be appropriate, thanks, I'll have one." Three drinks later we were both slightly inebriated, and hungry. We found ourselves a corner in a restaurant and ordered a peppercorn steak for me and grilled sole for her. We were famished, and ate without a word being spoken.

After we had boarded our connecting train, we talked about our favourite movies and actors, in a bid to keep the disquiet at bay. The train moved off around midnight, again eliciting huge relief from both of us.

"Time to hit the sack," I said.

Claire looked up at me, and I could not quite make out her expression. I picked up my toiletries and went to the washroom and got ready for bed. I came back to the cabin where Claire was sitting beside the window staring into emptiness, her face completely devoid of expression.

"Please look away, Claire, I'm going to change into my pyjamas."

There was not the slightest response and she continued to stare out of the window. I reckon it took me no more than ten seconds to change into my pyjamas, after which I climbed into the upper berth. Claire left the cabin, presumably to go to the washroom, and returned about ten minutes later. She barely glanced at me, and threw her toiletry bag on the berth below. And then she said, "Look away now, I'm going to change."

I dutifully turned away, and for just a moment was tempted to peep! Before I knew it, she had changed and was out of my sight, on the lower berth. We switched off our lights, and darkness reigned for an unspecified length of time.

Claire's voice broke in. "Tintin, I can't sleep. I'm scared." That really startled me.

"I don't know what I'm doing here with you. Why don't we both just jump off the train and hide away in the nearest town? Or why don't I just go back to Marty? Where the shit are we going, anyway? This plan ain't gonna work, is it?"

There was fear in her voice. I felt moved and recognised an urge to protect her. I controlled myself and said, "Claire, if I knew the answer to your questions, I'd be Superman. As it is, all I can do is be with you and support you as much as I can. I know that isn't much coming from a half-baked apology of an Englishman, but that is all I have to offer. Apart from maybe a comforting hug."

I felt stupid as soon as I finished and Claire's response simply confirmed my stupidity.

"Comfort me, eh? More likely you'll try and get your paws on me. No, thank you, I'm in no mood for romance or anything else."

I was irritated and it must have shown when I said, "Claire, for heaven's sake, that's the last thing I had on my mind. All I'd wanted —

"Oh, just cut the crap, will you?"

Her words lashed out at me and I fell silent, too annoyed to even respond. After a few minutes she had the grace to say, "Look, I'm sorry, I shouldn't have said that."

"No, you shouldn't."

And that was that for the night. I cannot remember when I dropped off to sleep, but it was much later.

I was woken up by the knock on the door. It was our breakfast, which was hot and delicious, consisting of fried eggs, toast, bacon, tomato and mushrooms, accompanied by a steaming kettle of coffee. Claire and I had the breakfast in silence and our eyes did not meet once. After the man had cleared the trolley away, Claire said to me tentatively, "I hope you slept well. I'm afraid I didn't."

I shrugged my shoulders in reply, saying nothing.

"Are you still mad at me? Look, I'm sorry. I can't remember when I last said sorry, but here it is for the records."

"Forget it. We can do better than fight with each other with all the problems that we have. I really don't know what is awaiting us."

"Tintin, I have been thinking most of the night. I know it's a wild idea, but it just might work, and I can't think of anything else, anyway."

"I agree, Claire. It sounds totally hare-brained, but I guess we are in a desperate situation, and this just has to work. Do you think it is time to start by ringing your contact?"

"We'll be arriving in Chicago soon, so I'd rather call from there."

It was just before 9 a.m. when we pulled into Chicago Union Station. We found refuge in a coffee shop. Claire looked at her watch and said, "I guess it's time to make that call. It is probably a bit early for them, but who cares." She rang the man whose number she had obtained from her mother.

"Is that Frank?"

I could hear the loud response from the man. "Who the fuck's callin' this early? I'm sleepin'. How d'ya get this number, anyway?"

"My name is Claire and I need to speak urgently with the Salamander. Tell your boss that I have vital information for him about Marty Nero, and I need to meet with him tomorrow." The man went silent and I thought he'd dropped back into a coma, but he did come back on the line with a grumpy, "Wait, I'll call you back."

Half an hour later Claire's phone rang and I could see the trepidation in her eyes as she answered. Her expression made it obvious that it was the great man himself. She introduced herself and proceeded to describe how Marty had double-crossed him, and details of some key bank accounts which harboured a lot of Marty's loot. It did not take long for her to explain her plan to him. At the end of the call Claire turned to me with real excitement in her eyes. It suddenly hit me that she could transform into a very attractive woman, when she allowed herself to smile or laugh, and when her eyes lit up. "It's on, Tintin! Il Salamandro is going to give us a fair hearing tomorrow. Meantime, let's live it up."

We had about five hours before catching the next connection and so we decided to spend that time in the city. Again, we debated the wisdom of venturing out, but decided that it was no better than lurking around within the station. Besides, we had already spent enough time in the restaurant and making calls, that if anyone was lying in wait, they would have given up and gone – or come looking for us. I suggested we visit the Hancock Tower, thanks to Mitch's joke, and we decided to walk the two miles in that lovely autumn morning. We ended up on the ninety-sixth floor of the building, having a drink and looking out over spectacular views of the city and Lake Michigan. On the way back we joined the locals and picked up the essential over-stuffed burger on the street and proceeded to wolf it down in the expected messy style. I could not help noticing that Claire's appetite was very healthy indeed. Her cheeks had filled out just a wee bit, and in the space of barely a week she was beginning to seem uncomfortably good-looking. I shook myself back to reality. We reached the station and boarded our train at 2.30 p.m. We left Chicago twenty minutes later.

⊕

DELVING THE HISTORIES

Looking back that was the very first time we both relaxed totally. We snoozed for an hour or so, and then had our tea, and then went over the plan yet again. It was around six o'clock when Claire exclaimed: "Enough of this, Tintin, let's get on to other stuff. Now, you were going to tell me all about your life story, and now's the time for the unedited version." And so I did – about my non-existent parents, wonderful Aunt Charlotte, forbidding grandmother, Jimmy, despicable Jack, scary Uncle Charles, my schooling years and finally, my *bete-noire*, Harriett. The unexpected death of my grandmother. Jimmy's suicide. And finally, the day I snapped. Claire was a good listener and was quite taken up with my story.

"Tintin, some things seem rather nebulous, you know. For example, the bit about your parents.

Why was your father such a rebel, and what really happened to him? Again, your mother giving you up, and vanishing from your world. Haven't you wondered, where she might be today?"

I realised that I had never questioned these facts, as that was what I had always been told. It hit me that someone hearing this for the first time could find weaknesses in my story.

"Claire, this is all I know, and when a child has been told something from the time he can remember, then I guess that is taken as gospel. My grandmother may have been more than capable of twisting the facts, but my Aunt Charlotte would never lie to me. She was obviously so extremely fond of her brother, and yet there was always an element of accusation when she spoke about how he had effectively dumped me in the care of his mother, while heading off on his adventures. You can see why I hate my parents. My mother I can still forgive, the poor wretch was widowed and penniless, confronted by this formidable and wealthy English aristocrat, but I can never forgive my father."

I must have sounded bitter and perhaps a bit emotional, and was startled when Claire reached across and put her hand on my shoulder, and gave it a little squeeze. I looked away. "Coming to the present then, have you any idea who is trying to get at you, and why?"

"I really can't understand what on earth's going on. Nothing seems to make any sense. Firstly, why would anybody want to kill me? Is it simply a case of mistaken identity, or is it something quite specific for me? Something tells me it is the latter, but I just cannot fathom it. Any ideas?"

Claire replied, "Actually, I reckon it is the former. Who on earth would want to try and murder a gormless guy like you? Unless of course, you have something of great value, that you're not aware of, and someone else is. Do you think you might be the owner of some unbelievable treasure, such as a Constable in your attic, which somebody has discovered?"

"No, I have absolutely nothing that could be worth anything." I shook my head. "Harriett seems an obvious suspect, but it beggars belief that she could be capable of this, particularly given the paltry sums involved. No, Claire, there is something more to this, but I'm damned if I know what."

Claire nodded. "Think hard and think meticulously, Tintin. The answer lies buried somewhere deep in your history." I nodded in agreement.

And then it was Claire's turn. "It's a sordid tale, mine. I'm originally Canadian. My mom grew up in a violent household in Quebec, and ran away at fifteen, escaping from a brutish father intent on abusing her. She ended up working as a waitress and took on any odd job she could find, until she got herself a boyfriend, and got pregnant with me. I arrived on May 7, 1985, and what she hoped would be her new life of happiness, ended abruptly when my father got killed in an accident.

"We then moved to Montreal to make a fresh start. Desperate, she started working in a lap dancing/strip club, and started making good money to support me. God alone knows what she went through for me. Perhaps predictably, she got picked up by this rich and handsome older man, who relocated us to Boston. He turned out to be with the mob, and had this sadistic son, by the name of Marty. There were times when my mom was on offer to other associates, and I was too young to know the significance of those random visitors. It was during this period that Mom got to meet some other gangland bigwigs, including Il Salamandro. She surreptitiously squirrelled away not just money, but also useful contact details. Poor Mom was kept a virtual prisoner, while she lavished all her earnings on me. She sent me to a private school, and encouraged me to read, read, read, from a very young age. She was the one who introduced me to the Tintin comics, who I believe was her favourite character when she was a little girl in Quebec. When I became of age, I remember her saying to me, 'Claire, my darling, we're born into this wicked world of men, who will always abuse us women. The one and only way to escape is through education.'

"The old man died, leaving his twisted son Marty in charge, and within a month he came to claim his prize – me! I had just got my degree from Johns Hopkins, which was one hell of an achievement, thanks mainly to my mom. She begged him to leave me alone, and I pleaded with him to let me go, to no avail. There was no question of running away, for we knew he would hunt us down. Going to the police was not an option, as we feared it would be a death sentence. I was a voracious reader, majored in English literature, with a head full of dreams, all for nothing. That monster reeled me in, like a frantic frenzied fish. I died that day, Tintin.

"In fact, I would most certainly have tried to escape much sooner, but he held the threat of getting to my mom, if ever I tried to get away. At least I had the reassurance that she was relatively OK, allowed to live her life without any further visitations. She opened a flower shop, which she worked all hours of the day, and made a reasonable living. We were allowed to meet just once a year, when I was allowed to fly to Boston and spend a couple of days together, under the watchful eyes of his henchmen. I think we both survived solely for this annual reunion. We never left home, just spent the whole time looking into each other's eyes, or holding hands." Claire's voice broke. "Mamma will have cooked for a week, all my favourite things, which took me back to my childhood.

"I have been a virtual prisoner like Mamma was. Alcohol, and later, Juanita, were my only friends. Many a time I considered sticking a knife into Marty's back when he was asleep, à la Tess, but could never muster up the courage. Finally, I decided it was either that, or risk running away, and I chose the latter. And here we are…"

After a short pause, she continued, "I just don't get it. How on earth did *you* come into the picture, you poor mutt?"

It was almost nine o'clock, and time to head for dinner. We had decided to go to the dining car, and just as we were about to leave our cabin, on an impulse, I put my arms around Claire, and she instinctively returned my embrace, burying her head on my shoulder. When she looked up, I saw a bewildered little girl. I blinked and looked away, not daring to say anything. She contemplated me for a second, and then turned away. The evening was almost like a dream. We enjoyed a delicious dinner, accompanied by a bottle of New Zealand Sauvignon Blanc, followed by a bottle of Argentine Malbec.

We fell silent as we re-entered our cabin. We went through the routine of changing into our night-wear, as we had done the night before, though this time I sat on the lower berth, looking out while Claire changed. There was a certain feel in the air that I cannot quite describe. I decided it was time to snap out of it and hit the sack. As I wished her goodnight, she put her hands on my shoulder. "Thanks for everything, Tintin." Before I could react, she leaned forwards and planted a quick kiss on my lips, and jumped into her bed. I wished her goodnight, acutely aware of her body, and this kiss was nothing like the first sterile interaction on the boat. I could not settle myself to sleep for a while.

The morning was a subdued affair, and we were both a bit anxious about what was to unfold. Would the Salamander come up trumps? Would he reject the plan and send us on our way? Worse, would he hand us over to Marty, in exchange for reparations and recompense? To me it seemed that if he was 'smart' the obvious thing to do would be to threaten mayhem on Marty, unless there was a handsome settlement, and throw us in as additional enticement. Yet again, I brought up the issue of being recognised and trapped by Marty's henchmen, but Claire reassured me that our hosts had guaranteed our protection – meaning if there were any unwelcome guests, they would take care of them.

PRELUDE 2

THE TALE OF THE REBELLIOUS YOUTH

The parents were proud, overjoyed, ecstatic. The gawky scamp had turned into a lean and striking young man, and had returned home with an honours degree from England. The extended family and the old friends descended on him with a vengeance. It was all celebration, until they suggested that it was time for him to get married to a nice girl (and there were many in line!) and then his mood turned dark.

After a day of silence and palpable tension in the house, he announced that he was intending to marry an English girl. Recrimination and tears had not the slightest effect on him. He failed to enlighten them of the fact that he and the girl had, in fact, spent a delirious week together, not a million miles away. Threatened with excommunication from the community, he laughed derisively. After a week of verbal battles and emotional blackmail, it was finally the parents who relented. They insisted that the wedding had to take place in the ancestral home where they lived, and after some argument, the young man agreed. He convinced them that he needed to return to England, to meet the girl's family and get their consent. And what if they threw him out on his ear? Why would any self-respecting English parents agree to sacrifice their daughter to a poor boy from an ex-colony?

These questions were posed by his father, challenges that were mixed with hope that that would indeed be the case. The boy just laughed and replied that she would happily leave her family for him. So the day arrived, when they would part company again. The parents pleaded with him, to promise to return, and not disappear into the decadent West. The boy left in high spirits, fully intending to keep his promise and return with his English bride-to-be.

6

TRAPPING THE PREDATOR

When hunted, the usual response of the prey is to flee to safety, and may be the most sensible. However, there are times when the only solution is to turn on the predator.

When we got off the train in Las Vegas, it was almost midday. We were greeted by a chauffeur in uniform, with the customary dark glasses expected of a man of his station. We were ushered into a stretch limo, something I had always fancied, although at that point I was not in much of a celebratory mood. Within a minute two others joined us in front, presumably part of our security detail! We drove off and we were invited to help ourselves to the bar, which contained a small selection of drinks and snacks. After about an hour or so, we found ourselves entering a walled compound with electrified fences and a massive wrought-iron gate. It was a warm and sun-drenched day and we seemed to be entering a new world altogether. Inside the compound we were surrounded by exotic tropical vegetation, with a tarmac road leading us to the front of a massive villa, built in European style. Armed men and dogs were much in evidence as we stepped out of the car. We stepped onto the marble floor of the portico and were admitted in through tall, large, beautifully carved wooden doors. It was magical in the way that, in a matter of a few minutes, we were transported from America to Europe!

Our host greeted us warmly and delivered the statutory Continental double kiss on Claire's cheeks. He then proceeded to shake my hand vigorously. He was far from what I had expected, short and rotund, with a cherubic smile, resembling an amiable housewife, more than a hardened gangland boss. But given the reception and the trappings, I was in no doubt at all about what he really was. After the usual visit to the washroom to freshen up, we gathered around a table in the cool shade, overlooking a large swimming pool.

"I am sorry that I am unable to introduce my family to you. I have a very strict rule about not mixing business with pleasure. In fact, I do not carry out any business at home, except in exceptional circumstances, as this one. This young lady has managed to convince me of the urgency of the situation and I must confess I could not resist the temptation of finally getting even with that piece of rat shit." Claire's reaction was a radiant smile. There was a pause as lunch was served.

The salad, the meats and the beverages were exquisite. I was interested to note that alcohol was not served. Almost as if he read my mind our host said, "I personally never drink alcohol during daylight hours and apply the same rule to all my visitors. You may think it unrefined, but I'm afraid that's the way it is."

"That is absolutely fine with us," said Claire. "Alcohol really is the least of our concerns at the moment. What did you think of our plan?"

The Salamander nodded, and gave us the thumbs up. I expected him to say something, but he maintained silence, expecting more from us.

Claire continued: "So, assuming that you have been through the logistics of my proposal, we can schedule this to happen the day after tomorrow?"

He nodded his assent. "Let's get on with the job. Now I want you to go ahead and make that phone call."

Claire punched the numbers in her phone.

"Hi, Mamma, it's me. Don't worry, I am fine and safe in the company of Signor Salamander. We have a plan to take care of Marty. I need you to do something for me. I want you to call Marty and tell him that you have heard from me. You need to convince him that I truly regret what happened and am scared for my life. If he promises to forgive me and return to the status quo, I would be prepared to return to him for good."

Claire's mother spoke rapidly and although I could not hear her exact words, Claire's reply made the gist of it clear. "But, Mamma, listen, there is nothing to worry about. I have arranged everything and Marty will never bother us again. So, you have to trust me on this." Claire then briefly outlined her plan and her mother seemed to come around.

"So, Mamma, this is why you have to make it work. Tell Marty that I am staying at the Luxor in Vegas, though you do not know the room number. If he asks about a man accompanying me, just say that I'm on my own, as far as you know, and that I did not mention anybody staying with me. If asked what I planned to do next, tell him I was planning to get to LA and stay with an old school friend. Obviously, you do not know the details of her name or where she stays. And Mamma, make sure you stay where you are and don't under any circumstances let Marty know where he can get at you. Do you get that, Mamma? On no account should you allow him to get anywhere near you. If he asks, tell him you're at home. I love you too, Mamma. I promise this will all be over soon and I'll be back for you." The conversation ended with Claire surreptitiously wiping her eyes.

We said our goodbyes, and parted company with the Salamander and his coterie. We were driven to the city in a less ostentatious car and the drive took over an hour. Claire and I both fell asleep, exhausted by the proceedings of the day. It was almost dark by the time we reached the Luxor. Despite having heard all about it and seen a fair amount of it on TV, I still marvelled at the sights and the sounds on the Strip, with all its legendary hotels – Caesar's Palace, Venetian, New York New York, MGM, Bellagio and finally the Luxor. We checked into adjacent rooms with an interconnecting door. An hour later, having showered and changed, we met for dinner in the restaurant on the ground floor. I was bewildered by the manic surroundings and while a part of me could understand the kind of excitement it might generate, the greater part of me just wished I was somewhere else – quiet. This was true pandemonium! I don't think we said very much during the dinner. I could sense some ongoing tension in Claire.

"Have you been here before with your boyfriend?" I said, trying to sound light-hearted, and failing.

Claire glowered. "Not for a long time and never had a desire to. I was his trophy to display, and I hate this place with a vengeance, for what it represents. This is the last place in the world Marty would think I would be hiding out."

"There is something wild and exciting about this place. Though my guess is that within a day I would be sick to the gills."

After a fairly modest dinner we retired to our respective rooms. No words were exchanged, just a nod and a perfunctory good-night, as we entered our respective rooms. Five minutes later I rang Claire in her room.

"Shall we fix a time to go down for breakfast? Say nine o'clock?"

"Yup, nine sounds fine."

"Goodnight then. Don't hesitate to knock on the door if you need anything."

"I won't need anything," she hissed. "And I have locked my door, in case you get ideas."

There was a touch of contempt in her voice, and I bristled at her misinterpretation of my innocent remark.

"You should be so lucky." I put down the phone before she could respond.

I lay in bed for the next half hour, going through the events of the last few days, still amazed that all this was happening to me in real life. Then I gave up on sleep, got up and dressed, and left the room. Although it was eleven o'clock, the place was still heaving. The slot machines, the gaming tables, the staff running around, the apparent sense of disportation – I found it all quite crazy. I left the hotel and went for a walk along the Strip and sampled some of the hotels, astonished by the dramatic creations and the sheer scale and size of the constructions. I returned to my room around 2 a.m. and collapsed into a dreamless slumber.

✟

PREY AND PREDATOR

I must have slept way beyond what I had planned, for I was woken up by the phone.

"Wake up, you lazy slob!"

"Bad morning to you, too," I said. "What time is it?"

"Ten, and we have things to do."

"*You,* not I. Have you called your boyfriend yet?" knowing that would annoy her.

"NO, and I was hoping to do it when you were present."

"Oh, well then. I'll order in the room. Why don't you come across in half an hour?"

Exactly half an hour later, there was a knock on the door. Claire looked rested, refreshed and quite fetching, wearing a light patterned top and a pair of dark blue jeans. I pretended to take no notice. I was still in my pyjamas, but had managed to get through the morning ablutions and even shave.

"I had a late night, wandering the streets."

Claire raised her eyebrows enquiringly, and I filled her in.

"Why didn't you let me know? I'd have come too."

"Not sure I wanted your company, the mood you were in."

She flushed, gave me a hard look and looked away.

I had made myself a cup of coffee, and made another cup for Claire. We sat in silence, just savouring the quiet and the hot aromatic drink. For a change, the quality of the filtered coffee (Costa Rican) was excellent. A few minutes later it was time to make the crucial call. Claire was distinctly uncomfortable and fidgety.

"Listen, no need to be jittery. Remember he cannot do anything to you, at least not at the moment."

"Yes, I know. I guess I am just worried that he might smell a rat. I'm afraid I might say something to tip him off."

"You have to be absolutely firm in your conviction and you are such a consummate performer, I have complete faith in you. Go for it, baby."

She looked at me gratefully and then picked up her phone and punched in his number.

"Marty, it's me." I could hear a veritable volcano of expletive eruptions from the other end! Claire crunched up her eyes, holding the phone an inch away from her ear.

"Listen, Marty, baby, I fucked up. I'll make it up to you, if that's the last thing I do. I don't know what got into me, and why I was wasting my time on that English jerk. You know I was drunk. When you threw me overboard, I really thought I had come to the end of the road, but heaven knows how we managed to survive."

I could hear Marty clearly. "And so you decided to run, you stupid bitch. You thought you could escape from Marty Nero, you really thought you could fuckin' escape Marty? You have no idea what is going to happen when I get my hands on you."

There was real panic in Claire's voice.

"Marty, please, give me a break. This is the first and last time this will ever happen. When I get back to you this time it'll all be changed and I swear you won't regret it. In fact, I would've come back to you the very next day, but for this fucking creep, who persuaded me to accompany him on the train. He convinced me that we could get away scot-free. On the train last night when I suggested that we split up and that I'd go back to you, he roughed me up a bit. That's not all, Marty, he raped me, and I could do nothing about it."

I started, as this was not in the script. I looked at Claire with obvious astonishment, a look that she refused to acknowledge, staring straight at the wall. I could hear Marty's expletives coming across thick and fast and he ended with, "I am going to make mincemeat of the motherfucker. I'm going to feed him alive to the rats, if it's the last thing I do. Just where the hell are you two right now, anyway?"

"We checked into the Luxor yesterday, but this guy's got this wild urge to drive across Death Valley to LA after dark. The guy's deranged. Now all I want is to get back with you, Marty. I'm so desperate I'm ready to try and run away. Shall I make a dash for the airport and catch the next flight to New York? I'm terrified he is going to have a sudden change of mind, and decide to drive off early."

"No, you dumb bitch, you don't fly anywhere. I'm already in Vegas, I flew in this morning. Fortunately, your mother had the sense to call me and let me know."

We both breathed a sigh of relief, as that was exactly what we had counted on.

"Marty, that's amazing. Can you come and get me right now? I just want to get away from this guy."

"I'll be there in an hour. Wait for me at the front. After I pick you up, I think we'll pay a visit to your new late boyfriend."

"Marty, no, please don't. Why not just forget him and get back to NY?" There was no way that Marty was going to deny himself the pleasure of dealing with me in his own unique way. The bait had been taken, but we still had to reel the fish in.

"Shut the fuck up and do as I say. Be down there in one hour sharp. If you can't give him the slip, at least call me from the rest room or something and let me know. OK? What's your room number?"

"8352. Before you go, Marty, describe the car you'll be in, just in case I have to make a dash for it."

It would be a black BMW X5 with the number plate MART1. The conversation ended with that. Looking at my surprised face, Claire remarked, "No, he didn't just hire a car with that plate, he owns it. The bastard maintains a car in each of the four cities he travels to regularly – apart from the three he owns in New York." The next call was to the Salamander to inform him about our progress, and most importantly the details of Marty's car.

Claire slumped on the sofa, drained by her effort. I looked at her with an obvious look of approval and gave her the thumbs up, which she acknowledged gratefully. We checked out of the Luxor. The nondescript 'hire' car that had been allocated, stood in readiness, having been delivered by one of the Salamander's drivers. We got in and I drove slowly out of the hotel, making sure we did not attract any attention. Claire's phone rang twenty minutes later. It was from Marty, and we ignored it. Claire then turned her phone off. We drove at a sedate speed and reached the designated hotel in Primm Valley, south of Las Vegas, on the I5, about an hour later.

After checking in to the resort hotel, we had a light lunch and then went to the poolside. Claire turned several heads, as we sauntered along the pool – or perhaps I did, as a fair proportion of the turning heads were female! I dived in and swam fifty lengths without breaking a sweat, as they say. I became aware of my new self, fitter and leaner. Claire did a few lengths and then stretched herself out. I took the sunbed next to her, and we must have looked the ideal couple, without a care in the world. We had already introduced ourselves as newly-weds, on a road trip. As it was getting to be dusk, we returned to the room, and fortified ourselves with a drink for what was to come. We could hear and see fireworks going off, and I realised that it was Halloween night! I had lost all track of dates and days.

At eight o'clock, it was time to make the crucial call. I could hear the fury in Marty's voice as he started with, "Just where the fuck have you been, you stupid —"

Before he could say anything more, Claire spoke in what appeared like a panicked whisper.

"Marty, shut up and listen. This maniac had a sudden change of mind, and checked out and dragged me off on his drive, just a few minutes after we spoke. I had no chance to call. We were heading for LA, and then he makes a sudden stop in this resort hotel in Primm Valley. I've been stuck with him all day. He is at the poolside and this was my first chance to call. So, his plan is to drive out soon and we'll probably reach LA at some goddamned unearthly hour. That's not all, the crazy sonofabitch wants to go off the road when it's dark and make love under the stars. I'm so scared, Marty, I don't know what to do."

"Fuckin' hell. Listen, don't panic, just play cool. Describe the car and tell me the name of the hotel you're staying in tonight."

"It's a Chevy Cruise, which is old and looks quite beat up. It's got a Nevada number plate starting 248 and the next three letters are UGM. As for the hotel in LA, do you think he tells me that kind of detail? I'll call and let you know."

"OK, you get in the car and go quietly with him. Pretend you are happy to be with him, and tell him you have decided to skip the country. I'll try and catch up on the I5, but don't worry if I do or I don't, because I'll sure as hell roast this motherfucker's ass in LA tomorrow. I swear to you this prick is going to get what's coming to him." He rang off.

We looked at each other and our expressions were a combination of relief, delight, apprehension and anxiety. Claire looked at her watch and then picked up her phone and punched in a number.

"*Buongiorno, signor.* Everything has gone according to plan so far. We are in the resort hotel in Primm Valley and Marty should be on the road, probably in a bit of a hurry to catch up with us. He should be heading for LA, and unless he is a clairvoyant, he should have no reason to stop here. Everything OK from your end?" I signed to Claire to turn on the speaker phone.

"Yes, *signorina*," came the distinct voice of the Salamander. "Your distress call to Nero was timed to perfection. Identification was no problem after you'd given us the details. He pulled into the Luxor, and jumped out, looking around for you, and flew into quite a temper, as you weren't there and hadn't called him. In the midst of his running around frantically, one of my men did exactly what we had planned, masquerading as one of the security guards inspecting the car, and using the opportunity to plant the device. From there on he was tailed by Jensen, you remember the tall blond guy you met at my place? So, if Marty is on your tail, so will Jensen be on his tail. So, you two can just relax where you are and wait."

We showered and came down to the poolside restaurant for a scrumptious dinner of seafood gumbo, Mexican lobster and jambalaya, washed down by two bottles of an excellent Californian Chardonnay. After all, we were honeymooners, weren't we?! Around ten we returned to the room, our high spirits now replaced by anxiety. By now, Marty, tailed by Jensen, should be almost half-way to LA. We made light conversation and tried to sound casual, but there was clear tension. It came to a head, when Claire, unable to keep up the pretence, snuggled up to me on the sofa. This was a nice surprise, I thought, under the circumstances.

The ring of the phone made us jump. It was the boss man himself. I turned on the speaker.

"How are you, *signorina*?" Claire was having difficulty breathing.

I intervened. "Thank you, sir, we are both in great form. Have you any news for us?"

"You are so English, young man. So, as you might guess, Marty was pushing his car a bit and frankly the last thing we wanted was for him to get a cop on his tail. Even worse, if a cop got on our tail, in which case he would have got away. Fortunately, neither of them got stopped. Anyway, just a few minutes ago, Marty's car reached a long stretch where there was no sign of a car for at least a mile on either side. Jensen, who was a safe distance behind, stopped his car and hit the detonator. That was the end of that. According to Jensen, the explosion was straight out of one of the *Die Hard* movies. That's the end of that lowlife skunk, and he'll never bother you again."

There was a sharp intake of breath from both of us and a couple of seconds of silence. Claire burst out, "*Signor*, that is the best news I have heard in my entire life. Can we be sure that Marty is gone?"

"Don't worry, *mia cara*, we are one hundred per cent sure. The little prick finally got what he deserved. You both can now relax and enjoy the rest of your lives!"

I joined in: "Don Salamandro, I don't know what else to call you, but this is fantastic and we are extremely grateful to you."

"No, actually, I am very grateful to the two of you. You gave me the chance to correct this injustice and eliminate this poisonous shit. I am now in a position to negotiate with his gang and recover some of my stolen goods, so to speak."

Claire chimed in, "I love you, Signor Salamandro! I know I can never repay you for this, but one day when I am safe and secure with my mother, I will invite you for the most lavish dinner you have ever had."

"Ah, my sweet girl, nothing will give this old man greater pleasure. And I would love to re-acquaint myself with your mamma. If in the meantime, however, you need any further help, just ask. I know you are heading to LA now and Jensen will pick up the car. You have a room booked at the DoubleTree Hilton, just off the San Bernadino Highway, easy to find. Just leave the keys in the car. So, wherever you are off to, just don't go back to New York! I wish you all the very best of luck, and the same to your young man from England!"

We laughed wildly and joked around for a little while. "Tintin, wasn't that a great Halloween present for Marty?! I'll celebrate this date with more zest than my own birthday from now on." I thought it sounded a bit macabre, but said nothing for fear of spoiling her mood. It was twelve-thirty when we collapsed, exhausted by the proceedings of the day. We slept late into the morning and arranged a late check-out. We finally left at three o'clock and ten minutes later we were on the I5. I had been reassured that this rather sad-looking car was actually nothing short of a racehorse, carefully camouflaged. Apparently, it housed a turbo-charged five-litre engine that was capable of topping 160 mph, if the occasion arose.

The traffic was moderate and I looked in the mirror as far back as I could and could see no sign of anything that looked like a police car. Partly because of my sense of liberation and partly because I wanted to test the theory, I floored the pedal. The response was mind-blowing; the car bucked like a spooked stallion and accelerated at an unbelievable rate. Claire screamed, "Tintin, what the fuck's wrong with you?" At the same time, she frantically looked around in both directions to see if we were under attack or under pursuit. I quickly slowed the car back down to a legal fifty-five, and explained that I had simply been putting the vehicle through its paces.

The rest of the drive to LA took under four hours and was punctuated by periods of silence, inexplicable laughter, anxiety and uncertainty. It slowly sank in that we had participated in cold-blooded murder; in fact we had actually planned and orchestrated it. There was a recurrent heart-sink sensation, mitigated by the inevitable counter-argument that it was pretty much self-defence. "You know, Claire, I'm getting a severe bout of guilty conscience. I have actively aided and abetted an act of murder, of a man whom I barely knew and who probably could not have harmed me if I had just skipped the country."

"What a load of crap, Tintin. This was an act of self-defence and retribution. Marty deserved this and much more for all his past crimes, that you have no clue about. Believe me, killing a cockroach would dismay me more than killing this fucking psycho."

Claire was right, of course, but I was still a bit taken aback by the vehemence and the animosity. She was almost manic, swinging from angry denunciation to hysterical laughter, and ended in the inevitable flood of tears. I had just parked the car when she broke down and was wracked by sobs. "Oh, Tintin, I have had a life of hell, and all of a sudden it is all over. It's actually all over. I can't believe it, I'm actually free." I put my arm around her and she buried her face on my shoulder and cried like a baby.

We got out of the car and made our way into the reception of the DoubleTree Hilton. We discovered we had a suite, and duly checked in. I had a quick shower, following which Claire ran a bath and slipped into it. I downed a couple of whiskies, following which there was a knock on the door. It was room service delivering two bottles of chilled champagne. I cracked open a bottle and filled two flutes, and knocked on the bathroom door. "Guess what? Champagne with the compliments of the Salamander. May I be so bold as to bring your drink to you?" I was excited, not least by the champagne!

At her invitation I walked in, only to be disappointed by the fact that only her head was visible, the rest of her submerged under a heavy layer of foam. I perched casually on the edge of the tub, sitting close to her foot end. We clinked glasses and drank the vintage champagne, which tasted heavenly. "In an ideal world I guess I would invite you to join me, Tintin! Unfortunately, that's not the kind of relationship we have. Though heaven knows why."

"Things can change, you know," I said with a very deliberate leer. Claire laughed, shook her head and waved me away.

We ordered room-service dinner, both in ultra-high spirits, slightly disorientated and drunk, on the edge of hysteria. Claire then turned on the music, and we danced with total abandon. Then I switched the music to jazz.

"So, tell me, Claire, am I Tintin, the comic boy-sleuth, or Rin Tin Tin the super-dog of the silver screen?"

Claire nuzzled my neck. "Both. The brains of one and the looks of the other. Up to you to choose the combo."

"Either way, endowed with both brains and looks, eh?"

Claire stuck a saucy tongue out at me. We hugged, we kissed and we crashed out, fully clothed.

7

MAYHEM IN PARADISE

*When pain yields place to luxury, it ushers in joy
that is well deserved. But be wary, weary traveller,
of lurking dangers!*

We surfaced late and ordered breakfast in the room.
For several minutes, we went back and forth debating
our next move. Claire was very keen to fly out to
Montreal ASAP to join her mother, but I counselled
against it. There were bound to be some repercussions
following Marty's 'accident' which obviously would
be seen for what it was – a hit. Someone in the
organisation could well connect it with Claire's
sudden disappearance, and start ferreting around.

The only sensible thing would be to lie low for a few months before returning to normal.

"But what the hell do I do, Tintin? Keep moving from hotel to hotel all over the country, looking over my shoulders? I need to go somewhere and forget this whole fucking thing, get it out of my system."

"Hey, I've got an idea. Why don't you join me on my round-the-world plan? I had thought of spending a couple of months here in America, but somehow I've lost the appetite for any more. I've decided to fly west from LA."

Claire considered it and shook her head. After a couple of seconds, she looked up with an animated expression. "What the fuck, Tintin, let's do it. Where did you have in mind?" And so, an hour later, we booked two business-class tickets to Nadi in Fiji! The rest of the day was spent getting a few travel essentials, and still we barely had any luggage to speak of. Claire spoke to her mother and gave her the good news of Marty's departure, followed by the news that she would be going abroad for three months. Then, she scurried into the bathroom mid-sentence. Curiosity got the better of me, and I sneaked over to the door and eavesdropped.

"Mamma, the time will fly and I'll be back before you know it. Meantime, you need to stay put and keep your head down. If by chance any of Marty's men call you, play dumb, and say you haven't heard from him or me since that last call you made to him. And don't worry about me, Mamma, I'll be much safer abroad. I just need to be away while the dust settles here. I'm going with Quentin, Mamma, who's been just amazing. He actually saved my life. The first real man I've met in my life." There was a pause as Claire listened to her mother. "Oh, please, Mamma, don't get carried away. Nothing of the kind, I hardly know him really, just that he is totally dependable and decent." A pause, and then, "To be honest, Mamma, I was fibbing when I said he was an ex-con, that was just to reassure you that I was safe with him. Now that Marty's gone, I can reveal that he is a bit of a wimp, but a true gentleman." I sneaked away before I was discovered.

We got a taxi to the airport, arriving well in time to board the flight at 22.30. I made my way to the duty-free shopping and I bought myself a bottle of Glenfiddich and a box of five Monte Cristo cigars. What the hell, why not? I toyed with the idea of buying John Le Carré's latest novel but then decided not to, because I knew I was in no state to settle down and read. Claire had wandered away and we met up after about twenty minutes.

"What have you got?" I showed her my purchases.

"I've got myself a bottle of pink gin, a bottle of White Linen and a tazer stun gun."

I looked at her aghast and she looked deadpan. And then she exploded into the most musical and delightful laugh I had ever heard or seen. Just for a moment she was completely transformed into a radiant, mischievous and beautiful creature.

"Tintin, your face…" She drowned in her mirth, eyes filling with tears. My horror turned to embarrassment, followed by profound amusement.

"Nothing that you would ever do would surprise me, Claire." She was mocking me, but I did not mind. We were both still on a bit of a high.

I looked up at the flight schedules displayed and noted that there was still half an hour to board. It was too early to drink, I told myself. She must have read my mind, for she nodded. "Not time for booze yet, buster." There was a sense of easy friendship between us and I wondered how long it would last.

Claire took out a magazine and devoted her attention to it. I wandered off for a few minutes and sat in a chair about twenty feet away, legs stretched and head thrown back, with eyes half-closed. Through my half-closed eye I could not help observing the new Claire, in stark contrast to the over made-up, highly strung, vicious, skeletal female that I had first met on the boat. In a dispassionate sort of a way I saw how attractive she was, her skin smooth and flawless, the expression totally relaxed, though the slight air of nervous excitement gave her cheeks a slight colour. Her hair was dishevelled, but did not detract from the overall effect. Poor kid, I thought to myself, a highly intelligent and sensitive girl, messed up by the events of her childhood, and then her 'slavery' at the hands of Marty. I wondered if she could ever retrieve herself and allow her scars to heal. All that crudeness, rudeness and callousness, were they ever curable? More importantly, where would she go from here on?

I shook the negative thoughts away and stood up and walked back to her. She continued to read a magazine, and without looking up, said, "Enjoy the scenery?"

I could feel myself beginning to redden, when she said, "It's all right, Tintin, I don't mind. It's a long time since any man looked at me with anything but lecherous eyes. So I take it as a compliment." Her eyes were firmly fixed on the magazine, but she was animated and her cheeks had coloured more.

I was at a loss to know what to say, but in the end managed, "I am sorry, I didn't mean to stare."

"Apology noted, registered and rejected, as there was no need for the same." She looked up and our eyes locked for what seemed a long time. I looked into the depths of her eyes, her mind and soul, and I relished what I saw. And suddenly the spell was broken when her lips curled and her expression hardened.

"Take it easy, lover boy. We are still in the shit, you're a burnt-out failure and I am a high-class whore on the run. So don't get carried away."

My jaws clenched and I managed a supercilious smile. "Don't worry, sweetheart, I have no illusions." A loaded silence fell, while she continued to read, or pretend to read. I looked out unfocussed, pretending to look at the runway and the flight that was landing. Our flight was announced and we boarded it.

Until then I had not even known that there was an Air Pacific, which was the national carrier of Fiji. The staff were charming. The stewardess looking after us was Polynesian, named Rigieta, well built, probably around five foot seven inches. She wore the colourful uniform of the carrier, in traditional style, a flower in her hair and a beautiful smile. She fussed over us as we settled into our business-class seats and I must say, my first taste of airborne luxury. One could virtually lie back and sleep with legs at full stretch.

By this time the frost had thawed between Claire and me, and we were both back to our erstwhile, light-hearted selves.

"This really is something, ain't it, Tintin?"

I concurred without hesitation. In fact we were the only two in the entire section. The orange juice arrived, followed by the champagne.

We chit-chatted for the next half hour or so, about fairly mindless things. Claire wanted to know what I had done in school, apart from the studies. Like most Americans she knew nothing about cricket, and I spent a little while explaining the game and its subtleties. She was amazed to hear about the five-day tests, and simply could not see the point of it. The one-day internationals, however, appealed to her, and she was prepared to concede that it might even begin to approach the excitement of a baseball game. My swimming prowess, of course, was already well known to her through painful experience, so I did not have to labour that point. Apart from these two, my third major interest was in reading works of fiction.

When talking about it, there was a look of wistful longing in her eyes. "You know, I loved to read as a child? I was quite simply unstoppable. I was always top of my class when it came to English. By the time I was twelve, I had graduated to reading Du Maurier and I was so proud of myself, but never mind me, my mother was a thousand times more proud of her little daughter. It was all literature and intellectual stuff for me, I was top of the class in speech and drama, in debating and public speaking. I was just such a happy little girl, why did it all have to go wrong? I hated my mother at the time and blamed her for all that went wrong. Yet now, when I am much older and looking back, I cannot tell you how grateful I am to her. She dragged herself through mud and slush to send me to the kind of school that she thought would get me the best education."

After a superb dinner, we drifted off. I woke up to a sensation of floating gently on a cloud, with a soft rendering of *Fleur de Lys* on piano. It crossed my mind that this is perhaps what heaven might feel like. I think I enjoyed the best night of my life on that flight. The outstanding service, the food and the drinks, combined with Claire's mood and high spirits, conspired to make the first part of the night quite delectable. And then the sleep that followed was deep and absolute. It was only the gentle whisper of the stewardess in my ear, announcing the arrival of the breakfast, which woke me. Claire was curled up and fast asleep, with her head cradled on a pillow against the window.

It was a lovely morning and we landed in Nadi International Airport a few minutes behind schedule. It took about half an hour to get through the immigration and of course we did not have any checked-in luggage, so we breezed straight through. The temperature was a balmy 23°C. We jumped into a taxi and I gave him the address of the hotel, which we reached a half hour later.

The resort hotel was delightful, with an abundance of foliage and exotic flowers. There were two extremely inviting open-air swimming pools. The reception was manned by an attractive young girl by the name of Jyoti, who welcomed us. Although the usual check-in time was 2 p.m., she pulled out all the stops and arranged for a room to be cleaned and ready within the hour. In the meantime we were invited to a complimentary breakfast, which I thought was extremely generous. We declined, however, and settled for some more coffee. Sitting in the garden at 7 a.m., listening to the birds and looking at the profusion of botanical delights, it felt like this was a continuation of the heaven I had experienced earlier on waking.

As if she had read my thoughts, Claire exclaimed: "I have spent an entire lifetime dreaming of this, Tintin. And now I'm here, thanks to you." We sat in absolute silence for the next five minutes, drinking in the beauty and just being in the moment. I had never felt so alive. I felt a sensation of deep and total contentment. We spent the rest of the day in a kind of haze. What was in no doubt was that we both for the first time in many days felt completely relaxed and at ease. Sometimes together, and sometimes separately we wandered on the beach, splashing in and out of the tepid sea. I went through periods of frenzied swimming, aware that my belly had regressed considerably, owing to the physical exertions of the previous fortnight. When Claire asked if I wanted to join her for lunch, I declined and jumped into the pool and proceeded to swim fifty lengths, while she sat at the poolside consuming everything in sight. At four o'clock I had had enough and was beginning to feel the effects of lack of food. I treated myself to a smoothie and informed Claire I was off to have a nap. She was sunning herself in a one-piece costume and I could not help noticing that she was filling it pretty well. With her shades on, I could not interpret her expression, as she contemplated me for a few seconds. "You go and do that. I'll soak up the sun a bit longer and get my nap right here."

I have no idea what time it was when I found myself being shaken gently. I was totally disorientated and for a moment did not know where I was.

"Wakey wakey, little boy. The time is seven o'clock, and I'm beginning to feel a bit peckish."

"You cannot be serious. How can a beanpole like you put away quite so much?"

"Precisely because I'm a beanpole. All my life I have been paranoid about my weight and yet look at me now, I don't give a fuck. What does it matter if I'm skinny and ugly or fat and ugly?"

"As a matter of fact, I'm not sure I want to be saying this. In a mere matter of a couple of weeks, you have gone from looking like a scarecrow to someone really quite attractive." I regretted it as soon as the words were out of my mouth. What was I thinking?

To my surprise, Claire blushed and looked away.

I rubbed my eyes and staggered out of bed. Half an hour later we were both showered and changed and ready to face the evening.

"Let's celebrate with a drink," said Claire, and pulled out a bottle of Ardbeg that she had bought at the duty-free. We sat and toasted, and savoured the whisky. It was an elegant, large room measuring probably around 300 square feet with a little lounge sofa at one corner, in front of which were wide glass doors, opening onto a balcony, giving us an uninhibited view of the sea. I opened the glass doors to allow the gentle breeze to waft in. Lights were twinkling all along the shore and the whole thing felt unreal. We talked about the recent events with a sense of disbelief. How on earth had we managed to escape our erstwhile hellish existence?

"This isn't really happening, is it? It's all going to blow up in our faces. Such nice things don't happen in real life, Tintin. I would happily spend the rest of my life outside America, if it weren't for my poor mom."

"I think you are over your nightmares. Your late ex-boyfriend is pushing up daisies and will not be troubling you any more. If anything, I'm the one who is still vulnerable, except I don't know why."

Claire looked at me with a curious expression and said, "There's something you're missing, aren't you? It must be something you can work out, if you think very carefully. The answer is probably sitting there staring at you." My mood turned gloomy instantly and it must have shown in my face.

"I guess it's safe to say that you should have nothing to fear right now, although what awaits you when you get back home is anybody's guess."

I nodded. "I intend to have the time of my life and while doing so try and work out what the hell is going on. If all else fails, I'll just go back home and confront Harriett, some of whose precious possessions are now in my custody."

There was a note of real eager curiosity in Claire's voice. "Tell me, Tintin, tell me. I want to hear all about you and your Harriett. She sounds like quite a character."

"Don't you dare call her *my Harriett!* She certainly is quite a character, preferably across an electrified barbed-wire fence."

Claire laughed aloud – I joined in – and her eyes were alight with anticipation, as she said, "I'm waiting."

"You've already heard a concise version of this. But I suppose you would like to hear more of the lurid details?" Claire nodded with a saucy grin.

"Okay, but I really need some food. So why don't we get going and I'll regale you with the tragic story that is my life, through dinner."

The restaurant was covered but open on all sides and looked out onto the beach. It was dusk, and the colours in the horizon subtly and silently exploded into a riot of contrasting shades that blended to perfection, a feat unique to nature. The soft white sand had turned to a startling shade of mauve, with a million undulations. Between the horizon and the sand, lay the vast expanse of the sea, which at that moment was somewhere between ultramarine and purple. The whole effect was magical, probably because my erstwhile fevered brain was finally at peace, and receptive to the boundless dividends of nature. I did not think life could get much better than this. I voiced my thoughts, to no one in particular, almost in a trance.

"That's almost poetic, Tintin."

I was quite chuffed by her complimentary tone, and the look of appreciation that accompanied it.

The menu looked extremely appetising, if unfamiliar. We decided to try 'kokoda', a kind of fish salad, for starters. It was perfect! For mains we had their traditional Fijian lamb stew with rice, which, combined with a bottle of Argentine Malbec, was simply outstanding. I narrated the story from the start, some of which, of course, I had revealed earlier. Claire was a good listener and seemed genuinely interested. Having had a couple of shots of the excellent whisky, I suppose my tongue was sufficiently loosened. We ate slowly, savouring every moment, and I continued to relate my chequered history.

"So tell me then, how do you fall so madly in love with someone, see nothing but the good in that person, only to find that everything you thought about that person was actually wrong?"

I took a long while to answer, feeling quite inadequate. "I don't know, Claire. You see, all my life I have craved for love, and all I received were those wonderful moments when my aunt visited. Even that disappeared with her untimely death. So, when I became infatuated with Harriett, I had absolutely no difficulty in translating that into an all-consuming love. More to the point, what did she see in me, I used to wonder. I attributed that to the fact that physically I was not unattractive – you may not believe that – and I was at the beginning of what might have seemed like a potentially high-powered corporate career in the pharmaceutical world. Alas, that was not to be, and with each setback Harriett's true nature unfolded. Like a horror story. I suppose that I was a gullible and vulnerable fool. Now I know for sure that she was after my inheritance. She stripped me of my sense of dignity, self-respect and self-confidence, the result being the progressive deterioration of myself over the last three years, both physically and mentally."

I was looking out to the sea during this monologue, not daring to meet Claire's eye. She leaned across and placed a hand on mine. "Hey, come on, Tintin, don't be hard on yourself. I have spent my entire life in the company of scum, in comparison to whom, you would be an angel. This Harriett sounds like a bitch you are well rid of, and she would never deserve someone like you."

Our eyes locked and I could see real sincerity and tenderness, which surprised me slightly. Our moment of connection was broken when Claire snapped back to her usual self. "Anyway, it's all over, so stop feeling sorry for yourself. Time to man up." She followed this with a little fake chuckle, which ended the conversation.

It must have been nearly ten when we strolled out of the restaurant. I said I wanted to go for a walk down along the beach and Claire went along with it. The darkness was intense and the stars were out in force. Lights twinkled along the beach and in the distance one could see the lights of the city. The breeze was gentle, and caressing, generating a continual flow of its soft fingers across my face and exposed forearms. We talked about impersonal matters like the beauty of unspoilt locations, global warming, climate change, and the ecovandalism by the human race. We talked about music and cinema, and it turned out we had some common favourites – Kate Winslet, Emma Thompson, Jennifer Lawrence, Nicole Kidman, Leonardo DiCaprio and Matthew McConaughey. In music we, however, agreed to disagree. Claire loved classical, Vivaldi in particular, whereas I was a jazz fan. We both agreed that Adele was the best thing going in pop.

At eleven we were back in our luxurious room and prepared to get ready for bed. The 'bed' was actually two large double beds together, which could easily accommodate four people. We took one each, without any fuss. Neither of us made any overtures towards the other. The lights went out.

"Thanks for being such a gentleman, Tintin. I know I'm not much comfort, but you need to realise that I have had a pretty shitty life so far. These last couple of days have been the best of my life and I have you to thank."

"Goodnight, Claire."

It was pitch-dark when I woke up the next morning, with no idea of how long I had been asleep – thanks to the blackout curtains. I fumbled for my watch and then lit up the dial to see it was nine thirty! This must have woken up Claire. "Good morning. What time is it?" She was just as surprised as I, when I told her. I made my way to the little lounge area and opened up the curtains, to reveal a slightly overcast day, which still could not spoil the beauty of the scene I beheld. I announced that I would make the morning hot drinks and Claire opted for tea. I made myself a coffee. A few minutes later we were both seated next to each other on the sofa, Claire with her legs sprawled over the side armrest and I with my legs stretched out onto a footstool. We sipped our drinks and stared out into the beyond.

"Isn't it weird, Tintin, that here we are for all intents and purposes, newly-weds on honeymoon? And yet what could be further from the truth? I have to keep pinching myself to make sure all this isn't just a lovely dream!"

"Yup, whatever the reality of the situation, at least we are putting up a reasonable show as honeymooners, except perhaps with one notable deficiency."

I looked at Claire with a telling look and she blushed and looked away.

"Shut up. You ain't gonna get it that easily!"

"I ain't getting it at all, I suspect."

She would not take the bait and I decided to back off before she relapsed into her former self.

We ordered breakfast in the room, which as expected turned out to be a sumptuous affair. I restricted myself, whereas Claire again did more than full justice. Around midday I decided to go for a run, leaving Claire by the poolside. It was two o'clock when I returned, determined to skip lunch. Claire gave me a look.

"You're going to fade away at this rate. Though I have to admit that you are beginning to look a lot fitter than you did when we first met."

"You should've seen me before I left England. Anyway, thanks for the compliment."

"Right, I think we have had enough of chilling. How about we go and look around the town this afternoon?"

"OK, give me half an hour to go and shower and change."

It was around two thirty when we reached Nadi city centre. It was a whole new experience for both of us, a great blend of the modern and traditional. We loved everything about it, even though it was clearly not the clean, hygienic world that we were used to. In place of that there was this sense of real life and colour. In particular we were both really taken up with the colourful Hindu temple. We were a bit hesitant about whether or not to enter the temple, but we were welcomed cordially and spent about half an hour admiring the idols and some of the rituals. The local shops and bazaars were a revelation and I just realised that for the last thirty-five years I had had so little experience of the rest of the world.

Almost as if she read my mind Claire blurted "Jesus, Tintin, I didn't even know such a world existed outside the US-of-FA!" No prizes for guessing what FA stood for. After that we wandered into a travel agency and on their recommendation booked ourselves into an activity tour the next day, and a sightseeing tour, which would end in a cultural experience. We meandered a bit more and around seven thirty decided to have dinner at a local Fijian restaurant. The food was delicious, but to my shame I cannot quite remember the names of some of the dishes. It was around nine thirty when we got back to the hotel.

I was feeling restless and wanted to go out for a walk, but Claire declined and went up to the room. I wandered along the beach for about ten minutes and slowly made my way back. Everything looked idyllic, calm and serene. It all looked too good to be true, and I thought about things that could possibly go wrong. Suddenly Jack materialised in my mind's eye.

I recalled his recent letter. Why had he written to me out of the blue? Could he actually have changed so much? Was I being uncharitable? Or was he playing a game? Did he have anything to do with Harriett? Acting on an impulse, I picked up my phone and punched in his number.

"Well, my dear brother, Jack! That letter of yours was quite a surprise."

"Quentin, I'll be damned. How and where the devil are you?"

"Fine, and Fiji, respectively. Who'd have thought we'd be even speaking to each other after all these years?"

"Worse luck, mate."

"For once we agree."

"All right, Quentin, I grant I was not the most affectionate of brothers and may have even been a bit of a bully."

"A bit of? Mate, that term was created with you in mind."

"OK, Quentin, time to put the past behind us. Can we wipe the slate clean and start again?"

"So what have you been up to, Jack, in these years? I heard on the grapevine that you had dropped out of Bristol and headed off to the States. I didn't hear much else beyond that, not of course that I would've been the least bit interested."

"*Touché!* As you know of course, after Gran died, I inherited the estate. I guess you must've been a bit cut up that you were left out of the will, but don't blame that on me. That's what the old lady decided to do and who am I to go against her wishes?" said with a slight taunt. Before I responded he continued, "Well, I spent three years in the States, wandering around and getting to know the sharp side of the business world. You know I never really had the ability or the inclination to go for academics. So when I got back, I set up a couple of businesses importing and exporting stuff to America, and touch wood, it's paid off. So before you ask, let me tell you, I am not short of a bob or two."

"Oh, I had no doubt about that, Jack. To be honest, I expected nothing more and nothing less from our illustrious grandmother. So good luck to you. I, on the other hand, have been going from mediocrity to something worse. I'm not sure you really would be interested in my rather dull existence."

"You really do underestimate me, Quentin. I'm not the same Jack of old, and I have learnt a few lessons and had a few knocks along the way, myself. Money fortunately has been plentiful, but I've been a loner all my life. Yes, a few women came into my life at regular intervals, but sadly no one I could really connect with. And you know, all the so-called friends have dropped out. Of course, I have drinking mates who work for me, but I know they'd dump me at the first opportunity, if they could. I'd give anything for a family. Whenever I thought of you, I assumed you'd be the ideal family man, married with three or four kids by now. So I genuinely am interested in your story."

I really could not believe my ears. I felt slightly ashamed that I was not charitable enough to even give him the benefit of the doubt.

"Fair enough, Jack. Let's exchange stories, but it's a bit late now and someone's waiting for me, so I can't stay too long."

I could almost see Jack's right eyebrow shoot up. "By that you mean someone of the fair sex? Your wife?"

"Not exactly. In fact not at all. I'm afraid my marriage went pear-shaped and the lady with me at the moment is really just a casual acquaintance. Not what you think."

"Hmm, I see... Quentin, I want you to know that I have been fond of you in my own twisted way. Perhaps that is just a reflection of the fact that I cared even less for all the other losers in my life."

"I don't believe that for one moment."

"So be it. Anyway, tell me more about yourself. To my eternal shame I realised that I'd never bothered to find out who your true parents were. I just knew that you had been adopted by Gran, having lost your parents and somehow thought of you as an unwanted brother, who was just a nuisance. Pretty awful of me, wasn't it?"

"Yes, it was actually!" I said with a note of lightness.

"Well, it'll be good to catch up and relax for a few minutes, so, carry on."

"Jack, I'm not sure I know much more than you do. My dad was supposed to be this wild youth, the older brother of Auntie Charlotte, your mum. Evidently, he abandoned the family and took off to India, where he had a liaison with my mother, I being the unwanted outcome. Since we are sharing confidences, let me tell you something I have never revealed to you. I absolutely hated both my real parents, for not being there for me. I don't know if you ever realised, but I was absolutely terrified of your dad. He seemed to loathe me, for reasons I never understood."

"My father was a man of strong feelings. At heart he was always a bit of a racist. The fact of finding a half-breed as his wife's nephew did not go down well. And of course, the obvious fact that my mum developed such a soft spot for you. It may seem odd coming from me, but in retrospect I don't think my parents should ever have got married. To each other, I mean. The last three years for them were pretty shitty. I don't know if you ever knew, and I hate saying this, but Mum had become an alcoholic!"

I jerked my head violently with a sharp intake of breath. "What crap!"

"I'm sorry, Quentin, to break this to you. There was more than one occasion when she would get violently drunk, and I mean violently."

"Hang on, Jack, what I understood was that it was she who was getting roughed up by Uncle Charles. I overheard a couple of conversations to that effect, between Aunt Charlotte and grandmother. Not to mention the times when she had a black eye or a bruise around the mouth, which she always put down to trips or falls, of course."

"That's quite true, but you could hardly blame a man for retaliating. If you had seen my dad as regularly as you had seen my mum, you will have seen him bearing even more impressive physical stigmata. In fact there was one occasion when she smashed a golf club into Dad's head, and it was a miracle that he escaped with just a contusion."

I was aghast, and too shaken to continue. "Jack, I need to get to bed. Shall we continue tomorrow?"

"Yes, of course. Again I apologise if this has come as a bit of a shock. At the end of the day there are just the two of us left from this family, and I think it is time to mend fences and get together."

"My friend and I are going to spend the day out and about. We should be back by the evening. We'll probably have dinner out before getting back. So shall we chat around the same time tomorrow?"

"Sounds good. I can't wait to hear about this new *platonic* friend of yours!"

With that we parted company and I went back to the room. Claire was away with the fairies and had no idea when I crawled into the adjacent bed. My mind was in a whirl and I could not sleep for a long time. At some point I must have gone to sleep, but it was a disturbed and restless affair.

I found Claire gently shaking my shoulder. "Wakey wakey, Tintin. You really sleep like a baby. It's nine o'clock, and the breakfast I ordered from the room service has just been delivered, as you can see and smell. We are going to be picked up in an hour, though of course, being a private excursion, we can be pretty flexible."

I said a bleary-eyed 'good morning' to her and stumbled towards the breakfast, laid out neatly on the table in front of the balcony.

"You will not believe who I spoke to last night after you'd gone to the room."

Claire didn't bat an eyelid. "Not Marty?"

We both burst into laughter. "No, I'm glad to say. Actually, it was Jack."

"Cousin Jack, evil Jack?"

"The very same. We had a good old pow-wow about our unhappy childhoods and I'm delighted to say that after so many years of ill feeling we have finally patched things up. Jack really is not at all the brute that he used to be, and now sounds almost half-decent."

"Well, well, I can't wait to meet the notorious, but now-dramatically-changed Jack," said Claire, with more than casual interest.

"You'd love each other, Claire. He's just your type. Filthy rich."

Claire was unfazed and ready for the challenge.

"He sounds much more interesting than you in every way! Joking apart, Tintin, I'll suspend judgment for the moment."

We then set off for the day, which turned out to be nothing short of spectacular. We snorkelled, we swam, we lazed and sunbathed. It was a first for both of us. The corals were magical. We were like children in the way we enjoyed the experience with complete abandon. After another delicious meal, we got back to the resort by seven. We changed and decided to spend the next half hour just chilling on our balcony, and enjoying the scene of Wailoaloa.

"I'm really curious to listen in on your conversation with your notorious cousin."

"Oh, I don't know, Claire, you might be disappointed. Or worse, you might be really impressed, and that would not go down well with me at all!"

"I'm already quite impressed with him, Tintin, from what you relate. There is something remarkably attractive about a bad apple that transforms into a sweet cherry."

"You'll find out for yourself if you travel with me all the way to England. Just don't go falling for his unquestionable charms. Saying that, you could do worse, if indeed he has turned a new leaf. He is extremely wealthy and you would be hard put to find an equivalent match, particularly one who could cosset you in the safety of Britain, where you could live happily ever after."

Claire gave me a curious look, which I could not interpret. She went into a bit of a trance, while I was trying to decipher her expression. I found the possibility of Claire getting together with Jack, distasteful, and I suddenly realised that I was feeling jealous of a man who didn't even exist in our world!

At seven forty-five we walked down to the bar. I called Jack, and turned on the speaker. After the initial hellos, I brought Claire into the chat.

"Claire, meet Jack."

"Delighted to meet you, Claire. I can sense that Quentin has developed an exquisite taste in women."

Claire flushed and replied, "Don't jump to conclusions, Jack. You could be disappointed."

"You must know, Claire, if Quentin hasn't already told you, I was really a bit of a shit in my younger days. Unlike your absolute gentleman sitting here."

"I did hear something about it!"

"Much as I regret my wild younger days, I guess some of us just have to learn things the hard way."

"Forget it, Jack, there is nothing to forgive. It's all forgotten, done and dusted. So, moving on then, you haven't updated me on the romantic side of your life. Not that I can forget the days in school, when wimps like me used to envy you your exploits!"

"Shut up, Quentin, I don't want to go there again. Whatever will Claire think of me? Anyway, moving on swiftly, I can't deny that I've had a few dalliances over the years, but never really found the right one for me. As a matter of fact I have been single and celibate for the last three years!"

"That must be quite some record for you. Now that you have all this wealth and the estate, don't you want an heir to bequeath it all to?"

"I used to think in my earlier days that having an heir was the most important thing for any man. But not anymore. I am now seriously thinking that I might leave everything to charity when I go."

"Jack, that is truly impressive. What happened to you, did you have a lobotomy or something?!" Had I gone too far?

Jack guffawed, and replied, "Don't blame you, Quentin, I guess it's time for my come-uppance."

Inevitably, the next question from Jack was about how Claire and I got together.

"That was something that happened rather unexpectedly. I just ran into her at a bar, we got talking and I guess we hit it off. She was looking for a career break and decided that this would be the right time to take it. And so here we are, slowly making our way around the world."

Claire chipped in, "That's it in a nutshell. And what about you, Jack? What do you do and where are you at the moment?"

"I run an international trading company, and I specialise in America and the Pacific islands. Right now I'm at home, but if I'd known Quentin was going to be there, and with you, I'd have come over like a shot. The fact is, Claire, I really wish to slow down, settle down and who knows, maybe even start a family."

It was nearly nine o'clock and Claire was obviously flagging. "Claire, why don't you head on to the room? I'll stay on a bit longer with Jack and catch up with stuff from the past."

"You go on, my lovely," said Jack. "It was an absolute pleasure to speak to you." With that, Claire sauntered off.

"I hope you haven't got lustful thoughts about her, Jack!" I said jokingly.

"I most certainly do, Quentin. But I don't stand a chance in hell competing with you." Again, I was taken aback by Jack's restraint and modesty.

"Speaking of which, Quentin, I remember you saying that your marriage hadn't worked out. Did it last long? I really cannot understand what kind of a woman would want to leave a safe haven like you."

I laughed. "That's because you never met Harriett, my wife from hell. We were married for nearly five years, but in reality it ran out of steam before the first year was out. Anyway, there is nothing more to be said, she is with a new boyfriend and I have happily escaped her attentions."

"So what's the story with you in terms of why you're way out in the Pacific, with an American broad you ran into casually? Something doesn't sound right here."

"It's a bit complicated. You might say we are on the run."

"You, on the run? Come on, don't bullshit me."

"As a matter of fact, yes, but the story sounds a bit too fantastic to believe. In any case there is probably not a lot of point involving you in all of this."

"You know, apart from being ra-ra rich, I do have fingers in many pies and some serious contacts. If you are in some sort of trouble, you might find yourself pleasantly surprised by the fact that I could help. And maybe, I will be absolved of some of the guilt of my past misdemeanours, if I help you out of whatever shit you've got yourself into."

I spent the next half hour going through the bare bones of what had happened to me, excluding Marty and related misadventures. "So here we are. I just need to decide what to do about the mysterious goings-on in my life."

Jack was silent for several seconds, while he digested all the facts. "Well, that is quite a story, and if I didn't know you better I'd say that is a tall tale! I hear what you say about your recently separated spouse, but quite honestly, I can't believe that she would get into such serious mischief, and all for a rather unimpressive inheritance. Having said that, if, as you suspect, her new boyfriend is of a certain class, you never know. To try and bump you off for this paltry sum of money must mean that they are pretty hard up. If that were the case, how is it possible that they arranged for a reception committee at JFK? No, this sounds a little more organised, though I confess I am baffled. Maybe you have something of value, that you are not aware of yourself?"

The exact same question that Claire had raised…

I had deliberately omitted to mention my little act of larceny, and the fact that I had hidden Harriett's little treasure, barely ten feet above her bedroom. And then it suddenly hit me. Was it not possible that amongst the various items I had quickly run my fingers through, there was maybe an item of very high value? Of course, that must be it! Harriett had tried her very level best to stop me in England, but without success. Once she came to know where I was headed, her boyfriend must have arranged the reception party, as Jack called it. That would clearly mean that this was no ordinary person. He must be a wide boy, with contacts in New York. Was it even possible that there was a link between him and Marty? No, that would be too fantastic.

All these thoughts raced through my head, when Jack interrupted. "A penny for your thoughts."

"I am flummoxed as to why anybody would want to abduct me or worse, kill me."

"Don't worry. As I said I have a fair amount of fire power here. I dare say we can work out a strategy to flush them out, but perhaps we can postpone that for the moment. I never thought I would be having this conversation with you, but let me confess, there are not many aspects of my childhood that I would like to talk about. Now that I have this chance, I feel I should capitalise. Would you mind? I hope it's not too late for you, but it would be nice to carry on a bit longer."

I acquiesced, recharged my glass and sat down, legs sprawled, eyes gazing into the dark sea, the sound of the waves undulating in my ears. Jack then started again.

"You know, Quentin, I was simply jealous of you throughout my childhood. I'm not sure why, but I can only attribute it to the fact that my mother seemed to care more for you than for me. You have no idea how hard I tried to please her and attract her love, but it never seemed to work. I fully accept that I was the reason for it – she was such a gentle and soft soul, whereas I was a real thug, no doubt the result of my paternal genes. Whatever the case, I really resented you, even though Gran was always on my side. And of course, so was my dad, who made no secret of the fact that he thought the sun rose from my backside! Somehow, that was not enough and I simply had to have what I perceived I was lacking – a mother's love. Does that make any sense?"

"I suppose it does. I admit I was less than charitable in my attribution of your reasons and motives. I make no secret of the fact I absolutely adored your mother. In fact, in my entire life, she was the sole source of light in an otherwise dark and miserable existence. Do you know it still hurts almost physically, when I think about her sudden and untimely death."

"You mean *their* untimely death? Don't forget I lost my dad, too."

"Of course, Jack, your loss was much greater."

"Oh well, all that is water under the bridge. I have wondered so many times over the years, how exactly did that happen? Was it just an accident, or was there foul play? Evidently, it was Mum who was driving when the accident happened. Could she have been that drunk? Do you know, I haven't got the answers to these questions. Gran just wanted the whole thing hushed up as soon as possible, and wouldn't tell me anything more than that it was just a very unfortunate accident. Do *you* know anything more?"

"No, I don't. Grandmother would not talk about it and most certainly would not answer any of my questions. She was never really the same after that, was she?"

"Gran always had a real soft corner for me, but as you say, she became all bitter and twisted after the accident. I suppose that's what must have led to a state of depression, which then led on to her jumping off the cliff."

"Really? You don't think it was an accident?"

"No, I am pretty sure. It was only a short time before that, when I had visited her. She was depressed as hell and would barely speak. I felt sorry for her, but honestly I couldn't stand being around in that morbid place, and decided to cut short my stay and leave after just one day. It was as I was taking my leave that she told me this and I will reproduce her words as best as I can.

"'Jack, there is something I have to tell you. Once I am gone, all of this will be yours. I have left nothing to Quentin, as I have never been able to accept him as a genuine member of the family. However, there is a charitable part of me which says I should not leave him completely out in the cold, even though he has done precious little to appeal to my better instincts. So, what I'd like you to do is to consider giving him a small settlement, perhaps a lump sum of say

£250,000. That is just a tiny part of the whole estate and you'll barely miss it. In fact, I did think of writing it in the will, but on balance felt that this would be much better coming as a gesture from you to him and that just might allow the ill-feeling between you to dissipate.'"

There was a prolonged silence as I digested this. I am ashamed to say that I felt nothing for my departed grandmother. Before I could say anything, Jack continued, "To my shame, Quentin, I could not get myself to part with even that small amount, and offered you a pittance just after the funeral. But now that fate has thrown us together, I'd like to make it right. Given the time lost and all that, I'd like to offer you half a million."

I drew a deep breath. "This is all a bit too much. Let me sleep on it. I fully appreciate your gesture, and let me be honest enough to say that the money will be a bit of a lifesaver at this juncture. I just need to convince myself that it's OK to take your money."

"Ever the upright and honest gentleman, aren't you? Do take your time, but remember this is not my money, it is part of our inheritance. You just happen to be the unfortunate bastard."

He then asked me about our plans for the next day.

"We're having a late start, doing a tour and going to a cultural village, which I believe is good entertainment. I think dinner may be included, and we won't be back till nine-ish. I could call you then."

"Perfect. Oh, by the way, I just remembered. Your mate from school, the snotty lad Harry something-or-the-other, tracked me down a couple of years ago and was looking to re-establish contact with you. I told him I had a vague idea you were living near Portsmouth. Did he ever get in touch?"

That was a real surprise. Harry should have had my contact details. Why did he not get in touch, I wondered. Soon, our chat drew to a close and we bade each other goodbye.

Claire was asleep, but she stirred. As I got under the cool sheets, she mumbled, "You clearly prefer spending time speaking with your cousin, than spending it in bed with me!"

"What do you expect, Ice Maiden?"

She chuckled, half asleep, and drifted away, leaving me still wondering about Harry.

The next morning we decided to go down to the restaurant for breakfast, which was laid open in style on the patio, overlooking the sea. I told Claire about the call with Jack, but she wasn't overly interested.

"Before getting into all this other stuff, you need to think about the shit that's going on in your life."

I contemplated her words. "You're right. I can't shake off the feeling that Harriett is in some way behind the mystery. I had this thought last night that the little pile of loot I stole from her might harbour something very valuable, something I overlooked."

"Tintin, why don't you try some fishing? Surprise your Harriett with a call out of the blue, and see what it is that she really wants. You might possibly even find out about her mysterious boyfriend. After all, what have you got to lose?"

I pondered this for a few seconds and realised that Claire's suggestion was not half bad. I looked at her and nodded approval. "I wonder what time it is over there. It should be late night, and she might be asleep. Actually, it would be fun to wake her and stir things up a bit!"

I paused for a couple more seconds, deciding what exactly to say to her, and then made the call. After about five seconds Harriett answered the call.

"Hope I woke you up, Harriett."

"Quentin? Where on earth are you? You've been gone weeks, and I've been worried sick."

"Yeah, right, cut the bullshit, will you? I've been enjoying life far too much to remember the likes of you. However, finally I'm at a bit of a loose end and I said to myself, why not call the old girl and give her a few minutes of my precious time!"

"I have no idea what's got into you. This is not you, it's someone else that's got into you. Can you please get serious for a change, and tell me where you are and what you're up to?"

"Never mind that. The question is, what exactly do you want of me? Why are you so desperate to make contact, after dropping me like a hot brick? If it's your little treasure you're worried about, I told you, I'll give you half of it and maybe even all of it if you simply behave yourself. What's the panic? Tell me something, who exactly is this mysterious boyfriend of yours, this Monty?"

There was such a long pause, that I momentarily wondered whether we had lost connection. "Never you mind. I know you're pissed off and I fully understand. I just want us to remain friends and move on in our lives. I'm sure you will find yourself your kind of a girl before too long. Why don't we just have a clean break, settle our affairs and call it a day?"

"Why, this is the first time in my life I have heard you sounding reasonable. This is not you, it's someone else using your voice!" I could hear the familiar sound of Harriett drawing in her breath through her clenched teeth and felt a thrill of satisfaction.

"OK, Harriett, let's bury the hatchet and all that. As for settling our affairs, I'm afraid that will have to wait until I return to the old country. And that could be some time away."

"For fuck's sake. Where are you, anyway? I know you haven't got much money, so how are you planning to sustain yourself? You haven't by any chance shacked up with some rich bitch, have you?"

I looked over to Claire, who had been listening to the exchanges, as I had the speaker phone turned on. I winked at her, in response to which she tilted her head and grimaced.

"Maybe I have, maybe I haven't. I'm on the other side of the world, in Fiji, where you can't get at me. Is there by any chance a high-value item that you may have stashed away, and are now keen to retrieve?"

There was a sharp intake of breath, followed by silence.

"I'm afraid you'll just have to wait it out until I decide to get back home. Let's call this retribution."

"Fuck you, Quentin —"

I disconnected.

"Well, she sounds like a real charmer. I can see she still has a hold on you." Was I imagining it or was there a touch of pique in Claire's voice?

"You're right, that little devil still has that effect on me. Don't for a moment think it's love or anything so sloppy. All that went a long time ago. It's more akin to the fear of opium for the ex-addict." After a minute of silence I said, "So we are no further forwards in terms of what exactly has been happening to me. And I still don't know the identity of the man who stole Harriett from me, may the Lord bless him!"

"Shit happens, Tintin, don't let it get to you. As you say, the important thing is that he took Harriett away and in a sense liberated you. For my money I'm betting that Jack is the bad guy. All you need to do is to find the motive."

We walked out to the foyer to find our tour guide waiting for us and a few minutes later we were off. The countryside was lush and green. The first stop was at the Garden of the Sleeping Giant, where we were treated to a veritable feast of orchids. Nearby we visited hot springs, where a mud bath was on offer, which we declined. After that we were driven to the Sigatoka Sand Dunes, where breathtaking views of the sea were on offer. From there we went to an archaeological site where artefacts over 2,000 years old were on show. This was followed by a visit to the Kula Eco Park, where we were captivated by some really exotic fauna and flora, which included beautiful birds, iguana and other reptiles. A late lunch followed and then we reached the Fiji Cultural Centre in the afternoon.

The initial introduction was in the form of a museum, which explained the history of the island. We were fascinated to learn that cannibalism was practised until just 150 years ago. It was difficult to imagine that these lovely, gentle people were capable of such acts not that long ago. I also found it very interesting that around forty per cent of the entire population of Fiji was constituted by people from the Indian subcontinent, brought in as indentured labour by the British.

"You must be really proud of that, Tintin."

"Nothing to do with me. I'm only half-British, and can't be blamed for the global exploitation carried out by the perfidious Albion, any more than you, for your American forebears, who only got around to abolishing slavery fifty years ago."

"*Touché*, but I'm technically a Canadian."

There was to be a cultural dance show and we had a half-hour break. We meandered around the beautiful gardens, populated by tropical trees and bushes. We came to a picturesque little stream and sat down on one of the benches, just taking in the atmosphere. There was a rustling of leaves behind us and I felt my heart lurch when I saw a figure jump out. It was a face from hell, with teeth bared, fiery red eyes protruding and an expression that can only be described as feral. But what was far more intimidating was the long spear that he held in his right hand, which was raised and all set to deliver a fatal thrust. The spear was pointed directly at the upper part of my chest, possibly the base of my neck. Claire let out a muzzled scream and grabbed my hand. We were in a state of paralysis, including our assailant. And then the penny dropped, and I let out a nervous cackle. Claire looked astonished for a couple of seconds before she realised that this was just part of the experience! I addressed the Fijian, saying, "Well done, my friend, you got us there."

The transformation was unbelievable. We now were looking at the most charming and friendly smile in the world, etched onto a typical Melanesian face with a strong jaw line. All he wore was his native Fijian costume, which exposed generous amounts of muscular flesh, all of which were very complimentary indeed. Michelangelo would have been delighted to be able to sculpt his figure.

"My name is Ratu, madam and sir. I'm sorry if I gave you a bit of a shock," the man said in excellent English, albeit accented. "I am one of the performers in the cultural show, but I do like to have a bit of fun on the side. I hope you weren't offended."

"I absolutely loved it," said Claire. "You know, I'm used to villains wielding guns, but I have to say

I have never ever in my life been quite so terrified as I was for those few seconds. I am delighted to make your acquaintance, particularly given your body characteristics." Claire's obviously saucy response invoked a slightly embarrassed laugh from Ratu.

I chipped in, "Ratu, I'm afraid that's the price you have to pay for your little prank. My wife, Claire here, has first claim on you!"

Ratu was now truly rattled and Claire burst out into a peal of laughter, which was most becoming.

"Thank you so much for visiting our centre and supporting our culture. I am going to be around all evening, so please don't hesitate to give me a shout if you need anything." With that he walked away.

The cultural show was most entertaining. Ratu was very much in the picture, being the lead dancer. The local Fijian beer enhanced our experience significantly. There was something bothering me and I could not get to the bottom of it. I remembered my promise to call Jack, and decided I couldn't be bothered. Claire was busy chatting to a small group of admirers she had acquired during the course of the afternoon. On an impulse, I called the driver, who should have been waiting for us.

"I wanted to say that we are going to be slightly late. Are you OK to wait?"

"Yes, sir, no problem. Did you meet your friends?"

"What friends?" I asked blankly.

"About an hour ago, two men arrived and asked if a couple from this resort had arrived. They said they were your friends, and I told them you were in the centre. Have they not come in?"

"Did they give their names, and can you describe what they looked like?"

"Both European, sir, but they didn't give me their names. They were both tall, but I don't know how to describe them. One man had a thin moustache."

"Anything else you can remember?"

"Err, yes, sir, the other man had a large, ugly nose!"

Bingo, my instinct was right. I thanked him and rang off.

I saw Ratu coming towards us, now dressed in normal clothes; a multi-coloured top and a pair of blue jeans. I intercepted him before he joined the group, saying, "Ratu, do you think you could do me the favour of lending your mobile phone? I just need to call my resort and will happily pay you for the call."

"Don't worry about payment, boss, it costs nothing."

I punched in the number of the resort, which I had memorised unwittingly. "Hello, good evening. My name is Quentin Grayling, and my wife and I are staying in room number —"

Before I could complete the sentence the man at the desk replied, "Yes, Mr Grayling, your room has been fully taken care of and the luggage has been dispatched. There is nothing to pay."

I thought the man must be having a seizure.

"What do you mean everything has been taken care of and luggage dispatched?"

"Your friend Mr Wilson rang and got your stuff collected. He told us that you will not be returning to the hotel, as you were travelling directly to your next hotel. His driver came around to pick up your stuff. Is that not right?"

I decided to bluff. "Yes, I guess so. Listen, did my friend come around and pay? I thought he was staying in a different hotel."

"No, sir, he called and settled by credit card. I'm not really sure where he was calling from. He is certainly not staying in our hotel."

"Did you tell him where we'd gone today?"

"Yes, sir. He wanted to know where to pick you up."

I thanked the man and stood there motionless, my mind in a whirl. Garlic-Nose was on the job! I had stepped out of the building to make my call, so when I finished I crossed the threshold of the door and beckoned to Ratu, who responded immediately. I took him outside where we could not be overheard.

"Ratu, we are in a spot of trouble. I need to find a way of getting out, but not through the normal exit. Can you help me? I will certainly make it worth your while."

Ratu's large eyes became even larger. He thought for a few seconds and then said, "Woman trouble, boss?"

"How did you guess? Anyway, can you help?"

"Of course, boss, I'll do anything for money!"

"So this is what I want you to do. My driver guide will be waiting outside in a black Toyota, number plate FQ587. Can you tell him that we will be staying on here after dinner and that we will be driven back to the hotel at night? Let him go, and once he's gone, you can suggest the best way for us to disappear."

Ratu went off to do my bidding and in the meantime I decided to update Claire on the developments. She was down to just two men who were in rapt attention when I intruded, "Boys, do you mind if I have a word with my wife?" They looked sheepish and apologised, making their way to the exit. There were still a few people about, so I gently led Claire to a corner and related the recent developments. She looked shocked.

"Tintin, do you think there's a chance you could be over-imagining things?"

I gave her a look that dispelled any such possibility. She realised how foolish her response was. "Just a thought."

Ratu returned in a few minutes, confirming that he had sent the driver away, who would have been more than pleased with the twenty-dollar tip I had handed to Ratu to pass on.

"So here is my plan, boss. If we walk a hundred metres along the little stream where I attacked you, there is a boat that belongs to the centre and is available to me. I can take the two of you down to join the Nadi river, which travels south-east to the sea. I can take you along there and drop you off at the mouth of the river, from where the two of you can walk to your resort, if you don't mind walking that is."

"Actually, you might be surprised to hear this, but we want to head to the airport!"

Claire was even more surprised than Ratu.

"Tintin, isn't this a bit precipitate? I was really looking forward to spending another couple of weeks on this beautiful island."

"I just don't think it's worth the risk. I think the sooner we are out of here the safer we are. I have a destination in mind where we could truly disappear. So, Ratu, can you manage to get us to the airport?"

"Hold on a second," said Claire. "There is the small matter of finding flights and getting tickets. Unless there is a really late-night flight, there is no chance that we will get out tonight. And we can't really risk hiding away for the night and getting to the airport in the morning because almost certainly they will be lying in wait."

Ratu looked askance.

"Oh, don't ask. There is history between these guys and Claire here," I said with a wink. Claire gave me a surprised look, which was not entirely benign.

"Ratu, can you find us a computer terminal that we could use right now?"

I was really glad that Claire had insisted we carry our passports.

Claire was right, there were no flights that night, the first one being late morning from Nadi. Finally, I hit upon a rather hare-brained plan, which might just work. There was a flight leaving from Suva early in the morning, and if we got going right away, there would be ample time to get there – it was a three-hour drive. The really curious thing was that the flight from Suva to Auckland would actually stop at Nadi, but being already inside the aircraft we would be safe. I never even considered the possibility that seats may not be available.

Ratu then revised his plan. He would take us in the boat not towards the sea but turning north-east towards the interior and would drop us off at the banks of the iconic Hindu temple (Siva Subramanya Temple, recalling the name with the help of Google). He would get a mate of his to meet us there with a car, where they would swap places. Ratu would then drive us to Suva. Claire looked truly bewildered by all that was going on, not really convinced that this hasty escape was necessary.

"Ratu, we really owe you big time, man. How much can we pay you for all this?"

"As much as you like, boss," said Ratu with a wicked smirk.

We were in the boat ten minutes later and Ratu took the oars, pulling strongly. Claire said, "Ratu, you are putting your beautiful muscles to really good work!" We all laughed. He was indeed doing a great job and the boat was moving apace. After about twenty minutes, I insisted on taking the oars. Claire looked suitably impressed, although my pace was nowhere near that of Ratu's. After another ten minutes he took charge again and finally in just over an hour we reached our destination. Ratu pulled the boat onto the shore and we clambered up to the road near the huge temple. The time was nearly nine o'clock and we were all famished. Fortunately, Ratu's friend was already there, parked in a quiet spot along the road. He was most curious to find out what was going on, but Ratu was not going to reveal the details. Claire handed a $50 bill to Ratu's friend for his efforts, and he was very grateful. As soon as he left, realising that we could not really carry on without nourishment, Ratu suggested we step into a nearby curry house. I have no idea if the food was as good as it tasted to us at that time. Replete, we left and snoozed in the car, while Ratu drove.

"I have not had such excitement in my life, boss! Now if I drive as I usually do, you will reach the airport too early. So I will go slow and aim to reach the airport by three o'clock, which would be a reasonable time for your six o'clock flight. That will give you some time to get some sleep."

So, we followed his instructions to the letter, and put our heads back and snoozed. I for one cannot remember the rest of the journey, until the moment Ratu brought the car to a halt. Claire was still asleep, her head comfortably resting on my shoulder, and I had to gently shake her awake. We got out and thanked Ratu profusely for his help. I then put a $100 bill in his hand and said, "Is that sufficient, do you think?"

Ratu looked at it and took a couple of seconds to answer. "If you say so, boss."

"I was just teasing, Ratu! That is no way enough for all that you have done for us." I handed him four more $100 bills and his eyes widened in grateful surprise.

"Thank you, sir, and lady." He turned to Claire, who bowled him over with a hug and a peck on his cheek.

We went to the ticketing counter and breathed a sigh of relief on finding plenty of seats. Using Claire's credit card, we bought two business-class tickets, despite my advice to try and be more frugal.

"Fuck it, Tintin, I have enough and more. I'm going to travel in style, and so will you."

From there on everything went smoothly and we left on time. It was just a short hop to Nadi, where we picked up the bulk of passengers on the flight. There was a part of me that was worried that they had somehow discovered our plans and made arrangements to board the flight at Nadi. Fortunately, no familiar face with a bulbous nose appeared, and I could only hope that we did not have other unwanted guests on the flight.

After we had settled in, around half an hour into the flight, Claire said to me, "So now, Tintin, please explain to me again how you reckon all this fits together."

"I'm damned if I know."

I wracked my brains through the flight, without coming to a reasonable explanation, for all that was happening. I also worried about – despite New

Zealand being a big country – for how long we could reasonably disappear. Sooner or later we would have to get back to our usual worlds, and then it would all kick off again. I must have dozed off and before I knew it, we had landed in Auckland. After a short stop, we flew on to Christchurch, our final destination. We arrived early afternoon. It was 6 November, a little over two weeks since I fled England, which seemed a lifetime away.

8

TRANQUIL PASSION DOWN UNDER

Love is but an evanescent dream
Love is merely an imaginary figment
Love is transient and unreal
Love is the only thing we live for

We had booked into the George, a beautiful hotel in Christchurch. From the moment we landed, we had been discussing how my stalkers might have found their way to Fiji. The answer, we agreed, was through someone who could access flight details. More to the point, who? Claire was pretty certain it had to be Harriett's lover, given that Harriett herself would be totally clueless about such matters.

As soon as we had checked in and got to our room, my phone rang. Jack.

"Quentin, where the hell are you? I was waiting for your call last night."

"Oh, sorry, we got tied up until quite late."

"Anyway, when you have a moment, I'd love to have another catch-up."

"Maybe when I get back to England."

"I have some news for you. You'll never guess who your wife's boyfriend is."

I held my breath, saying nothing, and Jack continued, "Remember that friend of yours I mentioned the other day, Harry, who pretended to be your best friend in school?"

I literally felt a tremor under my feet. "No way, that can't be true. I thought he was happily married."

"No doubt about it, I've had it all checked out. I ran into him at the London Boat Show, and we exchanged notes. He was extremely keen to reconnect with you, but had lost contact and wondered if I knew. I remembered you were working for that pharmaceutical company, and pointed him in that direction. Did he get in touch with you?"

"He did *not* get in touch with me, but obviously decided instead to focus on my wife, the bastard!"

"The question I ask myself is, why would he want to eliminate you, given that he already has what he wants, namely your wife?"

"I cannot for the life of me work any of this out. We were pretty thick in school, why would he harbour any ill-will towards me now? By the way, you said you might be able to help me out of the corner I'm in – is that still the case?"

There was a three-second silence.

"I have to be careful about what I promise. My sources tell me he is a cyber-expert, and moves around with a couple of enforcers by his side. Are you sure you haven't done something shady to upset this guy?"

I laughed out loud. "Do you even think that is possible? No, I've had nothing to do with Harry for years."

"I'll keep you updated if anything significant turns up, otherwise see you when you get back home. Just where the hell are you, anyway?"

"New Zealand."

"Wow! You certainly do get around, lover boy."

"Thanks, and we expect to be here for a few days, then take it as it comes. All very informal and unstructured."

Jack sounded positively jovial, saying, "Have fun, baby. I'll be in touch."

Claire and I looked at each other, and I made no effort to conceal my shock. "Harry! No, I can't believe it. He can't possibly have left his wife and child to go off with Harriett, whom he met for the first time at our wedding. It's just not Harry. Perhaps I need to contact my other best neglected friend Kevin, and see if he can shed any light on this. If things don't go well, I could perhaps get back to Jack for some assistance."

We just relaxed for the rest of the day, including a visit to the pool. There was a very good restaurant in the hotel, apart from which that first night was nondescript. The next day after breakfast, we made plans for the next week, which we decided to spend in Kaikoura, supposedly very picturesque and unspoilt. We spent that afternoon and the next day wandering around Christchurch, with its areas of post-earthquake construction and renovation, contrasting with the lovely gardens, the beautiful classical buildings and lovely houses. We found the food surprisingly delicious, and of course, the wine. Claire became totally captivated by their Sauvignon Blanc. The next day we rented a car and drove to Kaikoura.

Claire was like a child discovering new toys. She loved the experience of taking the wheel and driving on the 'wrong' side of the road. The route and the views were simply breathtaking. Nothing had prepared me for what we witnessed on reaching the town. It was one long curving beach, with mists swirling around, topped by scattered black clouds nuzzling snow-capped peaks! We had booked into a delightful little B&B at the southern end of the beach, a large room, which formed a separate annexe. I'd never seen Claire quite so excited and voluble. The long-dormant child in her had truly woken up. We went out for a long walk along the beach and ended the evening with a dinner at a fish restaurant, returning to our room at half past nine.

Claire was humming to herself, then turned to me and said, "Tintin, this has been the most magical day of my life. Thank you." I took her hand in mine and encircled her waist with the other arm, knowing I was taking my life into my hands.

"And can I possibly make it any better, Claire?" I said softly, but with a twinkle in my eye, giving her the option to reply any way she chose. To my massive surprise she threw her other arm round my neck and pulled me down. Everything came to a standstill, as our lips met and our bodies collided. And in the blink of an eyelid, like the chain reaction of an atomic reactor, our passions were unleashed. The explosion of the combination of cumulative stress, pent-up physical desire and emotional surrender created a veritable sexual storm. The first was followed by a second, more mellow one, and then complete and total bliss.

Exhausted and replete, I turned on the bedside lamp. "Gosh, it's nearly midnight. Two hours and counting!" I said, turning to Claire, whose head was cradled on my left shoulder. She turned scarlet and punched me gently. I marvelled at everything about her.

"Claire, I had no idea that it was even possible to go on a trip like this. I thought I was a man of the world, possibly a bit deprived, but what we have just been through has sent me into the stratosphere."

Claire looked up at me and her expression was one of pure love and joy. "Snap, Tintin. I thought I was dying, more than once. Having been used all my life like a passive vehicle, for the first time I felt like the world was mine, I felt like a conquering queen!"

I don't particularly wish to reproduce our cheesy conversation. We slept wrapped around each other.

It was predictably late when I stirred. The curtains were still drawn, so the room was dark. I stretched out only to discover that Claire was not beside me. I raised my groggy head to find her sitting right next to me, gazing at me with a look that immediately made my heart race. "Good morning, sweetheart." Claire said nothing, but just smiled, and I thought I had never seen anyone look quite so beautiful, serene and radiant. "You know it's rude to stare!" I followed on recklessly. Her smile widened and she stuck her tongue out at me, still saying nothing. In a sudden move I reached across, gripped her left arm and pulled her over.

"Tintin, for Pete's sake. You can't possibly —"

"I *can* possibly. Can you?" She nodded, and we did.

Those few days (five, six days…?) passed off in a wonderful haze. I am finding it hard to remember all the details in order other than that Claire and I spent absolutely idyllic days in and around Kaikoura and idyllic nights in our little annexe. We went out on long walks and climbs, with me including a brisk five-mile run most days. I had not been that fit for about twenty years. My belly had regressed, and my torso was correspondingly more muscular. Claire, by this time, was nothing short of stunning, at least to my eyes.

Early morning on the third day, when we stepped out of our room, the scene unfolded as if from a Disney film. High up, snow-capped mountains were gleaming in the rising sun, producing myriad mirrors of molten gold! Below we could see dense forests, greenish-black, in the shadow of the mountains. Further below were rolling clouds of mist, which descended all the way to the sea and the cream sands of the beach. The sea itself was restless, in a deep shade of blue, hurling itself continually on to the shores in explosions of white surf. Kaikoura was just delectable, delightful and dreamy, with very few tourists. That first boat trip was, by far, the most memorable boat trip of my life. There was a force-five wind, making the sea quite lively, and it was cold. The crew were as friendly as they possibly could be, jovial and witty. As soon as we boarded they provided us with heavy woollen over-coats. There was an air of real excitement, enhanced by the sheer beauty surrounding us. And then came the ultimate pleasure of seeing albatrosses at close range. Claire insisted that albatrosses were extinct, until she actually saw them. She was literally jumping for joy, overwhelmed by what we were experiencing. And then the dusky dolphins and the sperm whales! Followed by seals, giant northern petrels, shearwaters, Arctic terns...

This remote, unspoilt corner of the world had to be a piece of paradise, if ever there was one. We went on a few more boat trips that we found irresistible, often dumbstruck in sheer wonder.

We lost track of days and dates, until our kindly host said to us one morning at breakfast, "Well, I believe you love birds are checking out this morning. We hope to see you again, soon." With extreme reluctance we left Kaikoura and drove back. Another spectacular drive, this time with me behind the wheel, while Claire drank in the views and the surroundings.

"Tintin, I can't believe there could actually be a more beautiful or unspoilt place on earth." I wholeheartedly agreed.

We were back in Christchurch at the George that afternoon. We spent the evening wandering around, and ended up for dinner at a little restaurant not far from the seaside by the unusual name of 'Clink'. It was a perfect evening at the end of yet another perfect day and we sat out overlooking the beach and the sea, waiting for the menu. We ordered our cocktails first and told the waiter to come back in fifteen minutes for the order.

"Tintin, what exactly is going on between us?" said Claire, focussing her ravishing eyes on mine.

"Not a lot, as far as I can remember!" I said flippantly.

"Stop it! Be serious."

"I suppose we are enjoying each other massively, comfortable with each other and there is the safety net that nothing more needs to happen."

Claire's eyes clouded and she looked lost for a minute. "So we sail along having a lovely time together, but meaning not that much to each other. And what happens at the end?"

"Well, why don't we just carry on for the moment, until all this kerfuffle is sorted out. And then, if we feel we've exhausted each other and find not that much left to draw on, you can return home and reunite with your mother, to live a long and free life. To be fair, I won't hold it against you in the slightest, if you decide to call it a day and go home as soon as you're ready. It's unfair for me to expect you to hang around until I've dealt with my tribulations." Heartless words, thrown out casually. Claire looked startled and really hurt, before her usual self took possession.

"That's very reasonable of you, Tintin. But I don't feel I can leave you until your situation is sorted. I know in theory it is none of my business, but considering what you have done for me, there is no way that I'm going to be walking out on you. Besides, I might as well admit that you're pretty good in the sack! Who knows how long it'll be before I find another one to service me quite so adequately?" *Touché!* She certainly got me there.

"Claire, I'm touched by your loyalty, though as you said initially it really is not your problem. If, however, you are determined to stay, no one would be happier than me. You see," I said, miming Rex Harrison from the classic film, "I've grown accustomed to your face!"

The conversation moved on to other things and we decided we would head for Queenstown the next day. We went online and looked at flight timings. While waiting for the first course I called the hotel about arranging a shuttle to take us to the airport.

"Oh, by the way, sir, your friend came looking for you about an hour ago."

"Did the person give his name?"

"Mr Harry Richard, staying in room 648."

"Oh, yes. Could you leave a message with him to say that we will meet him at breakfast between nine and nine thirty?"

Claire and I looked at each other with a combination of trepidation and astonishment. "Looks like Jack was not fibbing after all. Harry is certainly the villain. There is only one thing to do, and that is to confront him tomorrow. I'll meet him one to one at breakfast tomorrow and have it all out. And that's as safe a place as any."

Claire looked dubious, and was not convinced of the safety of my plan. "Think about it, Tintin. The guy is just everywhere, virtually on your tail. And this time around, he has personally travelled here himself, all the way from England, presumably, because this time he doesn't want anyone else to fuck up."

"What do you suggest, Claire?"

"I have a better plan. Let's disappear, again. Let's head off to somewhere totally unexpected, like Singapore. I've always wanted to go there, anyway. We could sneak back into the hotel late tonight, collect our stuff and head off to the airport early in the morning. Your friend Harry will receive a little surprise at breakfast when he finds that the bird has flown. I know this is only postponing the inevitable, but it'll give us a chance to plan something, maybe some way to strike back."

I pondered Claire's suggestion and could see some merit in it. After some discussion I agreed to go along with this latest hare-brained plan. Fortunately, seats were still available, though we would have to purchase tickets on site, as it was past the deadline for online booking. We then proceeded to continue to drink after our dinner, which by the way was splendid, the star dish being a barramundi. I sent my compliments to the chef, in return for which we were rewarded with an additional exquisite little sorbet on the base of a finely cut kiwi fruit. When I asked the waiter where the chef was from, the answer almost knocked me off my chair.

"He is from Yorkshire, sir!"

Claire and I looked at each other and spontaneously burst into laughter.

"I thought the British could not cook," said Claire.

"So did I," I replied, to the considerable amusement of the Kiwi waiter.

We left as the restaurant was about to close, and sauntered along the beach. After killing as much time as we could, we took a taxi back to the hotel, arriving just after 1 a.m., hoping we would not run into Harry, or indeed Harriett. We managed to get to the lifts without attracting any attention and got into our room safely.

I asked the bellboy to come up and drop a message for Mr Richard in room 648. I wrote, "*Greetings, Harry, I heard you were looking for me. I can't believe my luck, running into you here of all the places! We had a very late night, so we may not be up in time for breakfast. So why don't we meet at the poolside restaurant at 1.30 p.m.?*"

We went to bed and dropped off, without any amorous excursions.

We were the first to check in for our flight and got through immigration easily. There was still a bit of nervousness in the air, until we were safely in the aircraft. Nonetheless I scanned every face that went by to see if there was anyone I could recognise. In particular the man with the garlic nose! That would certainly have spooked the hell out of me. Once we were safely in the aircraft, Claire let out a long sigh of relief, saying, "I feel like having a bit of fun."

"And how are the happy couple today?" asked the beaming stewardess.

"Very happy, thank you," I replied.

"Holiday, or any special occasion?"

"Holi —" I started.

"It's our honeymoon," interjected Claire. "Have you forgotten already?"

"Of course it is, I'm getting forgetful these days."

The girl looked confused, and recovered, saying, "Congratulations. I hope you have a wonderful trip."

"Unless we get divorced," said Claire, now really in the mood.

"Gosh, that would be amazing," I said.

The poor girl had no idea of what to say, but instead flashed an uncertain smile and beat a retreat.

"Do you think that was cruel, Tintin?"

"Not really cruel, just wicked."

The stewardess has clearly decided that we were indeed honeymooners and returned with a bottle of prosecco, which she cracked open for us, to everyone's delight. There was a little round of cheer as we raised a toast! We were pleased and relieved when we landed in Singapore. It was 6 p.m., on 15 November.

9

PARTING OF THE WAYS

There are a thousand reasons to part, some inevitable, some necessary, even wise, but sometimes it is sheer egocentric idiocy.

Claire and I checked into the Shangri-La Hotel in Singapore, which was very pleasant indeed. Extremely pleasant, in fact. Unable to concentrate on the flight, we had promised to each other that our first task would be to work out an action plan to deal with my residual problems. I was in more of a mood to put it off, but Claire was more sensible and focussed.

"Tintin, don't bury your head in the sand. There is something serious going on and you've got to sort it out. Whatever the hell Harry wants, you need to find out and deal with it."

I reluctantly agreed. We both acknowledged that he would probably have already come to know that we had flown to Singapore, using his cyber-expertise. The question was, should we wait for him to land up and look for us, or did we proactively contact him? We didn't quite resolve that, but at least I agreed that I would not put off the inevitable for too long. I sent a text message to Jack, asking if he could find out the contact numbers for Harry and Kevin. I got a prompt reply saying he would try.

"Now that that's all settled, Claire, I really want to let my hair down tonight. Who knows, this might be my last night in this world!" I thought I sounded jovial, but obviously I did not, for Claire gave me a smart slap.

"Shut up, Tintin. No such thing is going to happen, and you are not going to be stupid enough to meet him in a dark alley." My cheek was stinging, but I felt touched by her concern.

We ordered room service and by the time it arrived we were ready to eat our shoes. The switch to Chinese cuisine was actually quite agreeable. We wolfed down all of it with a bottle of Sauvignon Blanc, which had become our firm favourite. After dinner, we tried to play it cool, but it didn't last long. We jumped into bed and tried to force the life out of each other. It was just as I was about to lapse into sleep, at that twilight moment, when I heard Claire whisper, "Tintin, I so love you." I was not sure if that was real or just a dream.

The next morning was a subdued affair, with not much said. Perhaps we had both depleted all our reserves. I tried to lighten the mood, but Claire looked distinctly detached and unwilling to engage. I could not work her out. I woke up believing that the world had turned around for both of us and I experienced a bond and a longing in a way that I had never felt before. My previous peri-marital relationship with Harriett now seemed at best superficial, and at worst an illusion.

"Claire, I might as well declare —"

"No, don't say anything that we might both regret. What happened between us was a bit of fantasy created by extraordinary circumstances."

I was deflated, to say the least. "Claire, maybe you're right, maybe you're not. Whatever the case, what we have felt for each other is real and genuine and there is no earthly reason to deny it. Why not run with it and see where it goes? And last night when I heard you say —"

"That was sentimental crap. I did not mean it and you were a fool to take it to heart." Claire's face was flushed, and I realised that she was more angry with herself than with me. I was about to make counter-arguments, when good old pride stepped in and silence ensued.

"Anyway, we'd better proceed with our plan, and hope Harry calls before too long."

By the time we showered and got ready, it was eleven o'clock and we were absolutely starving. Again, we had breakfast in the room. And then we sat on the balcony, Claire in a kind of stupor, half awake, while I went online and worked out a plan, using the nearby Batam Island as my base. It is actually a part of Indonesia, but just a short ferry ride across from Singapore, and would provide a certain degree of anonymity that I found comforting. Within an hour I had chalked out a plan, with certain minor details to be filled in. I sat up resolutely and turned to look at Claire, who returned a languid look.

"Penny for your thoughts, Claire."

"Tintin, I'm afraid my entire concept of life has been thrown up into the air and I have no idea how it's all going to look when it falls back on the ground after last night. I don't know what to think, or what to feel, except that I simply want to be with you. I cannot understand how I could feel this way about another man. I'm supposed to hate men, all men." Claire had a look of bewilderment and trepidation in her eyes. I leaned across and kissed her and we held each other in silence for several seconds.

"You pretty much paraphrased my own feelings, because I haven't ever experienced the depth of feelings and emotions that I have done with you. And now we have found each other, I am almost terrified to think what this means in reality."

Claire's face fell and I felt genuine regret for what I had just said. "I guess you're right. It would be stupid to blow this up out of proportion. Perhaps the clue is in the fact that it took so long to happen. Maybe that should tell us that this is not going anywhere in the long run."

"Yes, Claire, that is probably the mature way to look at it. Anyway, we are in no tearing hurry to make any lasting decisions, given that there is still the little problem of a maniac running loose and trying to get rid of me."

Suddenly, the old, familiar Claire was back.

"Oh, shit, I had forgotten all about that. I know you've been thinking and planning, without necessarily involving me. I think I do have a right to know what exactly you are planning. I'll do whatever I can to help, given that I am eternally in your debt."

"Oh, shut up, Claire, you are not in my debt. You really must understand that I have *no* expectations whatsoever."

Claire's eyes went moist, and then her jaws clenched and she looked away. I continued, "Look, I'm really grateful that you are trying your level best to help me, but I'm afraid this is something I have to do on my own. You've already been through a lifetime of hell, and the last few weeks have been more than traumatic. You deserve your freedom and an unfettered life when you return home to your mother."

"Thanks for stating the obvious. Yes, I am delirious about my freedom and about the fact that I will be reunited with my mom and we will live together happily ever after. I can't believe that you're such a male chauvinist pig that you consider me a woman of no substance."

"Please don't misinterpret what I'm trying to say. I think you are absolutely magnificent. I just happened to drop into the scene, more by accident than design, and have given you little, apart from moral support. The whole scheme for eliminating Marty was thought up by you, with relatively little contribution from me. After all that, I think it would be grossly unfair for you to be burdened with my problem, which could well turn out to be as dangerous."

Claire looked mollified, but was clearly not happy. She stood up, saying, "OK, I'll leave you to your machinations. I am going to work off these calories in the pool." Her words were flat and businesslike and she avoided looking at me. As soon as she had gone into the room to collect her things, I turned my phone on. There were three missed calls and a message, which was the one I was waiting for.

"Hello, Quentin! I was disappointed we couldn't meet in Christchurch. A little bird tells me that you are now in Singapore. Believe it or not, I'm on my way to Singapore myself and I'd love to meet up tomorrow. We might as well sort out some outstanding issues that are of mutual interest. Your choice of where and when. Just make it some place that's pretty and quiet, preferably with plenty of booze and sexy girls!"

Oh yes, I said to myself, *I have just the place. Except there will be neither booze nor girls.* I texted him back.

"Bloomin' heck! My old friend Harry. How the devil are you keeping tabs on me? We are in Batam Island, which is just a short hop from Singapore, and there are several crossings a day. Once you decide what time you are setting off, give me a bell. I'll have you picked up from the ferry terminal. The driver will bring you over to where I'm staying in the south of the island. Looking forward to a productive meeting."

And then I decided to crack on with the second part of my plan, which was managing Harriett. I dialled her number and was rewarded with a prompt response. "Quentin, where are you now? Don't tell me you're going to do another runner! I guess you must have worked out by now that Harry is my boyfriend. He and I are in the airport lounge and due to depart in a while. He is looking forward to meeting up tomorrow. Why on earth have you moved to some godforsaken island?" She sounded upbeat, with an overtone of excitement.

"Actually, you'd be surprised, Harriett, this island is pretty impressive, though it's not exactly on the tourists' map. Will you be coming over tomorrow with Harry?"

"I don't think so. I'm going to chill out and enjoy Singapore, while you guys do the business. Listen, Quentin, Harry is really quite agreeable, as long as you let him have what he wants! That sounds a bit ridiculous, but that's exactly what I mean, because if you don't, I must warn you Harry can be quite difficult to deal with."

"Yes, I know exactly what you mean."

"If Harry finds us having this cosy chat, he might get the wrong idea. So, I must call off."

I was desperate to keep her engaged and knew the exact way to do it. "Harriett, don't you want to hear about my new love?"

There was a sharp intake of breath. "Oh yes, your new lady friend! Do tell me about this floozy you have managed to pick up!"

"Actually, she *is* a bit of a floozy. But you know what, she is bloody good in bed. I picked her up in a bar in New York and I thought I'd shake her off in a couple of days, but things turned out otherwise. In case you're wondering why I've still got her with me half-way across the world, you'll understand when I say she is paying for the whole shebang!"

"What the fuck? You mean you are worth all that? That's not the Quentin that I remember." There was derision and contempt in her voice.

"I am a different man. You won't recognise me. So much so, when this awful business is over, I'm still hoping that you might consider coming back to me. How long before Harry dumps you?"

"Quentin, to be honest, I don't know how long I'm going to carry on with…" she hesitated and continued, "your old friend and my new partner. I think I have learnt a few valuable lessons in the last couple of months."

"Harriett, you're getting emotional! I can't believe that after all this time you could be developing feelings for me again. After all that's happened, how exactly do you expect me to trust you again?"

"I know there is no way I can convince you, nor is there any reason for you to trust me. All I can say is, please leave the door open, and consider giving me a second chance."

"Well, Harriett, if that is really the case, then I guess things might just about work out between us. But don't hold your breath, and nor will I. But considering that we have this difficult bridge to cross, why don't you tell me what it's all about? What have I got that Harry wants so badly? It's not by any chance a lottery ticket or something, is it?"

"I really can't say anything. If Harry got the slightest inkling that I had said anything, I'd be really in for it. You'll know all about it tomorrow, anyway." A pause. "I'm so sorry I fucked up your life so badly."

"I agree wholeheartedly, Harriett," I said, sounding affable. "When we get out of this mess, we can make a go of it, so think positive."

"I have to go, as I can see Harry approaching. Bye."

I sat and ruminated over our conversation. Harriett back in my life? The very thought was intolerable! And then I heard the door shut and thought Claire had come back in. When I turned to look, there was no sign of Claire, either in the room or the bathroom, and I realised that the door shutting must have been her only just leaving for the pool. I wondered if she had overheard the conversation and felt a slight worry, but quickly put it out of my mind. What the hell? Serves her right for eavesdropping.

I then sat down and went over the plan, at least as far as I could. The recurring question of course was how I would deal with violence, of which there was a very high probability. If the plan failed, I was a goner. Funnily enough, I was not rattled and felt quite cool and composed. I looked at the time and realised I was peckish again. However, I was not prepared to give in to the urge and decided instead to go to the gym. I worked out for an hour and found myself drenched in sweat, which was most satisfying. After showering I went down to the poolside bar and ordered a plate of fish with a salad. Claire was on a sunbed under a parasol about twenty yards away, her eyes firmly shielded by a pair of shades, which ensured that I could not see whether she was awake or asleep, and if awake, where she was looking. I pretended to ignore her and finished my delicious lunch.

When I looked at my watch it was already three o'clock. It was warm and sultry and I contemplated my next move. I had decided to take the six o'clock ferry and hoped that I would not by sheer bad chance run into Harry or Harriett at the terminal. Most unlikely, I told myself. I knew Claire would be really miffed when I did apprise her of my plans. Oh, what the heck. I went up to the room and quickly put together a couple of things in a small shoulder bag. I then made myself a pot of tea and took it out to the balcony and sat there trying to enjoy the last few hours of unfettered freedom. Every time I thought about what was to come, there were alternating feelings of trepidation and quiet confidence. Looking back, I really was not the old Quentin at all; this was someone quite new, coolly confident and very agreeable! I must have dozed off.

I heard the door shut and looked at my watch. It was five twenty. I jumped up and turned to greet Claire. "You look like you had a good time down there."

Claire looked at me briefly with no expression and said, "Yes, thanks, just what I needed."

She sat down, looking out at the pool. I had been so preoccupied with what was to happen, that I had just brushed away the impact on Claire, of my unilateral actions.

"So, what's the plan for the rest of today, Claire?"

"As I don't seem to be involved in your plans, my plans don't concern you either."

"There is a very good reason for why I am not involving you in my dealings with Harry."

"Not to mention your recent *détente* with your wife!"

"Claire, for heaven's sake, you didn't really believe all that crap, did you?"

"What is there to believe? I heard what I heard, and whatever will happen, will happen. I ain't gonna lose any sleep over this." Claire's jaws were clenched.

"Why, Claire Gordon, I do believe you are jealous!"

"Fuck you, Tintin. You get on with your life and I'll get on with mine. It's time I went back home anyway. My mamma needs me, and I need her."

"Well, I suppose you'd better start looking for flights."

Claire flashed me a look which combined anger with real hurt. I desperately wanted to hear her express a desire for me, even while being aware of the fact that it was as much incumbent on me to express my feelings for her.

"Claire, Harriett means nothing to me. I just need to sort this out on my own and don't want you getting in the way."

"Fuck off, Tintin. What do I care?"

"I think the time has come for us to be realistic about our futures and think about getting back to our normal lives."

Claire was obviously wounded by my words. I hated myself at that point, but half believed myself.

"Yes, Quentin, I guess you are right. I'll never forget the fact that I owe my life to you. And so perhaps this is the best time to part company, with nothing but good memories." *Quentin*, not Tintin.

"There is no urgency to part though, is there?" I said playfully. "As soon as I finish my business with Harry, I'll be a free bird and the two of us can exploit each other's company to the maximum, and for as long as we want."

She controlled herself with difficulty, then got up and disappeared into the bathroom.

When Claire came out of the bathroom, her eyes were red and angry, but I could not weaken my resolve at this point. "Listen, Claire, I have to leave shortly. I'm going to be away for a night, maybe two nights. It's all arranged and I'm going to meet Harry tomorrow."

"As you please, Quentin."

Again, *Quentin*, not Tintin. That hurt, and I was annoyed that it hurt. I looked at Claire and felt the sensation of my heart sinking at the thought that I was losing her, and the realisation that I still felt a terrific sense of attraction towards her. It was all I could do to stop myself from grabbing her in my arms and smothering her with kisses.

"As soon as I'm back I'll explain exactly everything. The great mysteries of my life will be laid bare."

"Yeah, whatever. I'm not sure I'm that interested in your histories and mysteries. Are you at least going to tell me what exactly you have in mind?"

"You just have to trust me. I promise you won't regret it and when this whole thing is sorted out —"

"Well, don't be too sure of yourself."

She literally stomped away onto the balcony and shut the door firmly. I gritted my teeth. I grabbed my bag and headed out. Looking back, I can only marvel at the number of times we were back and forth, when dealing with our emotions, both painfully aware of the fragility of the situation, terrified of losing each other, but too proud and insecure to declare unconditional commitment.

I dropped in to a pharmacy not far from the ferry terminal and bought three pairs of latex gloves in anticipation of tomorrow. The crossing was uneventful. The boat was busy with locals, with a smattering of foreign faces, which included half a dozen Europeans and maybe twenty to thirty Chinese and Japanese. The rest looked like Singaporeans, Malaysians and Indonesians. The mood was distinctly upbeat and conversations animated. There were lots of smiles and laughs, none of which I could truly participate in, given the mood I was in. I realised with some apprehension, that this could be a potentially lethal encounter with my old 'friend'. The more I thought about it, the more I convinced myself that I would come out poorer than I might theoretically have become (does that make sense?), but alive. All I cared about now was to cut out my past altogether and start a fresh life with or without Claire. With Claire, definitely!

The crossing took a little over an hour. It was almost dark by the time we arrived in Batam Island. I walked off the gangway into the bustling port. There were any number of men accosting the arriving tourists, offering everything from trinkets to jewels to women to taxis. I spotted a young man whose face somehow appealed to me, displaying a keen eye and what I thought was an honest face. I signed to him and he bounded forwards, saying, "Good evening, sir, welcome to Batam. My name is Jintan. I can offer you the best taxi service on the island."

"Right now you can take me or direct me to the nearest decent hotel for tonight. I would like to hire you and your car for the whole day tomorrow. I have a business meeting in Barelang Ujung in the afternoon, which is a secret meeting. I would like you to take me to one of those stilt-houses which I would like to hire out for the day. I am sure you can arrange that for me. Once that is done, you can take off, and wait for my call. It may be late."

The man looked first distinctly puzzled and then a bit suspicious. "Yes, sir, no problem. I know a few people down that end who have stilt-houses for hire. I can make a call and fix one right now. But it will cost you, boss, that is a lot of driving."

I reassured him that cost would not be an issue and we agreed on the price he suggested, including a down payment of two million rupiahs, which amounted to a grand sum of one hundred pounds sterling.

By nine o'clock I was settled into a room in a moderately decent hotel about a couple of miles from the terminal. I had a couple of drinks at the bar and avoided contact with others at the bar, in particular a couple of women who seemed very open to developing a relationship. All I could think about was Claire and the way I had dealt with her. Far from cheering me up, the two drinks made me quite emotional and confused. At least the one good side effect of all that was that I was not fretting over what was to come the next day. I could not sleep, going over the various options. Just then, a text arrived from Jack, with both the phone numbers I'd asked for. Harry's number matched with the number Harry had texted from. Kevin's number was not one that I remembered from the past. A few minutes later, I got a call from Jack.

"Are you planning to contact your old friends then?"

"I just thought I might give them a call and see what's what. Just for your info, Harry turned up in Christchurch, looking for me. Fortunately, I managed to give him the slip and fly out to Singapore." My brain was on overdrive, and I was taking a calculated risk.

"You're fucking insane! So, what's the cunning plan? Or do you plan to keep flying round the world in circles until Harry comes over all dizzy and passes out?"

I burst out laughing. "Very good, Jack. I'm arranging to meet Harry tomorrow in a quiet corner of this place I'm staying at. It's called Batam Island, just a short hop from Singapore. I'll settle our problems once and for all. Basically, I don't intend to put up any resistance, just let him know he can have whatever it is he thinks I have. After all, if I don't know I've got it, I won't miss it."

"That sounds sensible, Quentin, but is it safe? How do you intend to protect yourself, if it gets physical? You can't really argue with a gun, particularly if there is more than one."

"That is just a risk I'll have to take. Logically, it would be madness to bump me off, when I'm happy to let him have what he wants."

"Play safe and hopefully there won't be any unpleasant surprises tomorrow. Let me know how it goes."

I remembered my idea of calling Kevin. It was nearly 2 a.m. locally, which meant it would have been around 6 p.m. (yesterday) in England. The realisation dawned, with a sense of shame and regret, that I had not spoken to Kevin for years, and now I was calling him in a moment of need. The phone rang and I was distinctly aware of my heart palpitating, and after ten rings I got my response. It was Kevin all right, the voice was deeper, but the accent had not changed and I would recognise it in a million years.

"Kevin McArdle. And who might you be, stranger, calling from a distant land?"

"Kevin, I'm that blot from your past. Can I start with an apology and ask you to forgive my despicable neglect of our friendship?"

There was a pause of two seconds. "Quentin? Long-lost Quentin, iconic arsehole Quentin! I'd given up on you, laddie." Kevin sounded positively jubilant.

"Kevin, I swear to you I *will* make amends. I have so much to tell you that I cannot even begin, nor should I because of the situation I am in. Suffice it to say, I'm calling from Singapore and am in a bit of a pickle."

"Oh dear, Quentin, I thought you had dug a bit of a hole around yourself when you married that

Harriett of yours. Surely you are not in deeper shit than that?!"

"I'm afraid I am, sport."

"How can I help you?"

"I'd like to know the current whereabouts of our dear school friend Harry. Would you have any idea?"

"Hmm, eh, I last had a chat with Harry a couple of years ago. He had moved to some place called Stubbington down south, located by the sea, I believe. He told me his marriage had broken down and he was on his own. However, I believe the business was doing very well, he was running a cyber-security firm and had contracts with companies in a number of European countries. From the sounds of it he was also exporting the contents of his private parts to the women around Stubbington!"

As always, Kevin delivered this in his deadpan style, and I exploded in mirth.

"Kevin, your sense of humour hasn't diminished! Thanks, mate, that's most useful. Did you think he had changed as a person since the days we knew him? Do you think he might have gone over to the dark side, to coin a phrase?"

There was a pause for a few seconds as Kevin considered. "To be honest, Quentin, I would say, pretty unlikely. Having said that, of course, we had not kept up our friendship the way it was in school. So, while I have no reason at all to believe otherwise, equally I could not confidently say that he hasn't gone dark. I am really curious, Quentin, what's going on between you and Harry?"

"I have difficulty believing this myself, Kevin, but it seems Harry is up to some seriously egregious activity against me. I can't say any more at this point, as I have things to sort out."

"Jesus, this sounds alarming. Can I do anything to help? Shall I speak to Harry and perhaps try and mediate? What about involving the police?"

"Kevin, do nothing, please. I'll sort everything out tomorrow and will soon let you know all about it. I must ring off now, but once more, my deepest apologies and thank you for your usual unstinting help."

"Quentin, listen to me carefully. You have always been my very best friend, although I often suspected that you preferred Harry. Seriously, if it would help, I am prepared to catch the next flight out to Singapore. I mean it."

I almost screamed down the phone. "Stop being so bloody nice, Kevin. Thank you from the bottom of my heart, but no thanks. And when I'm out of this mess, I *will* come back to haunt you for the rest of your life."

"Now you take care of yourself and don't get yourself into any danger, OK?"

"I'll be fine, don't worry. Now, I must say goodbye."

"Bye, Quentin, God bless."

I went over the conversation, ruminating over the fact that Harry had actually moved to Stubbington, which was all of seven miles from my home. Pure coincidence? Not bloody likely. What the hell did Harry want from me? More importantly, I needed to know how to defend myself, if indeed his plan was to take me out. And then the solution came to me, like a flash of lightning. I cast my mind back to when I was twelve, to that day when I was with Jimmy in the woods. I then went online and booked myself into a hotel close to the ferry terminal for the next night. It was probably around three o'clock when I finally fell into a disturbed slumber.

10

BLOODSHED IN THE ORIENT

Greed for gold is bad, but not inexcusable
Coveting another's is worse, but no crime
Stealing is a curse, sometimes justified
But most terrifying, unforgivable, is evil
Evil exists for itself, pure and simple

It was around nine o'clock when I finally got out of the hotel. I'd managed around five hours of sleep, and woke up feeling jet-lagged. I decided not to shave, and leave my hair tousled, so that I'd give the impression to Harry and co of being under the weather. Which was true. I had no appetite and skipped breakfast. I knew I ought to call Claire, but something was holding me back. Why didn't she call? Was she really not bothered? Was it stupid pride? Yes, in my case. What an idiot! Anyway, I had to carry out the distasteful task of texting Claire, like a coward.

My darling Claire

I should be back with you tomorrow sometime. And then you will know everything. My abject apologies, and hope you'll forgive me.

If I were to perish, and never turn up? Claire was smart, she would figure out the best course of action.

Our first halt was one that I requested at a local flea market. Jintan, my driver, took me to the one at Batuaji. I told him to wait in the taxi, and wandered around, fascinated by all the stuff which was there, but finally found what I was seeking. I bought three traditional Indonesian throwing knives. I felt an unusual mix of trepidation and thrill, not knowing how well I could handle them, and hoping against hope that I would not have to use them. I had them carefully wrapped up so that it would not be obvious to Jintan what the contents of the package were. We then went on our way, stopping for lunch at a little Korean restaurant. The food was delicious and fiery, a bit foreign to my untrained palate. It was about two o'clock when we reached our destination.

It was a row of three stilt-houses, which were reached by turning off from the main road onto a muddy path. The houses were out of sight of the main road, and camouflaged by trees on both sides. Jintan let me out. "It's that middle one, boss. You can stay as long as you like."

My phone rang and the voice was hoarse and unfamiliar. "Quentin, it's Harry. Sorry, I've lost my voice. Long time, no see!"

"I'd prefer to leave it even longer, like another fifty years, but unfortunately that's not to be."

"Now, now, Quentin, don't be like that. We'll have it all sorted out, nice and gentle."

"As per your suggestion, I've hired a stilt-house in the south of the island, but no booze or women, I'm afraid. I take it Harriett is with you?"

"Sadly no. I'm departing soon and should be in Batam in an hour."

"I presume you are going to be alone?"

"Of course. Surely, I don't need bodyguards, do I?"

"No, you don't. When you get off at the terminal, just head out to the nearby car rental. Give me a call and I'll give you the exact coordinates."

A sense of bitter disappointment, like bile, came up into my throat, at the thought of Harry's treachery. The next two hours were the most nerve-wracking in my life. I was really jittery and thought more than once about abandoning everything and making a run for it. I knew Claire would be waiting for me back in Singapore, probably equally jittery. She would have insisted on coming with me, but I had not given her the chance.

I set up the room in the way that I wanted it. I moved the double-seater settee to the right-hand corner of the room, straight across from the door. I moved the decrepit old desk so that it stood to the left of the door (from where I stood), about ten feet away. The room was more or less square. I moved two of the four chairs to either side of the desk, so they faced each other. The third chair I placed diagonally across the room. I then turned the fourth chair to face the wall, right next to the settee, and on this I placed the three knives. By this time I was actually shaking with fear and anticipation. The walls were of course constructed of wood and would be perfect for target practice. Over the next half hour I repeatedly threw the knives, stationing myself at the left corner of the room and aiming diagonally across, meaning that any marks on the wood would be out of sight for anyone who entered, located above the corner where the sofa was situated. There were two ceiling lamps, emitting a pretty poor light, and I decided that I would switch off the one at the back of the room, which would serve the double purpose of making the knife marks on the wood almost invisible and of course putting me in a position of some advantage, compared to the person who would enter, namely Harry.

I was thrilled to find that my throwing was accurate and consistent. More worrying was the speed with which I could mobilise, given that Harry would almost certainly be armed with a gun. What would I not have given for a gun (although I had never used one)? What did Harry want from me? The possibility that kept recurring in my mind was that I had won the lottery and they were after the winning ticket. But what if, hidden amongst all the jewellery I had rapidly gone through, there was an item of extreme value?

Harry's croaky voice came over the phone again, and I gave him the directions, which were fairly straightforward. I continued to practise, progressively increasing the speed of the throw, to the point where I thought it would be about as fast as I could get. I was acutely aware that there was a big difference between practising and delivering the real throw. That is the moment when people falter, hesitate, lose their nerve, and the outcome would be an inevitable disaster. I decided that I would stand with one knee on the chair facing the wall, still hiding the knives. I considered the possibility that on entry, Harry might decide to do a room search, or even a body search of me, in which case I might have to use one of the knives to immobilise the arm that was holding the gun. I thought hard, back to our schooldays, and remembered that Harry was left-handed, so I made a mental image of burying the knife into his left shoulder. At that point I was still not quite prepared to entertain the prospect of aiming for the heart.

It was an old and battered leather two-seater and I secreted an unused knife on the top edge, sitting between the hump of the soft backing and the rear ledge. I got rid of the bulb from the rear light. I secreted a second unused knife on the floor between the sofa and the wall, easy to reach if I sat on the chair with my legs astride. The third knife was the one I had been practising with, and was hoping not to have to use it. After some thought I decided to use that as a decoy, and slipped it into the holster which came with the set and strapped it round my shoulder. And then the wait.

I heard the car arrive and the doors open and close. Something happened at that point. I went into a trance, with zero emotion and no trepidation. I had decided that either this was going to be a done deal, meaning I gave up something of great value (which I knew and cared nothing about) or that I would be dead. I thought of Claire and felt a slight regret, but that was evanescent. She was safe, not embroiled in this mess.

Footsteps coming up the wooden stairs. A loud knock.

"Come in."

The door opened and in walked my old friend Garlic-Nose! Unsurprisingly, he held an unwavering gun, his face sporting a ghastly combination of a sadistic smile and a snarl. He waved his gun to indicate I should approach him, which I did. Ice cold. Not a word was spoken and he frisked me, as I had anticipated. With a grunt he stuck his left hand into my side and pulled out the knife and let out a throaty laugh.

"Are you even able to speak?" I said, lacing my words with as much sarcasm as I was capable of. He looked at me expressionlessly and then turned and walked back to the door. He nodded to the man outside, who was presumably waiting outside. "All clear." There was something oddly familiar about the voice and the diction.

"Yes, Harry, it's all clear and I have been disarmed. You can come in without fearing for your life," I said, continuing in the sarcastic mode. Garlic-Nose walked out.

And then my nemesis walked in, wearing a pair of large dark glasses and a baseball cap, and for a second I could not make out the face against the glare. I felt my heart do a somersault as I recognised the person.

Kevin McArdle.

✢

IN CONVERSATION WITH THE DEVIL

Kevin took off his cap and the glasses with his left hand, the right wielding a pistol. Before I could say anything, he exploded into a deafening and demonic laugh, which lasted a good five seconds.

"It's your old friend Kevin, you wanker. Got you, didn't I?"

My heart was pounding and all my sang-froid vanished at a stroke.

"Bleeding hell, yes, Kevin, I will admit it, you got me. But, why all the theatrics?"

"You'll soon find out. A man in my position needs all these trappings, I'm afraid. You know, I had planned to deal with you first in Fiji and then in Christchurch, and would've done, if you hadn't bolted like a pair of rabbits. I must say you managed to surprise me. What tipped you off?"

"Our hasty departure from Fiji was triggered by your minion, Garlic-Nose, who made such a lasting impression on me as I came out of JFK. When he turned up at the cultural centre, I knew there was no way that was a coincidence. And then I rang the hotel, to be informed that a mysterious friend had settled my room and was picking me up, which was most reassuring! And so we decamped."

"When you gave us the slip, I decided to go for plan B, which is where Harry came in. You know the tall guy you referred to as Garlic-Nose, he was the croaking voice of Harry. And just in case you're wondering, I am a cyber-expert, even if I say so myself. It was no big deal trailing you and locating the flights and hotels, wherever you went. Of course, you did give me a head start by telling Harriett you were in Fiji."

I groaned inwardly, cursing myself for never having suspected that there might have been someone impersonating poor Harry. I felt a pang of guilt as well for having cast aspersions on my dear friend, but there was really no time for any of that.

"Well, you need to know that I'm not quite alone in this, Kevin. You remember my bad cousin, Jack, whom we all hated in school? He is fully in the picture, and is on his way here even as we speak. We've had a bit of a *détente* and we are now a team."

The grin that appeared on Kevin's face was diabolical.

"Are you quite sure about that, Quentin?"

The voice was that of Jack's! I felt a spasm in my guts.

"Have you forgotten my exceptional talents at mimicry, you poor sod? I'm the Jack you've been speaking to all this time."

I shrugged my shoulders, trying to look nonchalant. "You certainly convinced me that you were Jack. Well, now that we are here, let's get on with it, shall we? What is it that you want from me?"

Kevin's laughter boomed again and his expression could be, charitably, described as ugly.

"All I need from you is a simple signature on the dotted line." He reached into his satchel and pulled out an envelope. He started moving forwards, but I quickly stepped towards him, in order to avoid him coming too close to my hidden weapons. He handed the envelope with his left hand, the right still clutching the gun pointing at me.

"What's the matter, Kevin? You scared of me or something?"

His expression got uglier and just for a moment I regretted that I might have overstepped the mark. Fortunately, he held himself in check.

"I suggest you simply sign on the dotted line where I have marked with a cross, and don't bother reading the document. I don't want you to waste your time on all the legal speak, because I'm going to tell you the contents of what you're signing over."

I stepped forward to the table and sat on the chair to the left, leaving the other one across the table to Kevin. I inspected the document, which was turned onto the last page and had a marked space for my signature, below which were two witnesses, both duly filled and signed.

"Don't worry about the other signatures, they are real people. And I believe I may have to get a notarising solicitor to countersign, which I am sure will not be a problem."

"And what exactly do you propose to do if I refuse to sign?"

"I shoot you, and you go to your grave without knowing what it's all about." Kevin put on a cherubic smile.

"All right then, Kevin, but before I sign I want to hear everything, and I mean absolutely everything."

Kevin sat himself down across the table, still holding the gun.

"I suppose you deserve to know. In school, I was always jealous of you, did you know that? You had the brains, the sporting ability and of course, that wealthy family. Oh yes, I know all about your unhappy childhood, boo-hoo! And your special relationship with Harry was infuriating and it took all of my skills to hide my resentment. I secretly enjoyed Jack's bullying of you. In fact it was when we left school, I decided to play one off against the other, and pick up the spoils of war, namely your entire inheritance. Who gave you two bastards the right to get all that wealth, anyway? I reckon I deserve it no less, and intend to get it.

"I got in touch with Jack nearly six years ago and established a working relationship with him, with my cyber-expertise. Gradually, I began to ferret out family details, and one day he revealed that he might potentially have to split the inheritance with you. That was the opportunity I was waiting for. I suggested this master plan which would ensure that he acquired all of it, and in return for my efforts, he would pay me a million quid. I had no idea then, just how much the actual amount would be.

"You see, Quentin, that grandmother of yours suddenly developed a conscience, soon after Jack's parents died in that so-called accident. Jack had always been her blue-eyed boy, and you were the wretched blot on the family landscape. A few years after his parents died, she started suggesting that the estate should be split equally between you, and Jack made no secret of the fact that that would only happen over his dead body. He went up and tried to reason with her, but to no avail. In fact things got quite heated and I think he may have blotted his copybook! He threatened her with physical violence and stormed out, believing she would never have the guts to do what she threatened. I guess he underestimated the old cow.

"About four years ago, Jack received a letter from her, in which she quite simply stated that she was intending to change her will, leaving the estate to be shared equally between the two of you. She was not cowed down by his rants and threats, and ended by saying she really needed to mend fences with the straight grandson she had wronged all these years. She said all the tragic truths of the past were contained in certain letters that she had sent to the solicitors, to be handed to you on her death.

"On my advice, Jack contacted the family solicitors in London, in an attempt to find out if there had been a change in the will. The lawyers flatly refused to engage with him. Jack also let slip the fact that the value of the inheritance would be over forty million, which came as a bit of a shock to my system. I had undersold myself; I should have asked for ten million! But having agreed a sum, I could not very well go back on it. I considered various options and thought I'd take another tack.

"I had already decided to infiltrate your camp, so to speak, and boy, was it a joyful piece of cake, going after Harriett! It was around March of 2017, that I engineered a meeting with her, and from there on there was no looking back. She couldn't wait to have it off with me, particularly when I dangled the inheritance in front of her. Soon she was sitting pretty in the knowledge that she would become the lady of the manor. I told her that I would get rid of Jack, making you the automatic heir, and then of course, eliminate you in due course, making her the beneficiary of the fortune – shared with me, naturally.

She went for it big time. And when I talked about eliminating you, she didn't bat an eyelid.

"If you thought that was interesting, you need to hear the rest. Jack called his grandmother a couple of times, cajoled, pleaded and threatened, all to no avail. In early December 2018, he got a letter from her informing him that she had formally altered the will in the way she had decided. He was white hot with fury. So that's when we finalised our plan. I offered to do the dirty deeds, for an increase in my share of the spoils, to ten million. The bloody prick, Jack actually argued and swore that it was too much! I did the only thing that seemed reasonable under the circumstances; I decided to have it all myself in due course.

"I took a flight to Aberdeen and hired a car, which I drove for nearly four hours, arriving at the manor around 2 a.m. Being a Saturday night the housekeepers would have been given the night off. I had to take a chance that nobody would see me and hopefully that was the case. I entered the house with Jack's key and immobilised the alarm, using the code he had given me. As I went up the stairs I suddenly realised that she could potentially be awake or have been alerted by my entry, in which case she could well be calling the police. I ran the next few steps up, turned left and dashed into her bedroom. She had just turned the lights on as I went in and was reaching out for the telephone when she saw me.

"She made a grab for the phone and started dialling, but before she could dial the second digit, I had reached her, snatched the phone off her hand and ripped it from the socket. That's when I saw the fear in her eyes and believe me that feeling was the next best thing to an orgasm. She began to struggle and yell so I slapped her hard and she fell silent. I then got her to get dressed and put on an appropriate coat for the cold of the night. It was January and freezing.

"'You see, old woman, there is no place in the world for rich fat cats like you. We all have a right to share, and have whatever we choose. People like you are a liability. So I have decided to kidnap you, and hold you for a nice, juicy ransom.' She was shaking with fear, but conveniently swallowed my stated intentions. We left the house in the dead of night, in total darkness, and I escorted her round to the passenger-side door of my car. I bent down and picked up the large rounded rock that I had strategically placed behind the tyre, stepped back and delivered the fatal blow to her right temple. I carried her, remembering to carry the rock as well with me, off to the edge of the cliff and I threw the rock down, followed by her limp body. Despite the sound of the waves I could hear her body strike the rocks. All that was left was for me to make my way back to Aberdeen."

I forced myself to stay calm and avoid any internal emotional reaction, but feigned horror and anger.

"You sadistic bastard. You killed the poor woman, just for the money?"

He looked at me pityingly, and said, "Is there any other reason? Oh, and I found a very interesting letter she had written to you, but not yet posted. I thought you might want to read it."

✚

25 December 2018

Dearest Quentin,

I have decided that you should be a joint heir to my estate in equal proportion to Jack. It is yours by right, you deserve it, and it may compensate in some small way for the way I have treated you all your life. Consider it my first real Christmas gift.

I do not need to justify my actions. I suspect Jack will not take this lightly, and I would strongly advise you to obtain maximum legal protection. I am even worried that Jack might resort to physical means of intimidation, and you need to prepare for that.

I have already posted a letter to our solicitors, Leadbetter & Barclay, in London, with my unequivocal instructions. I intend to follow up with a call to them next week to confirm the alteration to my will.

There are a few painful facts you have to get to grips with. I cannot reveal them at this moment, and they are best revealed by certain letters from the past, which will lay bare the *truth concerning you. I dispatched them to our solicitors a month ago, with instructions to deliver them to you on my demise.*

I am suffocated by guilt, of what I have been instrumental in, of having deprived you of crucial truths to do with your past and your origins. I no longer know what is right.

Your loving grandmother,
Winifred Grayling

Silence reigned for several seconds while my brain was absorbing and assimilating all that I had heard and read. Poor old Gran, murdered by a pair of psychopathic thugs. Why the hell had I gone off on that goddammed holiday to Tenerife? Would I have been able to prevent it happening?

And then the penny dropped. Harriett's sudden seduction and hastily arranged holiday to Tenerife in January 2019. So perfectly timed that I would not be around when Gran 'jumped' off the cliff, or at her funeral, where my presence could have been awkward, particularly if I'd got wind of the fact that the solicitors were holding letters for me. I could feel the fury rise within me, and it must have been obvious to see. Kevin's eyes gleamed with an unholy delight.

"Yes, you prick, you fell hook, line and sinker for the sudden resurgence of Harriett's love! We didn't want you anywhere near the funeral. You'll have to admit, it was a pretty smart move to relieve you of your mobile phone just as you were rushing for the airport. Harriett certainly got full marks for that. We also had a potentially more problematic situation with the solicitors, who were charged with probating the will. So Jack played the heartbroken grandson. Leadbetter said the will needed to be probated, but your presence was required, as a beneficiary. Evidently they also were in possession of correspondence that was to be handed over to you after the old lady's death. He told them that you were travelling abroad and hinted that you may well decide to emigrate. I was worried that they might try to contact you by post, so Harriett was charged with keeping a lookout for any letter addressed to you. Leadbetter wrote to you asking you to make an appointment to see them. Fortunately, Harriett intercepted it and we came up with a plan to reply on your behalf. We wrote to them to say that you were on a round-the-world trip and that you would see them on your return. Everything was settled, and Jack effectively became the lord of the manor and no one knew any better, except for Harriett and me.

"You know I had almost forgotten about the mysterious correspondence awaiting you with the solicitors. I wonder what dark secrets lie in there. Oh well, we will no doubt be able to claim the letters one way or the other. I have to say Harriett has been the perfect asset in all this. But I'm not finished yet. It was during the funeral that the stupid gypsy started playing up. That creep with whom you were supposed to have been so friendly? The one who used to turn up at the primary school when we were six years old? I hated you even then, living in that grand estate, while we plebs had to make do with our little terraced houses.

"So, coming back to the funeral, he was hovering around at the periphery, obviously not invited to the formal gathering. Fortunately there was just a handful of people apart from Jack, thanks to the fact that the old woman was a recluse. As the reading finished and Jack was walking away the little prick comes up to him, shakes his fist and says, 'You think I don't know what happened?'

"Jack brushed him off, but inside he was shaken. What if he had seen something?

"So, a few weeks later Jack repeated my exercise, this time landing in Dundee and hiring a car. He made it to the gypsy's cottage around six o'clock to find him sat in front of the fire and drinking rum. He was immediately on his guard and suspicious, but Jack put on an act and managed to disarm him, armed only with a bottle of an eighteen-year-old Arran malt. The gypsy's eyes evidently lit up when he saw this, something he could never afford. Over the next three hours he went on to consume a little more than half of that bottle of whisky, on top of the rum he had already imbibed.

"All this time, Jack regaled him with tall tales and humorous incidents, which may or may not have taken place. By nine o'clock the gypsy was pissed. Jack opened his bag and took out the heavy rubber hammer that he had brought for this specific exercise, which he duly carried out by a full-blooded blow to the back of his head. He fell on the spot, out for the count, but alive, and with no mark of trauma. Jack went to his car and brought out the old worn rope that he had brought with him and proceeded to hang the unconscious man from the nearest tree. An obvious suicide."

He looked at me with a combination of triumph and derision and I made no attempt to hide the total hatred and anger that I felt at that time. I felt as though there was a ball of fire inside me which was about to explode. "You bastards, you absolute fucking bastards."

"Wowee, finally Quentin swears! Finally Quentin shows evidence of balls! Finally is Quentin going to act like a man? And before you do anything, I won't hesitate to shoot you, because once you are dead, the estate falls to me indirectly, as I've explained. Of course, that would mean having to dispose of your body, never to be found, and the courts will accept your death after the usual statutory seven years or whatever. I can wait, but would rather not."

It was at that point that I knew what I was going to do, and all my rage and hatred suddenly morphed again into an icy calm. I got up slowly and casually, and stepped towards the settee.

"I had no idea that you could stoop to this level of criminal depravity. Is that all, or are there more victims?"

"Three more actually, but two of them have nothing to do with you. They got in the way of my business and would not see reason. But, guess who the third one was?" he said with a look of amusement. My blood ran cold, at the thought it might have been Harry. I shuddered, slightly exaggerating it, to give the impression of one in the process of being traumatised.

"Actually you'll approve of this one. Why, it's your dear cousin Jack!"

"What!?"

"Once everything was in place, I didn't really want him lording it as the default heir. The poor bugger fell down a flight of stairs, fully inebriated, and smashed his head. He was lucky to survive, but I'm afraid he is paralysed and will spend the rest of his days in full-time care. It was tempting to finish him off, but I thought it might be too much if both brothers died or disappeared, and I didn't want the solicitors to smell a rat. This way, Jack gets one half, Harriett the other, and I control both. Needless to say, I had arranged long ago to hold the power of attorney for Jack, as well as being his formal business partner. That's it in a nutshell. Did I make any mistakes?"

I held my head between my hands in deep distress and slowly walked towards the chair facing the wall.

"Now, come over and sign the fucking document. It basically states that you have left England for good, embraced Buddhism and intend to live out your life in the Far East; and you are leaving all your worldly possessions to your wife."

I turned and sat astride the chair, facing Kevin, and buried my face in my hands, with the words, "Poor Jimmy…"

I heard Kevin laugh with derision.

"You really are the fucking pits, you wimp. And all for some good-for-nothing gypsy!"

I pretended to wipe my eyes, but was ice cold inside, as I had always planned to be at this juncture.

"And what guarantee do I have that you will not shoot me after I have signed?"

"None at all. Either way I get what I want. If you sign, at least you have a hope that I might not kill you."

"If the end result is going to be the same, why don't you simply shoot me? Why do you need the signature?"

"Belt and braces. Get on with it."

"Tell me, why did Harriett refer to you as Monty?"

"The stupid bitch. I'm glad you didn't put two and two together. Don't quite remember my full name from school, do you?"

I thought hard and it came to me. "Kevin *Montrose* McArdle. Of course."

✛

VERMIN NO MORE

I stood up, my right hand casually moving over to the sofa and feeling the cold steel of the knife, simultaneously distracting Kevin with the words, "OK, but please put down that goddamned gun." I thought it worth a try, and it did work partially, with his hand resting loosely on the gun, with it pointing ninety degrees away from me. This was the moment. I forced myself into a trance, to avoid any tendency to falter, and went through the motion I had practised for the last three hours. My hand came up in one smooth motion, holding the knife at the ready, and by the time Kevin had registered what was happening, my arm was stretched above my head and the shoulder extended, the throw imminent. In what seemed like a blur, Kevin gripped the gun and swung it towards me at incredible speed. I can relive those moments as if they were happening in slow motion. The blade flew like an arrow, straight towards the right side of Kevin's chest, and as soon as I had released it I threw myself to the right, picking up the second knife from the floor. There was a loud explosion as Kevin's finger squeezed the trigger, but the bullet went harmlessly to the left of me, and my knife buried itself below his right clavicle. I could see the look of complete incredulity in his eyes and he was transfixed for about five seconds, during which he realised that he could not move his shooting arm, no doubt accompanied by the agony of having a knife buried into his chest. He made a hasty grab of the pistol with his left hand, with obvious intent. By this time, however, I was armed and in position, and this time the blade buried itself into the front of his chest, just below the lower end of the sternum. There was no second shot as his knees buckled and the gun fell from his hand. He slowly twisted to the right, still desperately trying to get his left hand on the gun. I leaped and stamped hard on his left hand, and he yelled in pain. I bent and retrieved the gun, retreated to my chair, which I pulled over, and sat three feet away from the monster.

"How does that feel, Kevin?" His face was contorted with pain and hatred; tears were trickling from his eyes. A thin line of drool exuded from one corner of his mouth.

"You got me, you actually got me," he said with undisguised disgust and admiration, in the midst of pain. "How do you propose to get away? My two boys will make sure you won't leave this place alive."

"You let me worry about that, Kevin, but you'll be long gone by then." I was experiencing a most bizarre combination of feelings of triumph, ecstasy, satisfaction and massive relief. "They heard one shot, which they will assume killed me. They have no idea that I'm the one here holding the gun, the one in the driving seat now."

Kevin winced and coughed up a small spurt of blood. "Quentin, please get me to a hospital. I promise you, I'll get out of your life for good. I swear it. You can have everything, I will sign whatever you like. Please just call for an ambulance."

"That's mighty generous of you! Now, why on earth would I want to risk any of that, when I have it all anyway?"

"Please, Quentin, I'm dying. If I do, you will be guilty of murder, and you won't get away with it. And even if you do, would you want to stain your unblemished life with my blood on your hands?"

I contemplated the content of his words and realised with a start that what he said was absolutely correct. I was still possessed by this abnormal calm, this state of icy emotional suspension.

"You are absolutely right, I'll just have to learn to live with it. And of course I will have all that money as inspiration to justify all my misdeeds."

Kevin starting blubbing incoherently, as his left arm collapsed under him. I stood up from my chair and went to stand directly above him, looking into his eyes.

"Tell me, how does it actually feel, to be dying? Was it really worth going through all this?"

In his final moments his real self re-emerged, contorting his face with fury. "May you rot in hell, you motherfucker..." His body convulsed a few times and Kevin died in agony and rage.

✠

There was complete silence for the next ten minutes. I left Kevin's body where it was and lay myself down on the sofa with the gun in my hand, concealed behind my right thigh. I lay on my side with my head angled back in a slightly abnormal position, to make it look like I was either unconscious or dead. I knew sooner or later Garlic-Nose would have to come in to check things out. I'm not sure how long it took, but it may have been twenty minutes before a knock sounded on the door. I let out a loud grunt, a sort of mixture of a groan and shout for help. Between the slits in my eyes I could see the door open and Garlic-Nose walked in holding up a pistol. There was a sharp intake of breath as he saw us both lying prostrate, Kevin in a pool of blood. I knew I was taking a big chance with the gun, as I had never fired one in my life, but again I was full of a calm confidence. As I had anticipated, Garlic-Nose dropped to his knees to check on Kevin, which was the cue for me to swiftly swing my arm around and point the pistol towards the man. Just as I said, "Drop the gun," he brought his right hand up, wielding the pistol towards me. The gun bucked in my hand and must have found its mark, as Garlic-Nose's arm dropped and he slowly sank to the floor.

I knew the wait would be much shorter this time, before the second henchman came to investigate. This time I decided to adopt a different tactic, and stood alongside the wall to the right of the door until the knock sounded. "Come in," I exclaimed loudly. The door opened and the man stepped in, holding a gun in his right hand, which, however, was of limited value as I was standing outside the line of his vision with my arm raised and gun pointing straight at his chest. "Drop it," I said. The man hesitated, his eyes taking in the scene of the two men lying in close proximity, obviously dead. There was a sharp intake of breath and he said, "What the fuck—"

"That's right, sunshine, your boss and his sidekick are both learning to play the harp!" He looked shocked, stood rooted to the spot, but dropped the gun.

"A pity you did that, I wish you had tried taking a shot at me, which would've allowed me to waste you with impunity."

"Hey, listen, boss, I'm just the odd-job man, running errands for Monty. I carry a gun and pretend to be his bodyguard, but never did any of his dirty jobs. Let me go, man, I swear I'll say nothing. I have a wife and four kids, man. Please let me go."

He was shaking and unless he was the best actor in the world, I believed he was telling the truth.

"Kick that gun towards me."

He complied. I made him kneel and turn to face the wall, holding his gun to the back of his head. I then picked up Kevin's gun, the one I had used on Garlic-Nose, and handed it to the man and asked him to grip it. I made him drop it and then kicked it away.

"I am going to ditch this gun not too far away, where it'll be found by the police. The prints if identified will be yours, and you will be the prime suspect. That is my insurance. Now I'm going to leave you here and you better hope you never cross my path again. Now hand me your passport, your mobile phone, wallet and the keys to the car."

"Oh, come on, man, I can't get nowhere without them. How do you expect me to get off the island?"

"Don't worry. At nine o'clock my driver will come and pick you up. You are not to say a word to him.

You can grunt, if you like. He will drop you off at the terminal and hand you your belongings. I suggest you take the next ferry back to Singapore, and the next flight out to London."

The man, whose name turned out to be Benjamin Matthews, handed over his passport, wallet, phone and the keys, which I deposited in my jacket pocket. I kept him kneeling and facing the wall away from the bodies, as I undertook the unpleasant job of emptying out the pockets of the erstwhile villains. I opened out the sheet I had brought in preparation, and dropped Kevin's gun (with Matthews' fingerprints) as well as Garlic-Nose's gun on it. The third gun I held in my right hand. I then dropped the passports, the wallets and the mobile telephones onto the sheet, and knotted it up. It made a bulky package, which I tucked under my left arm.

"So then, Benny boy, what's going to be the scene when you get back? Monty obviously had some businesses going and he must have other employees or associates. What will you tell them? Is there a likelihood that you might spill the beans to them, and they might come after me?"

Matthews looked blank, and it struck me that there was not much activity going on between his ears. So I explained the pitch, and then asked him to relate it back to me. He closed his eyes and recounted.

"I'll tell them that we split in Singapore, where I was supposed to wait for Monty and Kelso, who were going to meet someone on a nearby island. I was told it was some kind of arms deal. I waited for three days, but had no further contact with them, and I was getting no response to my calls. I panicked and took a flight back home to inform you guys of what had happened."

"And what do you think is likely to be their response? What happens to the business?"

"Nothing, man. Monty has one partner and a staff of five or six lowlife sods. He and his partner Morgan are like a pair of snakes watching each other all the time. If Monty dropped dead, no one would be happier than Morgan, because he then takes over the business. I'm not in favour with him, and will soon get kicked out of the outfit, or at least I hope so. I am sick to death of this whole business and just want to get out of it."

"Remember, I have your passport details and can track you down anytime. I'll have my men keeping an eye on you and your family, should you decide to get smart. So make sure you stick to the story and make absolutely sure there is no link to me. By the way, do you even know who I am? Do you know what Monty wanted from me?"

Matthews looked hesitant and looked away, shaking his head, then thought better of it and said, "Quentin? I never got your surname, unless that is your surname. As for what he wanted from you, I always assumed it was the dame, who I believe was your wife. I swear to you I have no interest in knowing anything else. If you fought over the woman and you killed Monty, good luck to you, man."

"Benny boy, I am leaving you now. Don't try anything foolish. Otherwise, you could end up facing the capital punishment, which is the usual sentence for murder in Indonesia." I almost felt sorry for the man, who looked like his world had come to an end. He looked at me awestruck and said, "You must be one helluva killer. Just how the hell did you manage to neutralise these two vicious thugs?"

"I knifed one and shot the other."

I shut the door and hastened down the steps. I jumped into the car and drove away, remembering to don a pair of gloves to avoid leaving fingerprints. I smiled to myself, wondering what Jintan would be thinking when the shit hit the fan. By then hopefully Matthews should be clear of the island. The last thing I wanted was Benny to be apprehended in Batam. When I reached the hotel, I parked the car and called Jintan.

"Actually, I don't need you tonight, but have a job for you in the morning. Can you come and meet me at the ferry terminal at eight thirty tomorrow morning? I need you to deliver something to one of the men, who is staying overnight at the house you took me to."

I checked into the hotel using Matthews' passport. Though there was little resemblance between us, the man at the reception was barely interested. Once in the room, I carefully removed Kevin's pistol and placed it inside a plastic bag, which I then placed in the safe-deposit locker and locked it. I asked for a small cardboard box, which the concierge found for me, and in it I packed Matthews' belongings and taped it securely. As soon as I let myself relax, Claire came flooding back into my consciousness. I should have rung to reassure her, but some stupid reluctance got in the way. I knew she would be worried about me (I hoped) and finally settled on sending her a text message.

Dearest Claire, mission accomplished! Can't wait to see you tomorrow, when I'll explain all the gory details.

I set my alarm for 4 a.m. I got up and had a quick wash. I put on a pair of gloves, opened the sheet, with all its incriminating evidence, and carefully wiped all fingerprints off, and then re-wrapped it into a tight bundle. Then, with my jacket slung over my left shoulder and the bundle firmly pressed against my side, I made my way to the front of the hotel. There was nobody at the reception, and the solitary man at the door was sat on his chair, half asleep. He started when he saw me and got up with a salute. "I just couldn't sleep, so I thought I would take a little walk." He smiled and nodded me on.

I walked swiftly for about fifteen minutes until I found myself in a quiet, dark spot close to the sea, with the waves lapping at the shore. I looked around and there was no sign of life. I quickly took out the bundle, opening it out carefully. I donned another pair of gloves, and threw the pistols and the phones one after the other, as far out into the sea as I could. That then left me with the sheet, which I dropped into one of the rubbish bins on the way back. I was fairly confident that all these items would vanish without any possible link to me. I kept the wallets with me for later disposal into a waste bin in Singapore.

I got ready and had an early breakfast, and checked out. It was just a short walk to the terminal. On the dot of eight thirty Jintan arrived. "Good morning, sir. Where did you stay last night?" I gave him the name of a hotel, which was located three miles away from the stilt-house, and told him they had arranged a taxi to drop me off here.

"Successful meeting, sir?"

"Jintan, don't talk about it, now or ever. It was a complete failure, because I was dealing with crooked gangsters. I was forced into a deal at a considerable loss to my business. Anyway, I was only too happy to get away from them. There were four men, from two different companies, and fortunately for me they were fighting between themselves by the time I left. Dangerous guys.

"So, here is a package which I promised to deliver to one of them this morning. His name is Ben Matthews, and he will be waiting at the stilt-house. Just go there and toot your horn, and he'll come down. Bring him to the ferry terminal and hand over the package. Remember, Jintan, these guys are dangerous. Don't get into conversation with them. I'll pay you for the whole thing."

Jintan gave me a shrewd look, and I knew he hadn't quite swallowed everything. I paid him ten million rupiahs, which made his jaw drop, and hopefully ensured his discretion. I knew that in due course he would have to 'help' the police with their enquiries, but I was confident that he was smart enough to keep his involvement minimal.

11

THE FALL OF THE SIREN

Women are wonderful creatures
Superior to men on almost every count
Women nurture and save the world
Women make men's lives worthwhile
Nothing can so appal as the evil woman

I caught the next ferry back to Singapore. All the while, since waking up, I had been tossing around various ideas on how to deal with Harriett. After much deliberation I dialled her number.

"Quentin, where the hell are you? I've been so worried. I've heard nothing from Monty! Did you not have your meeting yesterday?"

"We did, Harriett, and we came to a most amicable settlement, whereby I sign everything over to you, and in return your Monty allows me to live a quiet life in the Far East. I believe I'm now a devout Buddhist! Most magnanimous offer, I thought! The last I saw of Monty and his two minions was last night at a restaurant in the south of the island. Have you not heard from them?"

There was real panic in Harriett's voice. "Did they not tell you when they were heading back to Singapore? Why are you not all together?"

"To be perfectly honest, that's the last I ever want to see of Monty and his band of lowlifes. All I can remember is that when I left, all three of them were pissed out of their minds, delighted with the outcome of our so-called settlement."

"That's fantastic, I am so glad it's all gone off without any bloodshed. But that still doesn't explain where Monty has gone. Why isn't he answering my calls?"

"I haven't a clue, and really, I don't give a shit. I just never want to see any of them again, though I confess I wouldn't mind seeing you again."

"This is no time for that. I really need to get hold of Monty. If you hear anything, anything at all, please give me a call immediately."

I was shaking with laughter, inwardly! It was wonderful to see Harriett in the state that she was in. And then it suddenly hit me like a pile driver, the thought that I had killed two men yesterday. Killed two men. Killed two lowlife thugs. Killed two extremely tough, brutal, and ruthless lowlife thugs. I felt a sense of extreme elation, not one iota of regret or guilt.

"Harriett, I realise you haven't got the slightest interest in rekindling anything with me. However, there is still the small matter of your little treasure-trove."

"Shit, I had almost forgotten that, in all this kerfuffle. You can't just misappropriate my things. I'm prepared to go fifty-fifty on that." She ended on this generous note, no doubt expecting me to be bowled over by this act of extreme largesse.

"That seems fair enough. However, I am not going to tell you where I have secreted the stuff, unless and until we meet face to face."

"Have it your way. My first priority is to try and get hold of Monty and then I'll get back to you."

"Stop worrying. More than likely the three of them got hammered last night, celebrating the windfall. They are probably lying in a drunken stupor, and will no doubt get back to you soon."

Harriett's response indicated reassurance and I decided to press on. "So, there is this supposedly amazing dinner cruise that leaves at six this evening. If you are up for it, I could book us onto it. I can guarantee it will be an experience not to forget."

There was a short pause, after which Harriett replied, "All right, if you insist. But strictly on the condition that you come clean with where my stuff is stashed away."

"Done. I'll text you the address for the cruise. Can't wait to see you again." I tried, and I think I managed, to sound excited and convincing. I realised I had no clue what was going to happen this evening!

I sensed the worst as soon as I entered the room, which was completely dark, apart from a little bit of light filtering through from the balcony. I switched on the light and my worst fears were confirmed by the perfectly made bed and no sign of Claire. My heart sank at the thought Claire had left. Or maybe she was down in the bar? Maybe she had gone out for a walk? Bollocks. I knew she had gone. And then I found the note.

⊕

November 18, 2019

Dearest Tintin,

Sorry, I'm running away like a coward, which I guess is what I am. I know I can never repay you for saving my life, and standing by me through my darkest hours. You restored my faith in humanity and now I know that men are not evil by design or by birth. Now I know that there are men of honor like yourself. I also know that there is the possibility of true love between a man and a woman. Unfortunately, I also know that I am not destined for it, nor do I perhaps deserve it.

I would be lying if I said that I was not deeply

hurt by your refusal to allow me to participate in your plans to deal with your friend Harry. Maybe I would've contributed zilch, but at least I had a right to know. Yes, a right to know. After all that we have shared over the last few weeks, I think you owed me that and yet you denied me that. I felt totally let down and undervalued.

And then of course there is the question that we both broached in our own ways; what our nights of passion meant. Yes, maybe it was the beginning of a lifelong bond, but what are the chances of that? Just look around you – how many marriages that you know have lasted? Look at your own! Having said that, I also realise now that there is a realistic possibility of you reuniting with your Harriett. For all that you have done for me and for all that I owe you, I can't possibly hang around and jeopardise that reunion. So, when I put it all together, what do the stats say about my chances with you? Very poor odds, I would say.

But why not at least stay around and give it a go? That may be what you would say and I have asked myself that. The point is, Tintin, I have derived so much happiness from you and in your company that I do not want to take any risk of that experience, those loving moments, being sullied by our human failings. You deserve much better than me. This way I leave with nothing but profoundly happy memories, albeit with painful regret at the parting. But I am in little doubt that we will both ride this out and get back to our original lives. Don't forget that our origins are so different that it would've taken a monumental effort for either one of us to relocate to the other's scenario.

I was terrified that you might not return from your rendezvous, and could not sleep that first night. It was only when I got your text yesterday, that I got my life back. I scrambled to book my flight so I could be away first thing this morning. I was afraid that if I actually met with you, I wouldn't have the courage to escape. So, I am bidding you farewell, with an apology and an entreaty for you to think not too badly of me, and forgive me. I hope to be reunited with my mother tomorrow. If you ever feel like communicating with me, you have my number, which I intend to retain. I wish you a wonderful life, full of the happiness and love that you deserve.

Claire

✣

I sat, staring at absolutely nothing for the next five or ten minutes. Suddenly it hit me, and I felt an upsurge of deep sadness. I cursed and swore. This was my moment of triumph and Claire was not there to share it with me. All the way back to the hotel I had been fantasising about how I would greet Claire, how I would maul her, how I would make love to her, how I would rejoice with her. But no more. And then anger took over and I tried to smack her memory out of my thoughts. Who the hell cares? It would not have lasted anyway! Now I had my total freedom, why on earth did I need a millstone like her, around my neck? I was well rid of her. To hell with this cold, heartless American gangster's moll! In six months' time would I not look back and laugh?

Looking at my watch and noting the time, I wondered what my priorities were. My mind was in a whirl of conflicting emotions, with a part of me wanting to do a mad dash to the airport, to try and stop Claire – a bit like those movie clichés, where the hero would dash into the aircraft just as it was about to depart and reunite with his lady-love. No, I couldn't be distracted from what had to be accomplished. It was time to let go. I pulled out the envelope containing the letter from Gran which she had intended to send me, before she was so brutally murdered by Kevin. I re-read it slowly. All my animosity towards her melted away, and I felt nothing but a real deep pity and sorrow for her.

I sat, staring blindly, not daring to allow myself to feel anything. I still had a serious situation on hand. What deadly secrets did the remaining letters hold, the ones Gran had sent to the solicitors? I wondered what secrets they would reveal to me, that I did not already know. Then it dawned on me that I had a considerable amount of wealth – without impediments, and most importantly, Jack could do nothing about it!

It was five thirty-five when I reached the pier. It was a balmy evening with a gentle breeze and the whole place was festive. There was an air of *joie de vivre* which distinctly eluded me. I was getting a bit anxious about whether or not Harriett would turn up. At five forty-five I spied her getting out of a taxi. She looked stunning, much as I had expected. She wore a short purple dress which accentuated her voluptuous figure. We walked towards each other and I heaved an eternal sigh of relief, when I saw her broad smile, revealing a perfect set of teeth. I went forwards for a tentative hug, but was rewarded by a lingering kiss on my mouth!

"Why, Quentin, you look positively dishy. Where's the slob I last knew?" she said with a combination of mischief and humour.

"I got rid of that guy some time ago, Harriett. This is the new me, one that you may not be able to retrieve. Oh, by the way, you look absolutely ravishing. I might even try to seduce you tonight."

Harriett's eyes widened. "Quentin, what have you been up to? You sound different, too. But first, we have things to sort out."

"Why don't we board the ship, get ourselves a drink and then talk things over? Here, take this ticket and get on board, I'm just nipping to the kiosk to get myself a nice Cuban to celebrate." I did not want us to be seen boarding together.

The schooner was magnificent. I found Harriett ensconced in the luxurious lounge on the upper deck. We each were handed the customary glass of bubbly and we clinked glasses. We found ourselves facing each other, next to the window, overlooking the bay. It would have been magical, if Claire had been sat there in place of Harriett. Harriett pulled out her mobile phone, took a quick look and her face clouded over for a moment. Presumably no messages.

"Oh, by the way, Harriett, I forgot to tell you, I got a message from your boyfriend Monty, known to me as Kevin." Harriett looked at me with an expression that combined surprise with hope.

"Why the fuck didn't he contact me?"

"Relax, my guess was right, in that they did get rat-arsed last night and believe it or not Monty dropped his phone somewhere along the beach where they were splashing around late at night. Today, with some effort, he managed to get hold of the taxi driver whom I had arranged to pick them up. He discovered that the driver did indeed have my number and contacted me that way. I told him that you were getting a bit anxious about him and he just laughed in his usual way and told me to let you know they are all fine."

"Thank God, he's okay. What a fucking wally. So why isn't he back here yet?"

I shrugged. "He told me had come across a villa that he fancied and decided to buy it outright, to celebrate the acquisition of his ill-gotten wealth."

"You must be really pissed off by all this."

"The simple fact is, I really had no expectation of getting any of the estate, so I sure as hell am not going to miss it. And in any case, I'm more than happy to hand it all over on a platter, if only I would be allowed to live my life."

The vessel moved off gracefully and soon we were out on the bay, enjoying the Singapore shoreline by dusk. We were already on our second drinks and I was just beginning to feel a little heady. Knowing Harriett, I knew she would be stone-cold sober for at least the first four drinks.

"Right, you need to tell me where you've got my stuff."

"Harriett, I'm afraid you're in for a shock. You see, I had set up an ambush for your boyfriend and his mates. I confess, I was totally gob-smacked when I discovered that the real villain was not Harry, not even my cousin Jack, but my old friend Kevin, your Monty. Anyway, using a contact, I arranged with the local police in Batam to bug the room in which I was going to meet your man. I let Monty talk and implicate himself in his own shenanigans. It came as quite a surprise that I had inherited half the estate. Finally, when it came to me signing everything over, and Monty had pulled out his gun to persuade me, I pressed the buzzer and within seconds the police burst in. Monty was stupid enough to shoot one of the police dead, and I'm afraid he and his mates are currently the guests of the Indonesian Government. I'm told they can expect capital punishment, or a minimum of fifty years if they are lucky. Accomplices, like you, would not be dealt with kindly."

Harriett's expression slowly metamorphosed into one of fear, soon replaced by sheer despondency.

"So you see, Harriett, the game's over. I'm booked on the flight to London tomorrow and the moment I land there, I'll be effectively the official heir to the estate, given that Jack is not quite functional. In the meantime, I have enough to inform the British police of the truth about the murders of my grandmother and Jimmy Clayton, should I choose to. Again, you will be implicated pretty seriously." For a moment there was a flicker of defeat in her eyes; to be replaced within a moment by the usual defiance. She looked away and I could not read her eyes, all I could see was the clenched jaw, the downward droop of the corner of her mouth and the narrowed eyes. At that moment I would gladly have swapped a king cobra for Harriett.

"I never thought I would have to say this, Quentin, but I think you have won this battle. I can't believe Monty screwed up the way he did. He obviously mistook you for a dummy, and paid the price. To be honest, you really have become another person altogether – smart, fit and cool."

A slow elation was rising within me. "Let me get another drink to celebrate. Now that we've had a couple of glasses of bubbly, I reckon it's time to move on. Cab Sauv still your favourite?"

Harriett looked up at me expressionlessly and nodded. I made my way to the bar and got two large glasses of Australian Cabernet Sauvignon and came back to find Harriett lost in thought. I raised my glass in toast, but she grimaced and turned away. I almost felt sorry for her.

"Harriett, I've decided to return your little stash to you entirely. By my reckoning it might have amounted to some thirty or forty thousand, but that is small beer for me now."

"Fuck you, Quentin."

"Suit yourself. If you behave yourself, I might be moved to making a little settlement, which will keep you going for a few years."

Her eyes were on fire and for a moment I thought she was going to throw the wine in my face, but she controlled herself. "Think about it, while I pay a visit to the loo. You won't run away, will you?"

Harriett's expression suddenly softened and there was something unreadable in her eyes.

Just as I entered the toilet, something stopped me. Her expression. What did it mean? I had a sudden premonition of disaster and I turned back to the deck. I crossed over to the door on the other side, made my way in and carefully looked around the corner of the bar, and my blood froze. Harriett was in the act of emptying the contents of a phial into my glass of wine and in a flash the phial was back in her dainty little purse. I was shocked, but in retrospect I realised that nothing was beyond Harriett. I then went to the loo and took a leak as intended and sauntered back to my seat.

Harriett held up her glass, saying, "Sorry, I was

not in a mood to celebrate a few minutes ago. Now I see there is no point in crying over spilt milk. So, here goes." Winning smile! I picked up my glass and held it to my nose, pretending to savour the bouquet. "Hmm, this does smell just right."

I gently put my glass down. Harriett raised her right eyebrow in her typical 'what's up?' manner and I responded, "I'm feeling just a wee bit tiddly. As you know I could never hold my drink."

"No hurry, we have all night to celebrate."

"Maybe a little movement will help. How about it?" I said, inclining my head towards the dance floor. Four couples were on the floor, swaying to the music. Harriett looked reluctant but acquiesced.

We swayed on the floor and I was struck by how voluptuous Harriett really was. I thought to myself, what a waste of a human being she had turned out to be. She was applying herself to me physically in an overtly intimate and seductive manner, all the while trying to poison me! Was it something that would merely knock me out, or was she going all the way? I had no way of knowing, but it would not surprise me if murder indeed was her game.

After a few minutes Harriett whispered, "Oh Quentin, your body is to kill for! I think tonight is going to be one long night of seduction. Monty will never know, will he?" Her eyes were full of mischief and promise. We got back to our seats.

"In the last couple of weeks, I have been learning palmistry, Harriett."

"That's a load of mumbo jumbo, Quentin. Surely you don't believe in that crap?"

"You'd be surprised. For example, looking at your hands I could predict your lifespan, the number of marriages you will have, the number of children you will have, whether you will live in prosperity or poverty, and a few other things besides." I had little doubt that she would rise to the bait, and sure enough she did.

"Yeah, right… Let's see what you have to say about my hands."

Her glass was placed a mere six inches from mine and she placed both her hands on the table, palms upwards. I pretended to scrutinise her hands carefully. After about ten seconds I said, "Well, you'll be pleased to know that you are blessed with a long life, between eighty and ninety by my reckoning, looking at the length of this line that goes from the outer border of your left hand down to your wrist." Harriett peered curiously at the so-called life line that I was pointing to and looked up at me dubiously.

"Next, now let's look at your love life…"

I picked up my glass, looked up behind her and said, "Jesus, look who's here." Harriett jerked around, looking in the direction of where I was pointing with my left hand, and that was enough for me to swap the glasses. As she turned back, I grabbed my (her) glass, stood up and took a quick sip.

Harriett observed my action with relief and said, "Who the fuck's that, Quentin?"

"Give me a second," I said, and walked across to the table in the corner where two couples were sitting. I purposefully strolled towards them, bent down to the man nearest me, saying, "Oh heck, I'm really sorry, I thought you were someone else." They all looked astonished, and looked at me as if I was unhinged, which I suppose I was, at the time. I walked back to Harriett with a sheepish look.

"Wrong number. I could have sworn that was my friend Mitch from New York."

Harriett looked at me with a mixture of amusement and annoyance and said, "Sit down now and relax. Enough of this palmistry nonsense. How's the wine, anyway?"

In reply I took another sip and gave her the thumbs up. "Go easy on that. I don't want you collapsing on me."

Harriett took a gulp from her glass, the one meant for me. I felt a sudden tremor inside, and realised this could be cold-blooded murder. In a flash I knew I couldn't go through with it. She was just about to take a second sip, and I relented.

"Harriett, don't!"

"What the fuck do you mean?"

"That is the glass you spiked for me."

I've never seen such an expression of shock and terror on her face before.

"Jesus, I need to…"

She jumped up and scrambled, presumably to the loo. I knocked her glass over, so that it posed no danger to anyone. Several startled faces were looking in our direction.

"The lady is feeling sick. Probably had too much," I said with a light laugh, got up and followed in her steps. I accosted one of the stewardesses, and said, "The lady may need some help, would you mind just checking in the bathroom?"

I went and stationed myself outside the ladies' toilet, frantically hoping that the spike, whatever it was, would not prove lethal. I could hear the sounds of severe retching inside and hoped that the toxin would be egested completely. I heaved a sigh of relief when Harriett came out five minutes later, looking dishevelled, red-eyed and miserable. I took her by the arm and steered her to the open deck.

"So, what exactly were you trying to poison me with?"

"I don't know, Quentin. Monty gave it to me and told me I had to use it on you at any opportunity. He said it wouldn't be necessary, but only a back-up or fail-safe."

"You were trying to kill me in cold blood."

"No, I swear, I didn't know what it was. I was hoping it would just knock you out, long enough for me to get Monty to take charge of you."

"But you don't even know where Monty is!"

"I know, that was so confusing, I didn't know what else to do."

"You realise I could have let you drink the whole glass, and walked away without turning a hair?"

Harriett looked away and let out a sob.

"Why didn't you, Quentin? Anyone else would have done. After all, it was retribution."

"Perhaps that was my weakness. Heaven knows I was tempted to be permanently rid of you."

"My whole life is fucked beyond all recall. I don't know what to do." Harriett was truly and utterly in despair. This was no act. "I'm completely at your mercy, Quentin, I'll do whatever you want of me. Throw me overboard if you like."

"This is what we are going to do, Harriett, and if you comply, I'll let you go and we never see each other again. Firstly, please understand that the evidence of your involvement with Monty is overwhelming, making you an accomplice to multiple murder. It'll take very little inducement for me to shop you. Secondly, know that I hold all the cards, and I know that I have inherited the whole estate effectively, given Jack's state. I have enough firepower to fry you alive. Thirdly, realise that I actually will not hesitate to take you out, if you give me due cause. As you have noted, I'm not the same grovelling wimp you terrorised.

"Take the SIM out of your phone, and do not reinsert, unless it's an emergency, and I'm the only person you call. So, no phone until you get back to England. You'll be on the next available flight to Lisbon, which I will book for you, as soon as we dock. You are going to write out the statement I dictate, and sign it, as your confession. You have no choice but to trust that I won't hand it in. That will be my insurance against any future malfeasance. You will return to England after one week, and get back to our little abode in Portchester, where you will have received divorce papers, which you will sign unconditionally. I will, actually, grant you the full ownership of the house. That little strong-box of yours is sitting in the loft, near the water tank. It's all yours. I'll also transfer a grand into your account, for immediate expenses. Get yourself a new mobile, and text me the number. Then destroy the old SIM. You have to be available at all times. You will not make contact with Jack, or any of Monty's gang, under any circumstances. You will leave the house as soon as you have returned the papers to me, and find yourself a B&B on the south coast of the Isle of Wight. You then put your house on the market at seventy-five per cent of the market value, and stay put until it sells. Once all that is done, you leave the country and disappear. I suggest Portugal, to some little village out in the sticks. I will, however, have a private eye keep tabs on you, pretty much forever, so don't ever be tempted to get smart. Is all that clear?"

"Quentin, you are a truly good man, and I just can't..."

Harriett broke down. Her gratitude was quite pathetic.

12

TRIUMPHAL RETURN

Love of a mate may be extreme
Love of offspring may reign supreme
Love of siblings may be the best relationship
Only a fool forgets the treasure of friendship

Fortunately, a seat was available on the British Airways flight to London and I flew back home the next day. The journey was entirely unremarkable, not least because I remember nothing of it. All I remember, is thinking of Claire, reliving every moment we had spent together, how it could have been if only...

I walked out into a typically cold and wet November afternoon in London. I checked into one of those nondescript hotels near Heathrow Airport, with no clue as to what I was going to do for the rest of my life. Except think about Claire.

The next day I rang the family solicitors and made an appointment to see Mr Barclay, who turned out to be a convivial and cheerful soul. I deliberately avoided Leadbetter, who sounded like a pernickety character. "Welcome back, Mr Grayling. I trust you had a successful trip. When did you return?"

"Only yesterday."

"It was a terrible shock to hear about your dear cousin-brother Jack, so untimely and tragic. Is there any chance of recovery in the long term?"

I looked at him blankly.

"Oh, my goodness, you didn't know. Poor Mr Hillier had a dreadful accident, which has left him paralysed. He has been placed in a nursing home, obviously the best one available, given his financial status. I'll give you the details, as I'm sure you'd want to visit him."

"Oh my god! That's shocking. What kind of accident was he involved in?"

"Errr, I believe he fell down a flight of stairs."

"Oh dear, it wasn't alcohol-related was it? Jack did have a lamentable weakness for it."

"Errr, I couldn't really say, but I did hear something of the sort from his partner Mr McArdle, who also held his power of attorney. Do you know him?"

"I'm afraid I've had no contact with Jack for a long time, and I certainly don't know any of his associates."

"Mr Grayling, we need to settle certain matters, now that you are back in the country. We got a letter from Lady Grayling last December, instructing us to alter her will, so as to make yourself a joint heir, along with Mr Jack Hillier, who was originally supposed to be the sole heir. When Mr Leadbetter met Mr Hillier after your grandmother's death, he indicated that the two of you would comply with the terms without dispute. I presume you had agreed everything between yourselves?"

"Yes, we had indeed. Jack said that he would have it formalised, when I last spoke to him before I went on my journey."

"Given the subsequent events, I think it would be appropriate for you to take over the management of the estate, and obviously, we will ensure that Mr Hillier's interests are well protected, in terms of ensuring that he does have access to the best care, within the envelope of his share of the inheritance."

I tried to look sombre, and nodded gravely.

"Mr Barclay, may I suggest that the property *Gorm-Faire* remains in joint names, although I will be residing in it. The liquid wealth can be simply divided in two, and your firm can take charge of my cousin's half and administer it, without any hindrance from me. Does that meet with your approval?"

"That is more than fair. All the funds, bonds, stocks and shares have been sold and the proceeds, along with the residual cash, are in a holding account."

"Which amounts to…?"

"After paying out the inheritance tax, and our fees, forty-two million pounds and some change. So, as of tomorrow you will have full access to your own account, to the tune of approximately twenty-one million pounds. I understand you are married, Mr Grayling?"

"Technically, yes. Our marriage disintegrated, I'm afraid. In fact, I was coming to it next. Would you be able to draw up divorce papers and see it through?"

"No problem, we work closely with a partner firm that specialises in divorce. Will there be any likelihood of a contest, involving the inheritance?"

"No, our separation pre-dates my inheritance, and my spouse has accepted a settlement of all our current estate, with no further demands. It's all amicable."

"You are lucky indeed, that you have such a mature and understanding person to divorce!"

"One last thing, Mr Barclay. In the event of my cousin's demise, I wish to have no profit from his remnant share of the estate. I would like to donate it to five chosen charities, which I will nominate."

"Hats off to you, sir, for your generosity."

"Now, before I forget, I believe Lady Winifred had left some letters for me?"

Barclay disappeared for a few minutes and returned with a thick envelope, which he handed to me.

"Thank you, Mr Barclay. I shall now head off to the manor and see if the old place is in shape."

Before we parted company, he gave me the contact details of the nursing home, as well as the caretakers of the manor.

I knew what I had to do the next day, which was to contact the caretakers of the manor, Albert and Daisy. They were more than a little surprised to hear from me, when for the last year they had only dealt with Jack, though I believe they had only met him physically a couple of times. I instructed them to get the manor shipshape and direct all the bills to me. Fortunately, Daisy was computer literate and promised to communicate by email. I told them that I would drop in in about a couple of weeks. They said that the garden had all but disappeared into an overgrowth of grass and weed, but the woods were very much as they were. Again, I gave them leave to contact any local company and get them to spruce up the considerable exterior. They sounded sceptical about the potential costs, and hinted that they were not terribly well paid.

"I might as well ask you, Albert, how much are you getting paid?"

"Mr Grayling, I don't want to complain, but things are getting a little tight. Of course, we have a roof above our heads and that is worth a lot of mental peace. We also have the free use of the facilities, gas and electricity. Nevertheless, in terms of cash, we are getting £800 a month, which is not a huge amount. Of course, we are in our sixties and don't have any children, so there are no major expenses to speak of, excepting for our food and drink. All the same it would be nice to be able to save a little bit for a rainy day."

I was shocked and mortified that Jack was paying them a shoestring wage. Not that it came as much of a surprise.

"Listen, Albert, I am increasing your salary to £3,000 a month as of now. I sincerely apologise that you have been underpaid for so long, but as you will realise, I was not in charge then."

There was a gasp from the other side as Albert registered the import of my words. He was having difficulty with his words.

"Mr Grayling, Mr Grayling, sir, I... I... I do not know what to... to say!"

"Say nothing, Albert. And I want you to go out and rent yourself a nice little cottage nearby, where you can enjoy your days off. And don't stint, that rent will be in addition to your salary."

I then rang one of the local estate agents in Portchester and instructed them to put the house up for sale. I transferred £1,000 into Harriett's account. And then, the distasteful job of making contact with Jack. The nursing home was situated in Somerset, in the middle of nowhere, about a hundred miles away. The matron informed me that Mr Hillier was bed-bound and unable to comprehend, or hold a conversation. I felt a real sadness that this was Jack's fate, despite all his malevolence. And then I thought of Jimmy, and my feelings hardened. I decided there was no point in making a token visit.

Finally, I decided to carry out the most vital task, which I anticipated with a combination of real excitement and a little trepidation.

"Hello, Harry, this is the prodigal son, returning home."

Recognition was instantaneous.

"Bloody hell, it's my soul-mate Quincy! Have you developed brain-fever or something, that you're calling up old losers like me? But, what a lovely surprise!"

"I can't tell you just how sorry I am, Harry, for being such a prick, and neglecting you."

"What on earth have you been up to?"

"Well, Harry, I'm alive and kicking, but have been through an incredible roller-coaster in the last month. Suffice it to say, I'm out of the woods, and wanted to touch base with you."

"Quincy, you *are* a prick! Anyway, I'm so delighted to hear that all's well. So, can we look forward to seeing you anytime soon?"

"Yes, Harry, soon. I only rang to check that you were in town tomorrow. There is an important item that I have arranged to be delivered to your place tomorrow and wanted to make sure somebody would be there to receive it."

"Oh yes, don't worry, Quincy, I'm very much here. So, what is this interesting item that you have ordered? Something to bribe me with?"

"Ah, it's a little surprise, if you must know. I need your full address."

It was in Sunderland.

"Will you be home between eight and twelve tomorrow morning?"

"Yes, I will. And when do you intend to come and see us?"

"Patience, dear boy, patience. All will be revealed, but now I must dash. Bye for now."

"Bye, Quincy, and you take care."

Next, I booked myself into a hotel in Roker in Sunderland, not far from where Harry lived. And then I did something which I never thought possible. I took a cab to the nearest Jaguar Land-Rover dealer in West London and drove away with their latest XJ! OK, extravagant and unnecessary, I agree, but so what? I felt I deserved it. I then drove to an art gallery and bought a Soozy Lipsey painting for an impressive sum of money.

It was five o'clock when I checked out of the hotel. It did not bother me in the least that it was a long way to Sunderland, and I was still in a state of slight detachment from reality. The prospect of a long drive in my new Jag was thrilling. I still had very few clothes, or indeed very few of anything. I stopped on the way to get a bite in one of the motorway services. I got to the hotel in Roker, on the seafront, around nine thirty and walked directly over to the nearest pub, which was fairly busy, and ordered myself a pint of the local beer (produced by Vaux, a brewery almost 200 years old) followed by fish and chips. I got back to the hotel, checked in, and went to bed with a feeling of real eager anticipation. I could not banish Claire from my thoughts, but managed to keep pushing her out every time she crept in. I knew there would come a time when I would have to sort things out in my mind. But not today. The letters? I just could not generate the energy for that. I think, deep inside, it was trepidation. I slept like a baby.

☦

FRIENDSHIP RULES

It was a ten-minute walk from the hotel to Harry's place. I was up at seven, excited at the prospects of reuniting with Harry, but had to hold myself in check and not reach him too early on a Saturday. So, I ran, for an hour, along the seafront, and came back drenched in sweat. A quick shower followed by breakfast meant I was in good time to get going. I reached Harry's at nine thirty, and rang the bell, slightly breathless. I was holding the painting up high so that only my eyes were visible. The door opened, and Harry's strong, handsome face emerged.

I lowered the painting, and you should have seen Harry's face and expression! The widest possible grin cracked his face and he literally shouted, "Oh my god, Quincy, you sneaky bastard!"

I placed the painting down and we grabbed each other in a bear hug. "I'm sorry I've been such an arsehole, Harry."

"You have indeed. Hey, what the hell, the prodigal has returned, and that's all that matters."

"You, mate, are a gem, and I don't deserve you."

"Right again!"

I punched him playfully and hugged him again, mainly to conceal the tears which were threatening to reveal themselves.

Once in, Harry said, "What a wonderful surprise this will be for Jen, and the kids too. We are going to have one helluva celebration this weekend." He led me through the L-shaped lounge, into the kitchen, which led on to a utility room, which then opened on to a large, beautifully manicured rear garden. There was a little girl chasing an older boy, while a young woman, presumably Harry's wife, was inspecting a flower bed. Harry opened the door partially, and called out.

"Jenny, my sweet, just pop in, will you? I need to show you this crummy parcel that's just arrived. I can't believe Quincy would send us such crap!"

Jenny, walked towards the door, unable to see me behind it. "Jenny, I'd like you to meet the second most stupid man in the world, my dear friend Quincy, sadly christened Quentin, of whom you have heard so much!"

Jenny's eyes widened, and ignoring my outstretched hand, she stepped over and gave me a tight hug.

"I've so heard so much about you, Quentin. Only last night Harry was regaling me with all your school-time adventures. I so wished you had kept in touch."

"Jenny, I'm over the moon to have met you finally. As I have already said to Harry here, there really are no words to excuse my lapses, except to confess that I am by far the world's biggest moron, and don't really deserve the kind of reception I'm getting."

Jenny then summoned the two children, who came running in. When introduced, little Quincy stepped forwards and shook my hand, saying, "Were you named after me?" which drew a laugh from all of us. When her turn came Juliet promptly turned away and buried her face into her mother's skirt.

Now would be a good time to describe them as they were. Harry was my age, two inches shorter, with a handsome, elfin-like face, which had changed very little since I last saw him at my wedding. His eternally smiling face had added a few lines and crinkles, which looked most agreeable. He looked a picture of health and happiness. Jenny looked around five foot six, muscular, though slender. She had arresting cornflower-blue eyes and light brown hair. I can only describe her face as soft and gentle, with a small nose and pouting lips. Quincy was a strapping young lad, who must have been eight at that time, with a strong resemblance to Harry, although he had Jenny's nose. Juliet, who was all of four years old, was the prettiest little girl I had ever seen. She was a miniature version of Jenny and I felt an overwhelming urge to pick her up and squish her. It wasn't until the next day that she would allow me to do that.

That was a weekend of complete celebration. The wonderful family suspended all their other planned activities in my honour. Harry had decided that I was staying over with them, and ordered me to check out ASAP. What can I say? I offered to take them out for lunch, but Jenny declined, saying I would have to have my first meal at home with them. Harry was dying to find out the details of my post-marital life, but barely had a chance, because of my attention being competed for by the kids, as well as Jenny. By the time it was one o'clock I was totally and head over heels in love with this family. Claire did not even enter my thoughts!

Jenny had rustled up a delicious lunch, comprising of a smoked salmon starter, followed by a spicy pasta and an amazing salad. Finally, around four o'clock, after a hot cup of tea, I suggested that we all go out and get a bit of exercise to burn off the calories. The suggestion was received enthusiastically and we left. Just before we did, Harry ripped off the wrapping and revealed the painting. I was relieved that both of them immediately loved it.

As we left, I said, "My hotel's along the seafront just about fifteen minutes away. Let's walk down there, then I can nip in, collect my stuff and check out. If you're all feeling up to it, I could take you for a drive."

It was a pleasant day, sunny, but cool and a little fresh. That of course did not bother any of us, as we were all in high spirits. We sauntered down, reaching my hotel in due course. The kids wanted to get by the seaside, so I left Harry and Jenny with them. I quickly collected my things from the room and checked out, came to the car, opened the boot and deposited my belongings. I then walked across the road and yelled to Harry, who then rounded up his children and the lot of them came back to where I was standing. I took them across the road, back to my car and as we neared it, Quincy let out a whoop.

"Oh my god, it's a new Jaguar!" Juliet repeated his words verbatim, skipping after him. Harry got in beside me and the rest at the back.

"Quentin, this is a treat indeed. I never thought I would ever sit in a car like this in my life," said Jenny.

"Nor did I, Jenny, until yesterday. When I realised that this new windfall has left me rather better off than I had ever dreamed, I made a snap decision to go for it."

Taking Jenny's advice, I drove north along the coast, going through fairly built-up areas. Finally, we reached Whitley Bay, which had an attractive sandy beach, where we stopped. The kids were enjoying themselves running in and out of the water, while the three of us engaged in conversation.

"So, are you going to tell us about your misadventures in life, Quincy?"

"Quite boring, really. My marriage turned out to be a disaster, and Harriett took off with another man recently. I was made redundant just a few weeks ago and was at absolute rock bottom, with no money and nowhere to go. So, I flew away into the sunset, and then various things happened, which will take ages to relate. Then I inherit this fortune, which I have done nothing to deserve."

"Quincy, you really have been an idiot. An unhappy marriage, then unemployed and broke. All this time you could not be bothered to pick up the phone and contact the person who you used to claim as your best friend."

"It is no justification or excuse, but I do have an explanation. You see there was this sense of profound shame and reluctance to expose my so-called weaknesses. I was just being an ordinary dumb human being, trying to put on a brave front, trying to hide any sign of vulnerability. What's much worse is my attitude, which lost me so many years of valuable interaction with you and your wonderful family. But not any more."

"Yup, you have at last made amends, but you have to admit you really have behaved like a gigantic arsehole!"

Quincy chortled, but Jenny was outraged. "Harry!!"

"Oh, sorry, love, that just came out spontaneously, and is nothing more than a reflection of my deep affection for Quincy here."

"That's right, Jenny, this guy of yours can say or do absolutely anything to me and get away with it." I gave Harry's shoulders a squeeze. "Well, there you are, Harry, pretty much up to date. There are some more details, but they can wait."

We left at seven and a few minutes later I parked next to a fish restaurant and treated the family to dinner. Jenny chose a bottle of Gavi, which she shared with Harry. I thought I could restrict myself to one beer, being the driver, but Jenny thought otherwise, and so I had none. Harry just rolled his eyes and laughed. After we got home and the kids had been put to bed, Jenny came down to join us. Harry brought out a bottle of an eighteen-year-old Glenfiddich, and we sat and chatted late into the night. I told them that I had taken a round-the-world trip, giving them brief details about the places I had visited, without going into the specifics. When asked about any romantic developments in my life, I mentioned that I had met a girl during my trip, which looked promising, but had in the end fizzled out. It was past two o'clock in the morning when we went to bed.

The Sunday was a lazy affair. After breakfast I asked Harry if he was still working for the DVLA, to which he replied, "Good God, no, mate. Five years ago, I started up on my own and now run a successful online recruitment firm. The major advantage, of course, is that I mostly work from home. Jenny is a lecturer at the university and is very happy with her lot."

"Hey, Harry, does that mean you could take a few days off and accompany me on a road trip up north?"

"I don't see why not, as long as I have Internet access and can have a couple of hours working on my laptop."

So that was settled. Jenny seemed very happy with the suggestion, saying, "I think that's a great idea, as

Harry has not had a break for a few months now. Also, that means he'll be out of my hair for a bit!"

The children, however, were not so pleased at the thought that their father was going away on holiday, when they still had to go to school.

Harry soon appeased them, saying, "I know you'll miss me terribly, kids, but think of all the lovely presents you are going to get from Uncle Quincy here!"

To which Quincy retorted, "It's Uncle Quincy we'll miss, Dad, not you!"

The rest of the day was spent in rest and relaxation, with plenty of chatter, banter and general enjoyment. I insisted on taking them out for dinner again, to what my gracious hosts considered to be the best Indian restaurant in town. As it wasn't within walking distance, we took a taxi. The food was certainly excellent, suitably enhanced by two bottles of Chilean Merlot. The kids were in high spirits, never having had a dinner treat two nights running.

"You are spoiling them rotten, Quincy. I don't know that we will be able to cope with them once you leave."

"Not a problem, Harry, I'm more than happy to adopt them, if Jenny would allow it."

Jenny maintained a diplomatic silence, while Quincy interjected. "Yay! Does that mean we can ride in the Jag every day?"

When we reached home, the realisation that it was Sunday night put a damper on the children's spirits.

By this time, I had struck up a deep bond with both of them, who sat on either side of me, as we were having our coffees. When it was time for bed Quincy gave me a hug and Juliet clasped her little arms around my neck and kissed me on both cheeks. I felt a peculiar sensation, which was deep and visceral, something I had never known before, something very different from what I had felt with Claire, but just as powerful. The next morning Harry and I drove north.

SECRETS BETWEEN FRIENDS

I had said nothing to Harry about where exactly we were going, except for a vague 'take it as it comes'. I had given him an approximate duration of one week, give or take. I made my first halt at Bamburgh, a gorgeous little place with a spectacular beach. We spent that day and the next there. Harry put up a fight about sharing the expenses, but I emphatically overruled him, saying that this whole adventure was my treat to him, as an apology for the years of neglect. On the second day I invited Harry to join me for a long run and even though he was pretty fit, he was no match for me. After about half an hour, he stopped and turned back. I ran on for a full hour each way and returned to the hotel with a sense of achievement. It was only during my return run that Claire re-entered my thoughts. Almost on cue, I got a call from an unknown number, which turned out to be Harriett, in London, using her new phone. It was a short and terse conversation, which reassured me that everything was in motion as I had intended.

The next day I drove north, past Edinburgh, across the Firth of Forth and then north-east, to St Andrews. Harry was positively delirious at the thought of visiting the home of golf, which, apparently, he had wanted to do all his life. He had in fact taken up golf some ten years ago and had achieved a very respectable handicap of twelve. I had played golf very occasionally and was looking forward to the possibility of having a round on the hallowed course. Harry disabused me of that option, saying that a minimum handicap of twenty-four was required. When I queried this with the bartender at the pub we stopped at, he just laughed and said he would book us in, giving me a handicap of twenty-four. It was early afternoon by the time we booked into our luxury hotel overlooking the course. Harry kept pinching himself to ensure it was all real. We went for a long walk and on our return, I hit the gym for about forty-five minutes. A gourmet dinner followed and we went to bed, two very happy chappies.

The next morning, we got off to an early start, teeing off at 7 a.m. Because of my ability at games in school, I suppose, I turned out reasonably good at golf, despite not having played for years. Harry, of course, beat the spots off me, but nevertheless was impressed that I could play to a reasonable standard. After lunch we took a short kip and went out for another long walk, followed by another excellent dinner. I sneaked away for a few minutes and called Albert, warning him that we would be arriving the next day. The poor man was beginning to get flustered about their state of unpreparedness, but I calmed him down, reassuring him that we had no great expectations. I told him to have two bedrooms cleaned up and ready for us. If they could cook for us, that would be very welcome, but equally if that was a problem we would happily eat out. He was most indignant at that suggestion and absolutely insisted that we would have to have breakfast and dinner at home.

The next day we set off and by this time Harry had given up being curious about our destination. He was having such a good time that he had decided that a surprise would be better than knowing the destination. At one point he said, "Ah, we are going to Inverness, are we?" looking at the road signs. I refused to confirm this and a while later turned east, which would have negated his guess. It was early evening finally when we arrived at *Gorm-Faire*.

"Welcome to my estate!"

"Bloody hell," said Harry, looking around in awe as I drove down the drive.

Albert and Daisy were ready and waiting and nervous as hell. I think I managed to calm them down and convince them that I wasn't the terrifying 'lord of the manor' that they had experienced in Jack. Harry and I parted company into our respective rooms and had a couple of hours to ourselves. Harry was going to log into his computer and get on with some work. I was going to put my feet up, open the wide bay windows and contemplate my world. Conflicting emotions were hurtling around in my head, mostly nostalgia and tenderness relating to Aunt Charlotte, and Jimmy. Vivid and painful memories were flooding in. Are there still such people, with hearts of gold, in this world? There must be precious few, and I had lost two of the best; cheated of their presence. And then I thought, I still have Harry and his lovely family. And then Claire...

For dinner we were served the perfect haggis. Albert led me to the place I knew existed, but had never been into before, the cellar. I picked up a Bordeaux 1999, which did not disappoint. It was during coffee that I said, "Harry, there are things I have not told you. Awful things about myself, but I feel you are the one person from whom I should hide nothing."

"I knew there were bits that didn't quite hang together. However, it was not my place to question. On the other hand, if you do wish to confide, you will know that you have no truer friend. All the same, it's a risk you have to call."

I pondered over the potential risk and then said, "Yes, it's actually quite a risk. But I'm prepared to take it because there is one thing I have learned in the last few months and that is when something has to be achieved, and I mean absolutely has to be achieved, whatever the cost, then one has to go for it. But not tonight, mate, let us just enjoy the evening and get to bed. Tomorrow I will take you on a full conducted tour of the estate and at some point, spill the beans."

After breakfast we set out, and I walked Harry through most of the grounds, which covered approximately twenty-two acres. The wooded area was a lot thicker than what I remembered, quite wild and unkempt. Harry absolutely loved it. And then we walked along the edge of the cliff, looking down at the waves crashing on the rocks. I could almost imagine my grandmother's limp body lying broken on top of the rocks, washed by the foaming waves.

"My grandmother's body was found somewhere down there. Suicide, they said."

"The poor old lady must've been ever so lonely stuck in this wild place with no company. From what I remember you saying all those years ago, she was clearly not close to you."

I nodded, saying nothing.

We drove down to the nearest village to get a bite of lunch, after which I drove north along the coast for a bit and we returned to *Gorm-Faire* around four o'clock.

"*Gorm-Faire*; what on earth does it even mean, Quincy?"

"Blue horizon in Scottish Gaelic."

"Very appropriate indeed, except, more realistically it should've been called grey horizon."

"Quite right. A case of hope prevailing over reality."

After parking the car, I took him on a track that led to Jimmy's cottage. "You remember I used to speak about Jimmy? After my grandmother died, he hanged himself. I keep blaming myself for not having done something to pre-empt it or to prevent it. I'm going to see his old place, where I spent many happy hours when I was a kid."

The cottage was dilapidated and falling apart. I felt an intense sadness welling up and was controlling myself with some difficulty. Harry said absolutely nothing, but just put his arm around my shoulder and gave it a squeeze and that was enough. On the way back, I said to Harry, "Let's pour ourselves a drink and then I will get started." I decided that it would be better done after dark and out in the open. I told Albert to put on an early dinner and by seven-thirty we were done. I told the couple to finish their dinner and retire early to their quarters, saying that Harry and I would be going out for a walk.

By the time we left it was dark and chilly, but fortunately there was no wind. Without any further ado I started by giving him the full version of the truth.

"You see, Harry, I was stupidly infatuated with Harriett, who completely turned my head. She pretty much took control of my life and insisted that I had to ditch my earlier friends. To my eternal shame, I had already ditched you, when I thought I was riding high in that poxy little pharmaceutical job. So much for my character. Harriett was bad news in every possible way. I realised too late that there was no salvation for me, and the marriage had fallen apart, except I could not get rid of her. Unbeknown to me, she had started this affair with a mystery man, whose identity I will come to presently. Anyway, it all came to a crunch one day a few weeks ago, when I lost my job. Harriett completely lost it and threw me out of her life and our home. Something snapped inside my head, Harry, and I mean a major brain-crash, which at a stroke decimated a chunk of who I was, and liberated an altogether different side of me, which I never could have imagined, existed deep inside. With no prior thought or planning, I took off to New York. And that is how this story begins."

I went on to describe the first attempt on my life, followed by my experiences, all the way up to the time I left Singapore. Harry listened with rapt attention, with periodic intermittent exclamations. The explosion came, when I revealed the moment when Kevin walked into the stilt-house. Harry was incredulous, then furious. And then he went very silent, as I narrated the lethal interactions. "So, you see, Harry, I am not the benign, restrained and flaky lad you knew. I may have turned into a bit of a monster. I actively planned and killed Kevin, albeit in self-defence. And his assistant was collateral damage. Unplanned or otherwise, I almost disposed of Harriett. Last but not least, I colluded in the elimination of that American thug. There you have it. That's the new me."

The whole narration had taken just under two hours, during which time we had sauntered to the cliff edge and back, recharging our glasses a couple of times in between. In the dim light I could see Harry's face and I could discern a combination of dismay and shock. "That's a lot to take in. I wish you had never told me."

Nothing more was said as we went in and up to our respective bedrooms, which were side by side.

"Harry, whatever you decide to do with me, I will accept willingly. All I want to say is, thank God there are people like you still around."

I gave him a quick hug, which he did not quite reciprocate, and we parted.

13

PLUMBING THE ABYSS

How is it, when your brain tells you that you have everything in life and more, that you have eliminated all trials and tribulations, that your mind tells you otherwise, and casts you into a bottomless mine of despair?

Everything in my life had been resolved! I was the owner of an inheritance of some twenty-odd million pounds plus *Gorm-Faire*. I had no responsibilities or outgoings. There were no obligations. I had rediscovered my best friend in life. I was free to travel the world as I wished. As animals go, I had no known predators, and I was at the top of the food chain!

On the other hand, I had simply eliminated the love of my life. It hurt physically every time I thought of Claire. And I'd decided to make no contact with the wonderful Mitch and Matilda. Had they really been a part of my life at one time; when I needed them, and used them? And last but not least, I had lobbed an emotional bomb at Harry and Jenny, expecting them to pat me on my back and say 'there, there'.

Those were the rational thoughts ravaging my mind. Wait, was I sure I was back with Harry? He was so shocked by my acts, that he was pretty silent during our drive back. For the first time in my life I saw him gloomy and withdrawn. I stopped my car about fifty yards away from his place. When the parting came, he pre-empted me by saying, "Quincy, that was a lot to take in. I still wish you had said nothing to me about all this. Life would have been so much simpler."

My heart sank as I thought of the potential implications.

"Yes, Harry, you're right, but look at it from my standpoint. You are the only person in the world who has meant so much over the years. Confessing my crimes was an act of catharsis, an act of love, friendship and trust. I want you to judge me, and damn me if you must. Even if you report me to the law, I won't hold it against you, Harry. You are my judge and jury, and I'm ever so sorry to have landed this on you."

Harry looked pained. "Thanks for that, dear friend. I don't know that I can tell you at this moment what I'm going to do with this knowledge. I really will have to share this with Jenny, and I think I'm pretty sure what her response will be. Fuck it, Quincy, what have you landed all of us in? I'll be in touch. Or not, as the case maybe." With those final words Harry turned and walked away, towards his house.

I drove back north, arriving late. It was a stormy night and I had given my housekeepers the night off to go back to their little cottage. I knew I had to get down to the letters, but felt a distinct trepidation, adding to my general gloom. I got into bed and tried to sleep, but could not. After a couple of hours of tossing and turning I finally gave up and switched on my light. It was 2.42 a.m. I picked up the letters and got back into bed.

There were five of them, each one folded in three. I read them in order, from the top. My heart was racing and I took a few deep breaths, before taking the plunge.

⚚

THE CRY OF THE DYING UNICORN

4 October 1994

Quentin, my darling,

Quentin, my lovely boy, whom I have abandoned, rejected and neglected. How have I survived these years of separation, without losing my mind? I suppose I should be grateful

*for at least the times I have been able to spend
with you, albeit as your aunt, never able to give
you what was your due. I have no words to
apologise adequately and have no right to ask
for forgiveness. If there is a hell, believe me, I
have already experienced it in this very life. For
what I have deprived you of is so dreadful that I
will gladly accept consignment to a biblical hell.*

*Today, on your tenth birthday, I am sending
this letter to your grandmother for safekeeping,
to be given to you when you turn twenty-five. I
have no idea what is the right age at which to
deliver this bombshell, and can only hope that
by the time you read the contents of this letter,
you are mature enough to bear the impact of
the sad realities of life. If I am still alive, I will be
there for you, my head bowed in disgrace.*

*To begin with, you are very well aware of
my background, and the stern household in
which I grew up. You have had more than your
fair share of exposure to my formidable, bigoted
mother. Believe me, she was not much better
to me than she was to you. My father was my
refuge and my support, but like so many in his
position he was away a lot of the time, and of
course, died prematurely young. You will no
doubt be burning with curiosity about your
father, and I will come to that in a minute.*

*Throughout my childhood, apart from the
times when your grandfather came home, I lived*

a lonely life, even as you did. Jimmy Clayton was a godsend. He just materialised one day, and stayed ever since, eking out a living as our errand boy and later, the odd-job man. Despite my mother's strict proscription, I found every opportunity to slip away and play with him. Jimmy had a heart of gold and I believe would have given his life for me, if ever called on to do so. He had an extraordinary instinct and could look into the soul of any person he met. We were hugely devoted to each other, though I am ashamed to say that his devotion to me was probably far in excess of mine to him.

Enough of childhood moans. My real story begins when I went to Cambridge. I will not bore you with the details of my course, my surroundings or any other physical or material aspect of those three years. I met Charles Hillier in the first week of my stay there and we became instant friends. Charles was big, brash, and extroverted. Coming from my background and being introverted, I felt like a cosseted bird liberated into a minor gale. It was wonderful. I loved his company, but felt no stronger attraction than that, whereas he unfortunately developed a stronger attachment to me than I was aware of, or comfortable with. The third member of our trio was Drew Howell, a really sweet and gentle soul, who was very much the antithesis of Charles, but was totally under his spell.

Enter Avinash Krishnan. I met him at one of the regular Saturday-night parties in the social club, three months later. He stood in one corner, looking around uncertainly, with a pint of beer in his hand. He was beautiful. I suppose he was probably around six feet tall, and very slender, with a strong jaw and a pointed chin. His skin was the colour of café-au-lait, with a touch of copper. I walked up to him and introduced myself, and I still remember his exact words: "What a lovely apparition you make!" Big black eyes, wide mouth curling up at the corner and a set of beautiful white teeth. We became instant friends. Charles, who joined us later, entertained us both with his usual high spirts and low humour. From then on, we became a foursome.

I was very aware of my increasing affinity for Avinash, and was a bit worried about how Charles would react. To give Charles his due, he never ever displayed any jealousy or spite towards Avinash. There were occasions when his innate prejudice would break through. Like the time, when during a game of cricket on a wet outfield, Avi slipped and got a hefty dose of wet mud on his clothes. As they walked back at the end of the innings, where I was waiting for them, Avi gestured towards his clothes and said, "Do I look terrible?" Before I could respond, Charles interjected, "Oh I'm sure it's nothing that you are not used to, considering where you come from." I went for Charles with my metaphoric claws, but Avi, in his usual anodyne fashion, intervened and defused the situation.

Avinash was beautiful, not just in appearance, but within. He was full of grace, wisdom and compassion, all traits that were deficient in Charles, as I discovered over the years. In addition to all of that, Avi had a razor-sharp brain, which had facilitated his meteoric rise through school in rural south India to a scholarship to Cambridge. By the end of the first year, I was head over heels in love with him and to my eternal surprise, he reciprocated wholeheartedly. Unlike these days, Quentin, in our time, love, whilst being just as powerful as it is today, did not immediately lead to the physical intimacy that is taken for granted now. To be honest, I would have jumped into bed with Avi anytime, but it was he, with his sense of honour and propriety, who would not allow it.

We continued to be a foursome during the second year, although it was clear that Charles and Drew were becoming more peripheral. I cannot remember when exactly, but Charles did confront me and declared his love for me and asked me outright about my feelings for Avi. At the end of a difficult and emotional evening, Charles accepted my verdict and promised to get out of the way. To his credit he maintained our friendship, without any animosity towards Avi. He and Drew were pretty tight, and I wondered sometimes if there was something more between them. During the third year Avi and I became inseparable. The four of us did, however, meet for drinks and dinner every Thursday, something that stayed with us right to the end of our time there. Though Charles remained superficially affable and friendly, I was getting distinctly uncomfortable in his company. There was nothing overt, no harsh words or threats, just a lurking darkness in his eyes which unsettled me. When I mentioned it to Avi, he brushed it aside, saying it was all my imagination. Drew, on the other hand, was always his gentle, friendly self.

It was after graduation that Avinash had to return home to India. He explained that it would be more than a little challenging to get back to his orthodox community and convince his parents to accept a white British girl for a daughter-in-law. I had considerable trepidations and visions of things falling apart, but Avi was strong as a rock. He reassured me that whatever the ultimate stance of his parents, he would come back to marry me and no one else. I was long overdue a holiday abroad and of course, this was the perfect opportunity to visit India, something that I had wanted to do for a long time. And so it was, that the two of us flew out and landed in Goa, after a brief stop in Bombay, as it was then, in December 1983. Your grandmother was under the impression *that I was travelling in Europe with a couple of girls from university, though Charles knew.*

It was there, in the intoxicating atmosphere of the unspoilt beaches, that we finally gave ourselves to each other. Quentin, it is the memory of that one week that has kept me going all this while. If there is anything at all I could wish for you, I would wish that you experience the depth of that all-encompassing love that Avi and I felt and lived through during that week. Parting was devastating, but we were both upbeat, with a firm conviction that nothing would stand in the way of our future life together.

I returned to a freezing and dreary England. By the time I had settled back into Cambridge and found myself a temporary job as a teacher in a primary school, I was getting depressed. Charles was very much in evidence and came back into my life, albeit as a friend and nothing more. I was at pains to make him realise that and he seemed to accept me unconditionally. I told him about our plans to marry as soon as Avi returned, which I expected would be a couple of months away, around March/April time. I confided in him my considerable worries about my mother's reaction and how I was going to have to deal with it. I would be lying if I did not admit that Charles was hugely supportive.

A month later, I realised I was pregnant! Pregnant with you, my darling. Pregnant with my Avi's love-child. I was delirious with happiness, struggling with the fact that I could share it with nobody. We did not then have the same telecommunication facilities that you people take for granted so simply these days. I literally screamed in delight, announcing the news to the sky and the setting sun, almost hoping it would carry through across the world to Avi. Much as I had come to confide in Charles, this was a step too far. Something inside me warned me against it. One fine day I took off and went home to Scotland and my unsuspecting mother. I had left a letter for Charles saying there was an urgent family matter that I had to attend to, without giving any further details. I apologised and thanked him profusely for his support. I also left him the landline number at home, at which he could always reach me. I suggested that he should ring on a Thursday between 6 and 8 p.m., the routine we had established in the third year.

I dreaded what was going to happen when I reached home. Your grandmother was her usual majestic and cold self. After a peremptory kiss, she greeted me with the words, "Your father would have been very proud of your getting a first at Cambridge."

"And what about you, Mother?"

"Oh yes, I suppose I am too. I hope you are going to do something really useful with your *life. Time to get into society and meet some promising young man."*

"Mummy, I am pregnant."

I have never seen my mother lose control, or look so shocked and angry. With a huge effort she controlled herself and asked, "Oh, pray tell me, who is the procreator of this thing that you are carrying? Or are you unsure?" I should have known what to expect, but even so, I was wounded deeply. I wept, apologising all the while. Not for me the comforting arm of a loving mother.

Needless to say, revealing the fact that my would-be husband, your would-be father, was called Avinash Krishnan, from India, unleashed another round of vitriol. After a while she calmed down a little and asked me to relate in detail the circumstances leading up to the current debacle. I told her everything in detail, and reassured her that Avinash was not only the finest of men, but that he would be with us shortly. I said we would have a quiet civil wedding and go away (to the island of Santorini, I had decided, where we would stay) until the baby arrived. After that there would be no questions asked. Your grandmother's favoured option was for me to have an abortion, which I rejected so violently, that even she was shocked into silence. She went on to explore every possible avenue that would avoid getting Avi into our family, but finally admitted defeat. Even she could not think of a solution that would smooth everything over.

The next month was living hell for me, waiting for word from Avi. Charles would ring faithfully every Thursday, and kept my spirits up, but was unable to give me any news about Avi. Until that fateful day when he called, on a Monday, three days ahead of schedule, at 10 p.m. Mummy was already in bed and I was tossing about, unable to sleep, and trying with great difficulty to read a book. When the phone rang, I had an instant premonition of disaster and so it proved. It was Charles, in a state of agitation.

"Charlotte, I am so sorry to be the bearer of bad news. I have just received a letter from Avinash, the bastard. He has asked me to offer his profound apologies to you because he is unable to go through with the commitment. It turns out that his parents would not come around and he was threatened with effective excommunication, or the equivalent thereof, whereby he would have no further contact with the entire extended family. So, after much consideration, the creep decided that it would be in everyone's best interest if he broke off his connection with you. And that's not all, Charlotte, he has been engaged to his childhood sweetheart and the marriage is due to take place in two weeks. And he had the gall to tell *me to let you know that you are most cordially invited. He hopes you would understand and make a life for yourself."*

That, Quentin, was when my life effectively ended. What survived was just a shell. I went into a deep depression. Mother was almost triumphant with a look of 'I told you so' permanently etched on her face. I have little memory of the weeks that followed. Your grandmother declared that the only solution would be for me to have an abortion, but I firmly rejected this again. She then went on to create the myth of you being my brother's son. You see, Quentin, I did have an older brother, who unfortunately died even before I was born. Typhoid, I believe. Mother came up with this idea that I would have the baby in secret and once you were born, you would be officially 'adopted' by your grandmother, following the unfortunate demise of your father in India. There was, of course, nobody who would challenge this, because there were no other people in the know. We had no close relatives.

On the pretext of having taken up a short-term affiliation with an archaeological project, I headed off to Santorini, an island that had always fascinated me. It was there, Quentin, in the town of Oia, that you entered this world, my darling, as an orphan. I returned to Scotland, as the aunt who had rescued her nephew from some hell-hole in India, and in due course, we engaged a nanny to take care of you. Jimmy was over the moon to see me back, but he had a knowing look that told me that he guessed that you were mine.

Throughout this period, Charles continued to be my rock. The poor man did not even know that I was pregnant and remained in the dark until well after you had arrived. By this time Charles' regular calls were an established feature of my life and my mother was totally impressed by his devotion to me. Fond as I was of him, I simply could not consider him anything more than a friend. That was until Charles declared that he was coming over to meet my mother and ask for my hand. You were barely three months old then. The day Charles came over, we arranged for the nanny to take you away for the day. Charles was at his charming best and if your grandmother had any reservations at all, they were gone by the time Charles had left. With a heavy heart I decided that the best practical solution under the circumstances would be for me to marry Charles. My secret hope was that we could in due course adopt you, a prospect that seemed almost too good to be true. And it was.

We had a fairly quiet wedding, as Charles' family was small too. I was really surprised, and a little hurt, by Drew's behaviour on this *occasion of his best friend's wedding. He was distant, withdrawn and refused to engage in conversation. Again, I could not help wondering if he and Charles had been lovers. That was the last time I saw Drew, who simply dropped out of our lives from that day on. We went away to Paris on honeymoon and everything seemed to be going well, until I mentioned the possibility that we might consider adopting this unfortunate nephew of mine, who had been rescued from India. Quentin, I cannot tell you the violent response it elicited. Charles flew into a rage and said that there was no circumstance under which he would consider anything of the sort. He swore that his son (as if he knew that he would have a son) would be the heir to the estate and that you were not to be included in the equation. I was so shocked with the ferocity of his response that I backed down. To be honest, I was terrified. I knew then that it was a hopeless cause, but still hoped that at least we could be a happy family.*

The worst thing of all, Quentin, was the fact your grandmother was firmly in Charles' camp and decided to treat you like a pariah. I have shed tears of blood, my love, but all my pleas were of no avail in terms of softening my mother's cold heart. You will, of course, remember the rest of what was to follow. Jack came along within a year and the loving younger brother I had prayed for, turned out to be anything but. By this time, I realised that Charles was basically a mercenary and all the devotion he had shown to me was nothing more than an investment in the wealth of our family. He was clever, don't doubt that for a minute, in the way he played my mother. He was always solicitous around her and concerned about the family image and, of course, her well-being. It soon came to the point when I was becoming as much an outsider as you were. In the meantime, Jack was spoilt rotten by his father and his grandmother and soon came to believe that he was entitled to everything, and you, to nothing. It will come as no surprise to you that Jimmy was the real hero in all of this. He did everything in his power to keep you happy and me too, to the extent he could. Charles detested him, almost instinctively.

By the time you were five, my marriage to Charles had pretty much failed. Why did I not divorce him? That's the obvious thought that would be running through your mind. Believe me, it did come to a point where I considered it, but Mummy would not have it. But you know what, Quentin, I even went so far as to defy her and declare to Charles my intention to divorce. That was when the truly diabolical nature of Charles came to the fore. It was a winter's evening, when we were stuck indoors due to unseasonal snowfall. Jack had gone to bed, and with considerable trepidation and determination I raised the topic and suggested that we should separate and that that would be best all round. Charles lost his temper, which was a fairly regular occurrence, and slapped me around, which was also getting increasingly common. This time, however, I plucked up the courage to tell him that I was going to the police to report his abuse and that I would go ahead with the separation, whatever it took. It was then that he played his trump card.

There is no point in skirting around this, Quentin. He made the simple icy declaration that if I took this any further, he would kill you. I am not sure whether he suspected our real relationship or not, but what was abundantly clear was my bond with you. From his point of view, he saw you as a potential rival to Jack, and feared that once you grew up you could challenge him for your share of the estate. I pleaded with Charles and swore that you would not be in the picture. Indeed, my mother had already decided to will everything to Jack and leave you with a pittance. But Charles was having none of it, and swore that he would make you disappear, if I took the matter of divorce any further. And to think about it, why would he want to risk a divorce? I had little doubt that he was getting his share of women elsewhere, and *our physical relationship had ground to a halt years earlier. He was sitting on a goldmine, with you as the only potential threat, and I had come to know Charles well enough to realise that he really would carry out his threat. At that point, I caved in and became the miserable, cowering specimen that I am.*

What could I do, Quentin? Can I possibly ask for your forgiveness? If you have just turned twenty-five and I am still alive, please give me the chance to meet you and smother you with my love. If at that stage you are willing to accept me, I am prepared to go in front of the whole world and declare you as my first son. Together we will stand up to Charles and Jack. On the other hand, if I am gone by then – and I suspect that will be the case – please, please look after yourself. You are a wonderful human being and you should not take on the likes of Jack and your Uncle Charles. Just accept the injustice and blame it all on me. Get away from this putrid and poisonous family and make a life for yourself, away from hatred and deceit. I have thought frequently of taking my own life, but I cannot bear the thought of losing you, and withdrawing what little love and protection I offer. And don't ever forget, Jimmy is the one true soul that you can depend on. He knows everything, and loves us regardless. His is the truly unconditional love that people speak about, that you will never find again.

And finally, what of your father? In this day and age, it is commonplace for children to trace their missing parents. I have already told you your father's name, and will now let you know that he came from a town in southern India by the name of Madurai. I know nothing more, Quentin, and I feel so helpless and incompetent. Should I not have at least let him know that he has a wonderful son? Have I done you both a great injustice in not letting him know? I have no answers, my love, only apologies. If you do decide to try and trace him, please do so with my blessings. By the time you read this, you will be grown up enough to know the pitfalls and dangers of such an enterprise. However, if you do find him, I pray to the God I have no faith in, that you will find happiness with each other. My feeling towards him has remained one of extreme and immutable love, albeit interspersed with spikes of extreme anger and, dare I say it, hatred. Please do not approach him with the negatives. Indeed, if the predominant emotions are negative, please do not proceed. I have dreamed of the day when our paths might cross, and I would pretend that I was lucky to escape his attentions, tell him of my perfect marriage to Charles, and then spring the news of your arrival in the world all those years ago. But no, my child, no more lies and pretence. Tell him all.

How I wish I had given you up for adoption, that you may have found truly loving parents. It was my selfishness, combined with the naïve hope of being able to adopt you myself, that trapped you into this loveless family. Farewell, dear heart. My love and blessings will keep you from harm, away from hatred and bitterness. Have a wonderful life, and never spend a moment regretting the absence of your useless parents.

Your ever-loving mother,
Charlotte

✠

I cried. I howled. Charlotte was my mother! The aunt I had worshipped and considered an angel in human form, was indeed not just that, but my very own mother. The monumental injustice that had been inflicted on both of us was crushing me like an avalanche and I did not know how to deal with this explosion of emotions, which combined extreme grief and sorrow with incandescent rage. How could my poor mother have possibly been inflicted with two awful men in her life, not to mention a heartless and conniving mother? I had, to date, harboured a distant and nebulous hatred for a father whom I knew nothing about, but now I felt a real black hatred for the man who promised the world to my mother and then deserted her, leaving her with one sorry specimen for a son. The other had cheated and manipulated her, controlled her, abused her, and essentially destroyed her life. In a frenzy I picked up the next letter.

✠

THE SCREAM OF ANGUISH

13 March 1997

My dearest treasure, Quentin,

I have little time, and must write what I have to. I have spent the last four hours in the very depths of despair, which have come to a head, knowing now, what I do. I also know what I must do. You will by now have read the letter I wrote you on your tenth birthday. If that shocked you, this will rock you to the core, my darling. You will now be twenty-five, and old enough to handle the egregious truths of your past.

Yesterday, I received a bombshell, in the form of a letter from Drew Howell, a sort of dying confession. It was a short scrawl which I could barely decipher, and I need you to read it before I go any further.

✠

2 March 1997

Dear Charlotte,

May God have mercy on me for what I have inflicted on you. It was all for the one great love of my life, my Charlie. You see, I was in love with him from the moment I laid eyes on him. I don't think you had the slightest suspicion, you were so besotted by that poor bugger Avi.

I'm dying, Charlotte, and cannot go to my grave without clearing my conscience, far too late though it may be. Charlie was a cruel and deceitful man, who toyed with my feelings and exploited my sexual weakness. We were lovers during our third year, but all the time he lusted after you and your wealth. I was unfortunately under his spell, but even more importantly, I became terrified of his temper. When Avi returned to Cambridge in '84, he would not let me meet him. He told me that he and you had decided to split up, which sounded impossible to me, but who was I to question. The thing that has haunted me all these years is the act which I had to undertake for him. A couple of days before that fateful weekend when Avi disappeared, I saw Charlie having an animated conversation with Avi, at a distance. I was determined to finally meet up with Avi and I approached them. Avi was in high spirits and grabbed me in a bear hug, but I could see Charlie was not pleased. Before we had exchanged a few words, Charlie interjected, saying he and Avi had things to buy and pack for their weekend outing. Just as we parted, Avi turned to me, and asked if I could do him the favour of getting a stamp and posting a letter, which he handed to me.

I had barely walked a hundred yards, when Charles came rushing up to me, and said, "Drew, that letter is NOT to be posted. I want you to ditch it in the first rubbish bin you pass. You get it? If I find you haven't done it..."

The look on his face was the epitome of evil and malice. I can still see it. I wish I had either had the guts to post it, or the sense to ditch it, but I did neither. I held on to it, overcome by curiosity about what Avi could have written to you. That evening I read it and it most certainly was not the letter of someone breaking up. When Charles told me Avi had departed the country post-haste, after that weekend, I was even more troubled, but could do nothing. Charlie could sense that I was suspicious, but had no proof of anything, but nevertheless he warned me never to talk about Avi again. I only came to your wedding at your insistence, but could not face you, knowing what I had done.

I attach that letter, and beseech you to forgive me. I am paying for the sins of consorting with the Devil.

Yours sincerely,
Drew

✛

7 April 1984

My darling, my eternal love, my very own Charlotte,

I am decomposing, physically and mentally, without you. It has been five months since our journey through Elysium began, on the warm shores of the Arabian Sea. It has all come good my lovely, my parents are now on board and cannot wait to get their first glimpse of you. There were a few other things I had to sort out, hence the delay in getting back here. If you are annoyed, I fully understand and apologise from the very depths of my heart. Missed you horribly, and yet I have been feeling on top of the world, in the knowledge of what is to come. To spend the rest of my life with you seems almost unbelievable, too good to be true, to coin a cliché.

When I got back to Cambridge, there was, of course, no sign of you and I assumed that you had gone back to Scotland and was wondering what would be the most discreet way of contacting you. Fortunately for me, good old Charles, the third member of our gang, was on hand. Indeed, it was curious that I ran into him almost within a couple of hours of getting here, almost as if it was fated to be so. It was from him I learnt that you were in considerable trouble at home, with your formidable (your words, not mine) mother! Charles filled in all the details about how you were holding out resolutely, and refusing to budge from your total and complete commitment to me. Even thinking about it gives me the goosebumps!

Charles, bless his soul, has been a pillar of strength. I confess I was really down in the dumps for the first couple of days, but thanks to his encouragement and cheerful company, I have managed to regain my spirits. And of course, today my spirits soared, on the receipt of your news. Charles tells me that finally your mother has come round, and looks like I could be meeting her as early as Monday. Bless Charles for being such a friend and a most reliable go-between. I have thought a dozen times of calling you at home, in the hope that you might pick it up and I could just hear your voice even for a few seconds. However, Charles has strictly forbidden it, on the grounds that things are so fragile at home for you that any such intrusion could have a profoundly adverse effect.

I am on tenterhooks, my darling, and was not sure how I would get through this upcoming weekend, but again Charles has come to the rescue. He is taking me to a little cottage in Dorset and we are going to have a weekend of hiking, eating, and drinking. Oh, dear God, how I shall miss you, but we are almost there. I

am floating on air as I write these words to you. Until we meet, to resume our journey through Valhalla, your very own, yours and yours alone,
    Avi

✟

I sat, stunned! This was the father I had hated all along! But then, what happened, what became of him? Before I drowned myself in a sea of questions, I knew the answers would follow in the second part of my mother's letter. My *mother's* letter, *my mother Charlotte.*

✟

This, my love, was the letter to me from Avi, your poor, innocent father, written just a few months before you were born, Quentin. I felt disembowelled, heartbroken and utterly hopeless. Then I was gripped by a rage, which would only be assuaged by getting the truth out of Charles. That evening he was in his usual foul mood after a couple of drinks, and I confronted him with Drew's letter. He looked shocked, but instantly turned nasty, and started taunting me about my old love, 'Chavvy Avi', as he referred to him. It came to a point, when I could just not take it any more, when he referred to you in even more disparaging terms. I lost it, Quentin.

I screamed at Charles, "Tell me what really happened with Avi, you monster. You'll never be even a fraction of the man Avi was, and your Jack will never be a fraction of Quentin, who happens to be Avi's and mine!"

I could have bitten my tongue off, but it was too late. I was expecting and ready for an explosion, but Charles went completely silent for a minute, and then his expression turned devilish, his voice, a whisper. "I knew it, you slut. In that case, you need to know what really happened to Chavvy Avi. You're going to love this, you bitch."

My blood ran cold, my darling Quentin, and when I looked at Charles' look of triumph, I knew there was a terrible truth about to emerge.

"So, what do you suppose happened to poor lover boy?"

"You tricked him into some awful situation, didn't you? Did you tell him I was engaged, or worse, dead? How did you get him to pull out, you monster?"

"Get him to pull out? Not a chance. That fucking hero would have gone to hell and back to stay true to you. Nah, there was only one way, and I took it."

"Oh, dear God, you don't mean—"

"Oh yes I do! For a bugger with brains coming out of his ears, he had remarkably little ability to see the obvious. It was a piece of cake. We were partying at the top of the cliffs of Dorset one minute, and he is over and out the next. He never even saw it coming."

I threw myself at Charles with all my pent-up fury, but I was no match for him, apart from managing to scratch his face. He knocked me down and all I could do was yell and swear. He looked at me with complete contempt, and ended, saying, "Just in case you think you can use my confession, think again. I'll claim you just made it up and of course it's your word against mine. Not to mention, what I might do to that brown bastard of yours."

I know I've reached the point of no return, Quentin. Remorse is literally eating me alive, because of what I inflicted on that beautiful, wonderful man, who showed me the meaning of love. How could I accept Charles' word and accept losing Avi? Why did I not even make an effort to contact him, particularly knowing I was carrying his child? These thoughts have driven me insane, and I have come to the only decision I can. I'm sure this will rid you of any negative feelings you might have had towards your father. The one date I would like to etch into your brain is 6 September 1962, the day when Avi was born, three months after me, half a world away.

Don't think of me too harshly, my love. It was my weakness, that I did not have total *faith in your father, as I should have done. Whatever, there is no escaping the fact that I was responsible for depriving you not just the truth about your wonderful father, but also the love of a mother, who was around you all the time, but unwilling to accept her ultimate responsibility. I am not worthy of your love, and most certainly not worthy of your father's. I am bereft, eviscerated and filled with nothing more than a vacuum. There is one ineluctable path which beckons. All I pray for is for you to have a happy and fulfilling life, abundant in love.*

Your ever-loving mother,
Charlotte

✝

The horror of what had transpired all those years ago hit me like a sledgehammer. I shouted myself hoarse and yelled into the night. With dreadful clarity I realised that my father was a gem, one in a million. He was a lamb to the slaughter, Charles the butcher. The injustice inflicted on my parents was too awful to comprehend. I was worn out, but had to press on with the last letter.

PENITENCE TOO LATE

20 December 2018

My dear Quentin
What you have read will have shocked you

to the core of your existence. I apologise for that. I apologise for many more things. Indeed, I apologise for everything that I have been instrumental in inflicting on your life. I would not expect you to forgive and indeed, would insist that you do not forgive my trespasses. I do not deserve it.

Charlotte sent me that first letter in 1994, asking me to give it to you when you turned twenty-five. The others followed in 1997, posted the day before she died. I took it upon myself not to give it to you when you turned twenty-five, because I was terrified of what that truth might do to you, and more selfishly, of how you might turn on your vicious, scheming grandmother. I cringe, even from asking forgiveness.

Charlotte's second and last letter to you broke my heart, and heaven knows what it will do to you. When I read it, I was filled with such a sense of shame that I cannot describe. That poor Avinash was a lamb to the slaughter; no, slaughter is too kind a word, it was capital treachery and murder most foul.

From these letters, Quentin, you now know the reality of your birth and parentage. If I have to apologise to you, I have to apologise a hundredfold to your mother and my daughter, whom I have systematically neglected and abused. And infinitely more to that poor innocent, who was your father. Realisation has come to me so late, that I know that no reparations can be made and only look forward to my own punishment, be it in this life or in the hereafter.

I have spent my entire life being proud of my heritage, my lineage, my name and title and family. Your arrival as a child of love, with an Indian father, was something I was entirely unable to accept. Where Charlotte considered it a tragedy that your father 'abandoned' her, I considered it a minor triumph. It would have been bad enough having you as a stain on the family, but imagine actually having to accept your father as the son-in-law. Such was the degree of my bigotry.

Being the blinded, despotic character that I was, I was wholly taken in by Charles Hillier, the Devil in disguise. Unlike normal women with maternal instincts, I was a cold-blooded reptilian character. Instead of forgiving my lovely daughter and supporting her, I threw her to the wolves, or should I say, the king of the wolves, Charles. And then I continued to compound my crimes by pampering his seed in the form of Jack. It was plain as day that he was as evil as you were good. Where he was spoilt and rotten to the core, you were pure and unsullied. Yet, my despicable bias and prejudice overcame the obvious facts that were staring me in the eyes. For that I can never forgive myself, nor should you.

Quentin, I will not tarry. There is a certain sense of urgency about apprising you of all the facts. Charlotte meant you to have these letters when you turned twenty-five. I am afraid I have taken it upon myself not to follow her instructions, heaven forgive me. Instead, I am instructing our family solicitors to hand them all over to you on my death, which I pray will not be too distant. The horror of what Charlotte went through and what I had inflicted on her, became explosively clear to me when I read the letter. But by then it was all too late, far too late.

Quentin, my child, Charlotte rang me in a state of extreme agitation on 13 March 1997. The date is imprinted in my mind. This was late at night, and she was whispering, and was clearly terrified. Presumably of Charles. She said she was sending me a letter meant for you, along with another letter from your father to her, which would explain everything. She said she would call the next day, and she ended with, "Mummy, I'm setting it all straight tomorrow. No more misery, no more lies."

The next day, sometime in the evening, I got that fateful call from Charlotte. She sounded wild, almost manic. She said she had persuaded Charles to lead them to the very spot where he had pushed your father, Avinash, over the cliff back in 1984. Quentin, I was shocked to my core and was literally speechless. I knew Charles was bad, but this was beyond the pale. I was terrified of what Charles would do to her, but she laughed hysterically, saying I should worry about what she was going to do to Charles. "I've persuaded him to bring us to the hallowed spot, where I've paid my respects to my betrayed love. Charles is heavily inebriated and depending on me to drive. I'm in the car, Mother, in the driving seat, and as soon as Charles gets back in, I'm going to take the same route he sent Avi through. Goodbye, Mother, and if there is any conscience left in you, please take care of my little boy."

I felt my world collapsing around me, and it did. I was fraught, distraught, but could not contact Charlotte, who must have turned her phone off. I contacted the police, but without knowing where exactly they were it was futile. I stayed up all night, trying in vain to contact her. It was the next day that I got word of the fatal accident in Dorset. Autopsy revealed that both your parents had high levels of alcohol in their blood, and the verdict was 'death by misadventure'.

The truth hit me hard, but I had to keep on top of everything. Of course. Weakness was not something I could contemplate, never mind show. Even knowing the truth, I could not get myself to accept my own folly, my role in all this. Nevertheless, I was determined to make amends, and you may have noticed a certain softening of my attitude. I did, of course, have to alter my will, and had to force myself to divide the estate equally between you and Jack. All the while, I could not get rid of my overriding fondness for Jack, who enjoyed a considerable monthly allowance from me. Even though it was you who came to me during the term holidays. Even later, as young men, you always made it a point to visit this old woman at least twice a year, whereas Jack could never be bothered, except when he wanted to wheedle more money out of me. I did ask myself whether your visits were not more inspired by that wastrel, Jimmy.

It was sometime in the summer of 2007, when Jack visited me without warning. He demanded an advance of £100,000 against his inheritance, to fund this fantastic project he was embarking on. Frankly I would have given it to him, but for his attitude and arrogance. He was not asking, he was demanding. When I indicated that I was not impressed, Jack threatened me with physical harm! If there is one thing you might remember, Quentin, I was never one to be bullied, and I sent him away with a flea in his ear. He actually did look as if he was going to assault me for a few seconds, before good sense prevailed. He must have known that any such act could seriously damage his inheritance. He stopped visiting, *but what was really hurtful was the way he behaved. He blatantly threw in my face the fact that the inheritance was his sooner or later, and bullied me into increasing his monthly allowance at frequent intervals.*

It was when you invited me to your wedding, Quentin, that I finally made the decision I should have made long ago. By this time, it was clear Jack was rotten to the core. I'm sorry I did not attend, but I felt too ashamed. Much better that I played the role of the unfeeling grandmother. I rewrote my will and left the estate to be shared equally between the two of you. I informed Jack about it only a few days ago, and he was furious, but realised it was a fait accompli, as the solicitors had already done the needful. He basically threatened to harm you, Quentin, which both angered and scared me. I warned Jack that if he did not behave himself, I would not hesitate to cut him out completely. I am hoping that this would be a real incentive for him to control his obnoxious self.

I hope to continue to see you, Quentin, as frequently as possible, along with your wife, and who knows, children. If anyone deserves luck and happiness it is you. I know not how long I'll survive, but I have this premonition that my time is approaching. I'll say no more. I'll end with a repetition of my previous apologies, and one more – for deciding unilaterally that these

letters bearing the awful truths, should only reach you on my death.
    Your 'loving' grandmother,
    Winifred Grayling

☦

I was in a state of shock and unable to think or feel. I am not sure how long it lasted. Those five letters, interspersed by nearly twenty-five years, were incendiary, by any measure. Each searing fact went through my mind over and over again until I thought my head would explode.

It was six in the morning. I put on a T-shirt, a pair of shorts and my trainers. I went out and started running, with a back-pack containing a six-pack of lemonade. I tried to banish all thought, kill all emotion, and keep running. After an hour or so I alternated periods of walking with running. I have no idea what route I took or what direction I was going in. I returned sometime in the afternoon and collapsed into bed. I woke up the next morning, having slept for sixteen hours. I was emotionally drained and felt brain-dead.

Over the next few days, I set up direct debits to about twenty charities dealing with children, women and the poor in Africa, Asia and South America, to the tune of £10,000 a month. I set up a 'Jimmy Clayton Endowment' of £3,000 a year for two bright children from the lowest social class, in the school I'd been to. I set up a 'Charlotte Grayling Endowment' of £5,000 a year for the most promising economically disadvantaged student at the Cambridge college Charlotte had attended. Through this period, I sank progressively deeper into a morass of an ever-darkening abyss. The man who had everything, not a care in the world, was in a state of abject and complete depression, with a sense of possessing nothing of value. All the material wealth I had amassed recently was of no relevance, in the face of the vacuum in my life, created by all the people I cared for, being sucked out. I had cleverly engineered all of it myself, pretty much unaided.

Claire haunted me, day and night. I was determined not to give in. Harry had gone silent, and I understood entirely. Mitch and Matilda kept interrupting my thoughts, but again some inexplicable ennui would not allow me to make that call. I should have been furious with myself, and taken the steps necessary to reinstate some meaning in my life, but I could not muster up the energy. I wandered like a ghost in *Gorm-Faire*, sometimes spending hours staring at the sea. I did think of going over the cliff, to be relieved of the need to do anything, to escape from the black beast, but some little spark of life kept me from that act of finality.

⚚

THE FIRST RAY OF LIGHT

Nights merged into day and vice versa, with little difference for me. My housekeepers tried their level best to draw me out, but without success. I had lost the will to live and the will to die, being stuck in limbo land. Initially, alcohol was my friend, but soon I lost interest in even that. I can't even remember the arrival of the new year, 2020. Occasionally, the phone would ring, but I could not be bothered to answer. Not infrequently I would crawl out of bed in the middle of the night and wander around the estate.

I cannot quite remember the date, but it must have been six weeks since that fateful evening when I had revealed all to Harry. I was aroused from my light slumber sometime in the afternoon, by a loud knocking on the door to my bedroom. Before I could respond, the door opened and two figures walked in. Harry and Jenny.

"What are you two doing here?"

They looked at each other without saying a word, marched up to my bed, got hold of me from either side and dragged me out. I was outraged, but could not be bothered to resist and I stumbled along with them to the sofa set that adorned the other end of my bedroom. They pulled the curtains open, allowing in a flood of sunlight, which made me wince.

"Quincy, you prize idiot, get a grip," said Harry with a mixture of mock anger and genuine concern. "Do you know how many times we've rung and ended up just speaking to your man, Albert? You've got to snap out of this."

There was no stopping them. I did not have the energy to resist. They insisted on hanging around in my bedroom until I had a shower and got myself dressed to go out and face the world. The three of us sat out in the porch, with tea and cakes. They were determined to break through my barrier. I refused to respond to all their coaxing and cajoling.

"Jen, you must hear this. That time when just the three of us were practising cricket that first year we met in school. I was bowling to Kevin, and Quentin was keeping wicket, when cleverclogs Daniel from the year above, came strutting along. He told Quentin to stop being a woose, standing ten feet behind the wicket, and would show us how it was done. He stood barely two feet behind the wicket, while I charged in and bowled. Kevin missed the ball, the ball missed the wicket, Daniel missed the ball, and the ball got Daniel in the balls! And Quentin at first slip, collapsed and wet himself!!!"

Jenny and Harry exploded in laughter and a second later I collapsed, and almost wet myself. We laughed like it seemed forever, with tears running down our faces. These two angels had come to my rescue, away from the epistolary nightmare which had engulfed me. It was uninhibited disportation that evening, with our housekeepers in splendid form, turning out an amazing dinner. We wandered around the estate in the darkness, singing, exchanging stories and cracking dirty jokes, which, to my surprised delight, Jenny fully appreciated and participated in. I had no idea when we crashed out.

The next morning was predictably late in arriving and was imbued with the inevitable hangover. After plenty of hydration and a wholesome lunch, we felt restored.

"How can I thank you enough, Harry? Does this mean that Jenny is OK with me, too?"

Harry nodded. "We had a few late-night discussions about it and finally agreed that what you did was nothing more than self-defence. That's all there is to it."

I felt a huge weight lifted off my shoulders. I decided to tell them about the letters which had been the final trigger for my depression. I related the events in temporal sequence, frequently having to stop to control my emotions. Harry and Jenny were mesmerised, shocked and appalled in equal measure. Their support and understanding that evening, meant more to me than I can ever say. I am not sure that I would have ever got back on track, but for them.

They left the next day, with a firm agreement that we would meet up for one weekend every month, barring accidents. I promised them that I would not succumb to any negativity or self-pity. I swore to myself that I was going to put things right in my own life.

My next task was to re-establish contact with Mitch and Matilda, which was not difficult to do. The time in New York was eight in the evening and I knew they would be home, getting their kids ready for bed.

"Mitch, how are you, mate?"

There was a two-second pause.

"Quentin! It's been months since you've been gone and we'd given up on you and Claire. Matilda and I have remembered you every goddamn night, wondering where you were and if you were safe. Why have you made no contact, man?"

"Mitch I have no excuses. Suffice it to say I have been through a real torrid time, and am only just surfacing. And just in case you think otherwise, you have been in my thoughts just as frequently."

"Matilda, baby, you'll never guess who's on the line. Sir Quentin, the knight of the round table!"

I heard a squeal of delight in the background and Matilda came on the line. "Quentin, honey, we've been so worried about you and Claire. Are you both OK?"

"Yes, Matilda, we are both out of all danger. Not a day has gone by without my thinking of you and Mitch and your generosity."

Mitch came back on the line. "Quentin, I need to tell you, there was no end of excitement in New York a few days after you left. The tabloids were full of news of a gangland killing of a certain Marty Nero. Does the name ring a bell?"

"Ah, yes, that sounds vaguely familiar."

"Bullshit, you know what I'm talking about. I don't know how the two of you managed it, but hats off to you. Speaking of which, how's Claire?"

"I'm not sure, Mitch. I'm afraid we parted company a little while ago and we haven't been in touch."

Mitch must have turned the speaker phone on, for I heard Matilda exclaim, "Oh no, Quentin, how could you let that happen?"

"I've asked myself that a million times and really cannot find a good enough answer. I guess we fell in love, but couldn't persuade ourselves that we had. So we both decided to play it safe and withdraw. Ever since then, all I have been able to think about is how to get Claire back into my life, or how to get myself back into her life. I've been fighting myself, and then kind of went into a bit of a depressed state, but thanks to a couple of really good friends, I have come to my senses. I'm going to get back with Claire, but I'm still working out a way to do it."

There was a pause of a few seconds and then Matilda chimed in, "Damn it, Mitch, we can't hide this any longer. Claire has been in touch with us since she returned. In fact, she came and stayed with us for a weekend, loaded with gifts for the whole family. She was pretty down, and wouldn't answer any questions about anything that might have taken place between you, except to say that it was all a big mistake. She did say that her own danger was all very much in the past and that Marty's shadow was out of her life. However, she claimed she didn't know what had transpired in your life, since you parted company, and that you basically didn't want her hanging around. And then she went back to Montreal, where she is staying with her mother. She made us promise that we wouldn't tell you anything about her, whenever you made contact. I'm sorry to be going against her wishes, but can't really keep it from you."

"I'm going to make this right and I'm going to make this something special. If you speak to Claire, do let her know that I am back in England, and right as rain, but don't, on any account, repeat anything of my feelings, please."

Before ringing off, I remembered to ask for Claire's mother's landline number.

⊕

My next task was daunting. With determination I pursued my aim, with the University of Cambridge, in tracing the home address of my late father. In the end, the only thing that worked was when I revealed the fact that I was actually his son, desperately trying to trace my lineage. The address was in a city by the name of Madurai, which I had heard of, but knew little about. A quick look up in Google surprised me by its geography and history. It was a city with a population of nearly 1.5 million, magnificent architecture and history going back over 2,000 years. Again, using the Internet and communication technologies at my disposal, I was able to locate the telephone number of one T. Krishnan, living at that address. This *had* to be my grandfather and I only hoped he was still alive. Using Internet translation to Tamil, I gleaned that grandfather was *Thatha* and grandmother was *paati*.

As soon as I woke up the next morning, I rang the number with considerable nervous excitement. The time in India would be around 2 p.m. The phone rang for a good thirty seconds and just as I was about to give up, it was answered by a female voice.

"Hello…" She lapsed into what I presumed was Tamil.

"Could I speak to Mr Krishnan, please?"

"Who is talking?"

"Is that Mrs Krishnan?"

"Yes. Who is talking?"

I had intended to reveal myself to my grandfather, but decided I could not hold out any longer.

"You do not know me—"

Mrs Krishnan interjected, slightly breathless, "Avinash, Avinasha?"

I could hear the tears in her voice and sat myself down, truly shaken.

"I am Avinash's son."

My grandmother was struggling at the other end and was obviously trying to summon her husband between sobs, her voice choking. Then I heard a man's voice. "Who is this?"

"I am your long lost-grandson, Avinash's son."

"Don't play the fool with us, you blighter. We are old people and we haven't seen our son for over thirty years. We still don't know where he is. How can we know that you are the grandson?"

"I'm so sorry to have to spring this on you like this, sir. All I can say is that your son and my father died in 1984, the year I was born. I did not know the truth about my own father until recently and I have only just managed to trace him back to you. I don't blame you if you don't believe me, but please give me a chance to let you know the full story and then you can decide for yourself."

After a pause he responded by saying, "Are you on WhatsApp?"

That certainly surprised me, coming from someone I imagined would not be au fait with modern communications, and instantly felt ashamed of myself. "Yes, of course I am. Please make a note of my number, which in fact is the one I'm calling from."

"Unfortunately this landline of ours does not display the number of incoming calls. So please give me your number."

I read it out and he duly noted it down and ended the conversation by saying, "I'm going to call you back in three hours from my mobile, and we can talk at length then."

I fretted for the next three hours, waiting for the time to go by. My phone rang and I answered after the first ring, to find my grandfather's voice at the other end.

"You have given us both a big shock and my wife has not stopped crying. You seem to have convinced her just by your voice that you are indeed our grandson, but I am not so sure. So go ahead and tell me your story."

I told him the details as far as I knew, of Avinash's stay at Cambridge, his burgeoning relationship and love for my mother, their parting, at the end of 1983, Avinash's return to England in the spring of 1984 and the treachery that followed. When it came to telling them about his death, I was choking up and could barely speak. I was going to spare them the details and just tell them that he had died in an accident. I told them that he had gone rock climbing on his own, as his friend who was supposed to join him was unable to make it. My father had evidently fallen to his death and it was only weeks later that his body was found, but without any identifying features. My mother came to know subsequently through the mutual friend, by which time she was six months pregnant. She had kept that secret to herself and had revealed the truth to me in a letter, which I received after her death.

The old man listened patiently, with periodic interjections, asking very relevant questions, and I was seriously worried that he might find enough holes in the story to cast suspicion on the real cause of death. I could see no point in distressing them further with the appalling details of his murder by his supposed best friend. It was then that he surprised me with another request

"So, Quentin Grayling, as you call yourself, I would like you to turn on the video!"

Why had I not thought about this simple measure? I was dying to get a look at them, and no doubt the feeling was reciprocal. They had turned their video on before I did and I saw an elderly couple, in traditional south Indian attire. The camera had been positioned in such a way that they were both clearly visible. My grandfather looked wonderfully distinguished, but he had a frown, underlining his real doubt and anxiety. My grandmother had a round, kindly face with big eyes that were brimming with tears and her lips were quivering.

I turned on my video and the old man gasped. The lady burst into tears. My grandfather exclaimed, "Avinash, my Avinash is alive again. You don't need to provide any more evidence, my child. Our prayers have been answered. We have lived through thirty-five years of hell, wondering when we would see our son again. The bitterness of the news of his death has been overcome by the sweetness of your entry into our lives!" At this point he dissolved into tears, and my eyes were swimming.

Over the next week I spoke to them every day. My grandfather had a remarkable command of English, although heavily accented. My grandmother too had a surprisingly impressive vocabulary. It was humbling to realise within myself that I could barely manage a smattering of French. They were insistent that I had to take the next flight out to go and see them, which indeed is what I would have done, except that I had a better proposition for them.

The next few months seemed to drag on forever, as I waited for the divorce to go through. COVID-19 laid the world low in February and March saw the introduction of our first lockdown. I visited Harry and family at every safe opportunity, and I spoke to Matilda and Mitch once a month. I video-called my grandparents once a week, and that was a high point for all three of us. In April I decided to write my story, and made a tentative start. Finally, in July, the Decree Absolute arrived, and I was free of Harriett. I had one final conversation with her. She had moved to a town called Moura in Portugal, and was running a café. I reiterated my warning about having her under surveillance, which was entirely untrue, of course. She was a broken woman, but I could not generate any sympathy, considering her misdemeanours. I never heard from her again.

The next morning at nine o'clock I decided to take the plunge. I gambled on the fact that at this time of the day Claire's mother was likely to be at home by herself, while Claire was out working, or whatever. A female voice answered after four rings, a voice very similar to Claire's.

"I'm trying to get in touch with Claire."

"This is Claire's mother, she's not at home. May I know who's calling?"

I heaved a huge sigh of relief and said, "Mrs Gordon, we have not met. My name is Quentin Grayling."

There was a sharp intake of breath at the other end and she came back, "Quentin, whom she called Tintin? I thought you were—"

"You're right to think what you did, but I was an idiot, for letting Claire go. After this painful separation, I now know how I feel about her, but I have no idea what she feels about me or thinks of me. I deliberately rang at this time in order to be able to speak to you, and to apologise to you for having treated your beautiful daughter rather shabbily."

"No, don't say that. Claire still talks of you as her knight in shining armour and quite simply adores you. She blames herself for whatever it was that caused you to part company, and partly feels that she is not good enough for you, what with her background and all."

"That is utter rubbish, Mrs Gordon. Claire is good enough for the cream of the cream, but without any further ado, let me ask you outright – do you think she would entertain me again in her life?"

"Yes, yes, yes! This poor child of mine has seen nothing but misery all her life, until you entered it. She had a taste of heaven before it was all taken away again. What would I not give to see the two of you back together?" She was clearly in tears, and I felt a lump in my throat.

"In that case, I have a plan. One that is slightly risky, but I don't care. I want you to surprise Claire this evening, saying that you are taking her for a mystery holiday during the first two weeks of August. Refuse to give her any more details for the moment and do not take no for an answer. You will receive two tickets to this mystery location, and I will be there to surprise Claire."

"Bless you, Quentin, I have prayed for this all my life. Please call me Lucy. I am so truly, absolutely excited. I don't know how I'm going to keep this from Claire."

"Lucy, you must. Right, now to the business and logistics. Firstly, you will both need the antibody test against COVID-19 and certificate of vaccination. Next…"

We exchanged email IDs and said our goodbyes.

I was alive again!

14

HOMECOMING OF THE ASYMPTOTE

The time is nigh, to arouse yourself, discard self-pity, throw off the mental shackles, and embrace life in all its glory and misery!

I arrived in Santorini on 1 August 2020. Santorini, where my darling mother had brought me into this world in secrecy and disgrace, pining for her lover, betrayed and murdered by his friend. The weather was delightful and the island was more beautiful than I had ever imagined. I was almost manic, in love with everything around me. I had booked accommodation in Hotel Perivolas, which was stunning in every possible sense. I was able to get all the rooms that I wanted. I spent that day and the next just wandering around the delectable little towns of Oia and Fira. I could not get enough of it.

There I was standing against the pristine, white-washed walls of this incredibly beautiful, tiny island, watching a sunset like no other. The Aegean Sea was dead calm, offering no clues to the caldera that lay under its surface. There was not a cloud in sight, except to the far north. The sun went through every nuance of colour, from gold to orange and then finally blood red, all the while enlarging. The wisps of cloud in the north produced an astonishing array of colours, reflecting the dying rays of the sun. I stood there long after the sun had set, thanking the kindly destiny that had allowed me to be privy to this spectacle.

Claire and Lucy arrived on the 3rd, and the flight, routed through London, landed on time at just after 5 p.m. I was more nervous, than I had been prior to my final tryst with Kevin. After what seemed an age, I saw Claire and fought to tear my eyes away from her, to take in the presence of her mother next to her. Lucy was an inch shorter and would have been a striking woman, but for her slight stoop and lined face. Life had not been kind to her. I waved when they were about twenty feet away.

Claire looked at me blankly for a couple of seconds before recognition dawned. Her eyes widened, a slightly shocked expression appeared, before her face cracked into a delighted grin. We ran towards each other, and tried our best to squeeze the life out of each other, before our mouths met in what must have been the show of the day in the airport! When we prised ourselves apart, I looked around to find myself being inspected by Lucy.

"Why, Quentin, Claire never told me what a dishy hunk you were!" she exclaimed. We hugged and she kissed me on both cheeks.

Claire finally found her voice and said, "Tintin, what a coincidence..."

I went down on my left knee and pulled out the two-carat diamond ring, set in platinum, which I had purchased the day before, from one of the dozens of shops selling exquisite, if expensive, jewellery. And then I made my proposal, in front of a few dozen people, who were enjoying the scene thoroughly.

"Claire, will you forget my failings, forgive the secrets I am still to reveal, and marry me?"

For the first time since our very first meeting, I witnessed Claire weep; and I mean, truly cry. I think Lucy was crying as well, but my eyes were solely and utterly and immovably on Claire's beautiful face. Through the tears she managed to convey her consent without uttering a word. I slipped the ring on her finger.

The drive to the hotel was nothing short of a dream and I have never seen two happier people than Claire and Lucy. Then came the realisation that there was one more hurdle to cross. I felt a sinking sensation in the pit of my stomach, at the thought of having to tell Claire the full story of what transpired after we parted company in Singapore. There was a momentary temptation to fudge the facts, but I instantly decided against it. No way would I go through this marriage, never mind a lifetime, without letting Claire into the darkest recesses of my mind. I simply had to tell her about Kevin and Harriett.

By nine o'clock the three of us were seated for dinner, with a divine view to savour. Lucy had never set foot outside the US (except for Toronto and Montreal) and the two of them simply could not get over the sheer beauty of Santorini and its pint-sized elegance, in contrast with the megalithic and nondescript cities of America. At the end of a wonderful dinner, I made my announcement.

"Claire, sweetheart, our wedding is arranged for the 7th, which gives you three clear days. Hope that will be enough," I said with a mischievous smile.

"Oh my god, Tintin, I really cannot take all this in, it just seems too unreal. Of course, I'll be ready for it, I'm ready for it tonight."

Lucy interjected, "Enough, you two. Quentin, I'm over the moon, and like Claire, I'm finding it hard to take it all in."

"Claire, I do need a little time with you to update you on certain events that occurred after you left Singapore."

That lowered the tone distinctly and Claire's face clouded. "Tintin, please tell me it's not—"

"No, don't second-guess me, sweetheart. You need to listen to the full story. Lucy, I'm sorry but do you mind if I take Claire away for an hour or two?"

"Of course, not, Quentin, you go right ahead. In fact, I'm really not expecting to see Claire again, until the morning at the very earliest," replied Lucy, with a lewd wink.

Claire blushed. "Oh, shut up, Mamma, you'll be lucky to see me in the morning."

Claire and I sat in my room overlooking the sea, with a bottle of Cognac and two glasses, which I charged. We toasted and then I started filling her in. I left nothing out. Claire was shaken, but not shocked.

"Now, knowing what I've done, Claire, are you disappointed in me? Is this going to make you want to reconsider my proposal?"

"Tintin, listen, what you did was, in my book, self-defence. More than that, I have to admit to a sense of profound admiration and almost a sense of awe at what you accomplished. You've simply rid the world of a couple of people who are nothing more than vermin!"

Then I went on to relate the rest of my story, but when it came to the last bit of it, I decided I could not go through with it. "Claire, the story of my parents is too traumatic for me to relate, as it makes my blood boil. It makes my soul cry. I'm going to ask you to read these letters."

It took Claire about twenty minutes to read them all, and from the third minute onwards she was unable to hold back the tears. At the end of it she put her arms around me and buried her face into my shoulder and we both wept.

"Tintin, you had the most wonderful parents, both snatched away from you. How on earth can there be so much cruelty? I look back at my own life and you know, it was nothing compared to the misery that your mother lived through. The cruelty, the horror, it's all too much."

"This had been a day of real fear for me. I first feared that you might reject me at the airport. My second fear was that on listening to the story you just heard you might be persuaded to reconsider taking me for a life partner. And now I cannot believe there is a happier man in this world."

"Reject you? Just try and make me." That was the trigger which unleashed our dormant passion, which lasted late into the night.

The three of us spent the next day in Oia, and Claire did all the shopping that she needed for the wedding, which included a cream silk wedding dress. I made an excuse and escaped in the middle of the day to get to the airport, where I received Harry, Jenny, Quincy and Juliet. The excitement was palpable as we met and hugged. The parents were just as animated and voluble as the children. We travelled back to the hotel by taxi, but I got off in the town to rejoin Claire and Lucy. A little later I made my excuses again and took myself back to the airport, where I breathlessly awaited the arrival of Mitch, Matilda, Nelson and

Toni. The atmosphere was almost electric as they came through and I reunited with them, hugging each one with real fervour. The trip back to the hotel was noisy and boisterous.

We met for dinner at nine, this time the whole group. When introduced to Claire, Harry turned to me, saying, "Quentin, how did a toad like you land a beauty like this one?" And so on, the banter went and everybody was having the time of their lives. That included the four children who wisely decided to ditch the adults and escape into their own special world.

The late night was followed by another long night of love and a late morning. Everybody was off doing their own thing in the town, while I slipped off to the airport to receive the last three guests, whose flights landed just an hour apart. The first was Juanita, who looked radiant, but bewildered. The other two were my grandparents. By the time they arrived, the airport staff had pretty much grown to know me and expect histrionics, and they were not disappointed. Both my grandparents were in tears, and kept calling me Avinash, before correcting themselves. For the first time I was with my own family.

Our wedding on 7 August was the crowning moment of my life.

✚

We now have two children whom we have named Charlotte Lucy and Avinash Jimmy. Harry and his family are regular visitors, and less frequently, Lucy, Juanita, Matilda and Mitch. Claire and I visit my father's humble origins in Madurai once a year to enjoy time with my delightful grandparents, who have visited us in Scotland twice. *Gorm-Faire* is humming with life and bubbling with *joie de vivre*.

AFTERWORD

I first started creating this novel in 1997, on a round-the-world trip, which formed a kind of skeleton on which I built the story. The original intention was to have it written and published at the start of the new millennium – and here we are in 2022! In these twenty-odd years, I have repeatedly thought about changing various bits, but in the end kept coming back to the original plot, with little deviation. That more or less convinced me that I had probably got it together as best as I could. The disastrous COVID-19 pandemic turned out to be the catalyst that succeeded in getting me to complete the novel.

Having been a keen reader all my life, I have been influenced by a few brilliant writers, whose identities I will not divulge at this moment, preferring to let the reader do some guess work. Some of my own experiences have crept into the book, inevitably.

However, I have very deliberately not used or recreated any person that I have encountered in real life.

The 'quotes' in italics at the beginning of the book, and each chapter thereafter, are entirely my own. I wrote them in retrospect after having written the book, to create a fore-taste, an atmosphere, of what is to come.

I am indebted to the living treasures of my life, my immediate family, who are acknowledged at the beginning. I love them dearly, and they have made my life worthwhile, and have defined me. Inaya, aka Figgy, my first granddaughter, arrived on the scene in April 2021, well after completion of the book, but she has acted as a trigger to my decision to pledge my profits to charity, using nothing more than her pure innocence and radiance. I am grateful to my trustworthy and highly efficient secretary, Linda Martin, for her unfailing typing skills.

For myself, I am going to make an attempt to remain hidden under my *nom-de-plume*, though I realise it will not be for long. Having completed my first novel, I am ready to embark on my second. Hopefully this one will not take another twenty years to come to fruition.